I0818610

Erik Hanssen huddled under the heavy wooden table. Around him, the ground shook as wave after wave of missiles struck the barren desert, bringing pieces of brick and mortar down from the wall above his head. His granddaughter, Anna, huddled next to him.

"It's gonna be okay, hon," he said as she cried on his shoulder.

"I'm scared. Where's mommy?" Anna asked.

Erik cringed. *How do you explain death to a nine-year-old?*

"She's in a better place now, sweetie," he replied, fighting back tears. "She's with God."

"Will we see her soon?" she asked.

"I don't know, honey. I don't know."

QUOTE GOES HERE
—Attribution Goes Here

I can honestly say that nothing like it has ever been written and, God willing, nothing else ever will be.
—My editor

We said we would publish this when Duke Nukem Forever®[1] shipped. I guess that was a bad call.
—My publisher

Some stories are elegant in their simplicity. Others are just simple.
—Anonymous reviewer

It made us want to improve our products to better compete.
—The vacuum cleaner company down the street

As much as it pains me to say it, some rules were meant to be broken.
—Author of "Any Idiot Can Write"

This novel has single-handedly contributed more to global warming than any other book in the history of publishing.
—Guy Montag

If you prick me, do I not bleed? If I read this, do I not retch?
—Actor on the set of Merchant of Venice

It is impossible to estimate the impact his book had on me.
—Victim, great book avalanche of 2023

I never knew cats could be suicidal until I read this book to mine.
—The crazy cat lady

---

[1]Duke Nukem Forever is a registered trademark of Gearbox Software.

Patriots:
Enemies From Within

A novel by
David A. Gatwood

Published by Gatwood Publishing.

Printed in the United States of America.

ISBN: 978-1-940809-03-8

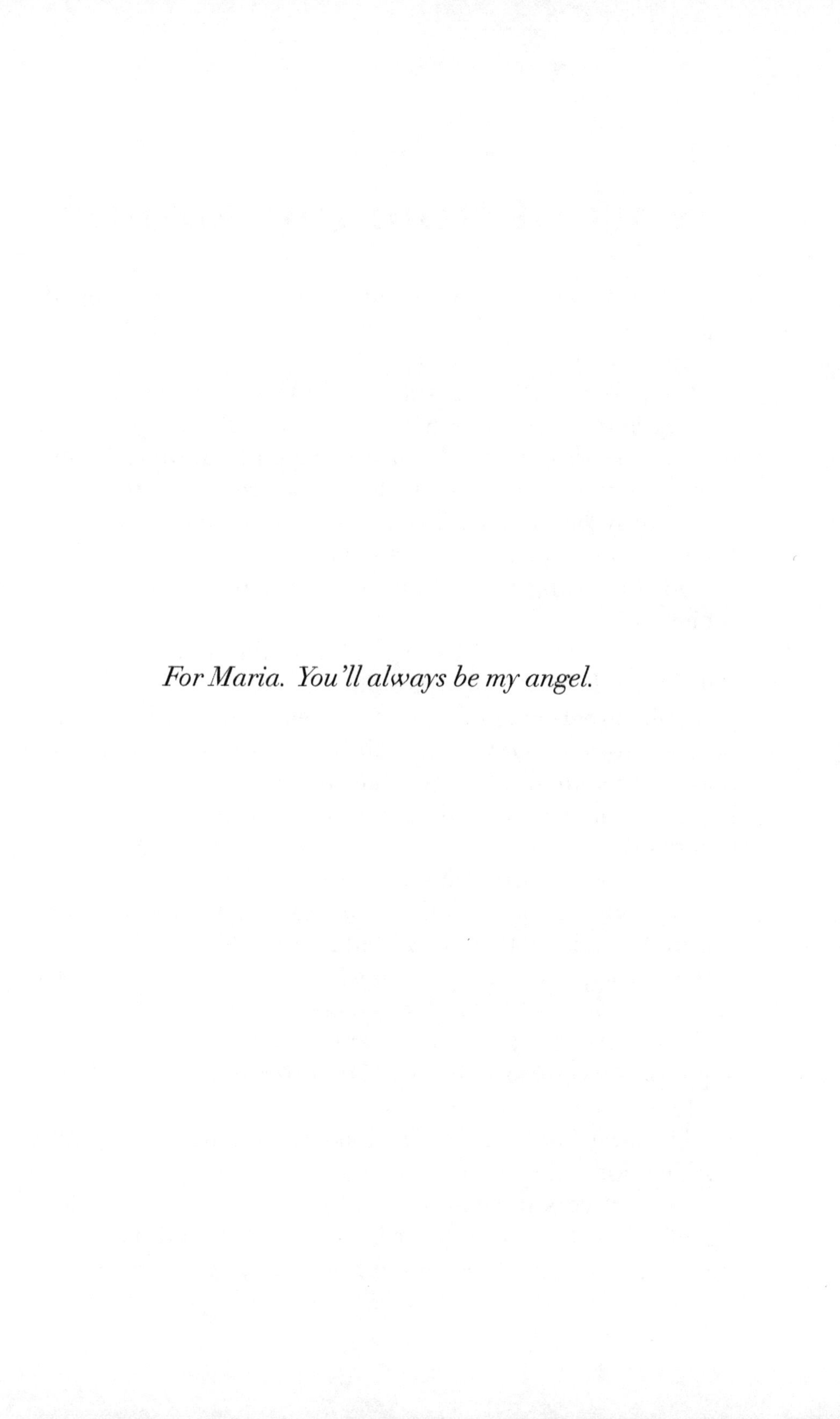

For Maria. You'll always be my angel.

A Word from the Author:

A few years ago, I woke up one morning and had the urge to write a novel. Two years and lots of delays later, "Traitors in Waiting" was born.

Long before that novel was finished, however, I was driving across Highway 280 at De Anza Boulevard in Cupertino, heading to work, having recently muttered something about how I'd love to live in a private island nation where only intelligent, world-wise people lived. Suddenly, I had an idea for a story in which a family of super-geniuses ended up raising a mentally retarded child in just such a society.

A few hours later, I was thinking about starting a new book, with Traitors only fractionally finished, when another possible direction surfaced—the idea of combining the two books into one. However, I didn't want to clutter the first book with something quite that unexpected or unusual, so it hit me that this would be a good start for a second book in a trilogy.

This book is the second in that series of three books. Unlike most trilogies, this book does not pick up where the first one left off. Instead, after providing a fair amount of backstory, it picks up somewhere between the first two chapters and the third chapter, then continues in parallel with the first book, telling events from the perspective of some of the opposing forces. The third book similarly parallels the first two stories.

The first book in the Patriots series, "Traitors in Waiting", explores the great colonial war from the perspective of military officers born and raised in a loyalist Earth colony, who find out, much to their horror, that the military is being manipulated by traitors in high-ranking positions.

The second book, “Enemies From Within”, treats the story from the perspective of a colonist and his friends.

The third book, “Beyond the Veil”, tells the truth behind the war.

After the book, be sure to read “Closing Thoughts”, where I ruin it for everybody by explaining everything you wanted to know about the story, and probably a lot of things you never wanted to know.

Special Thanks:

LIST OF PEOPLE
GOES HERE

Prologue:

January 17, 2391

Marc watched Kurt step to the podium before a crowd of about two hundred people in the crew mess of Portable Base 3. It was a crudely constructed ship for its time, but in many ways, it was an incredible achievement. From the very first sketch, it was designed to be a giant, space-borne research facility with all the amenities. Like most government projects, when push came to shove, they cut all the amenities....

The crew mess was one of the amenities. It looked like a filthy soup kitchen in a dark alley in Brooklyn, but it got the job done... *barely*.

Kurt Lawrence was the base commander, so when he spoke, everyone's ears perked up, but few more so than those of his closest advisors, Marc Hanssen and Kimberly Kurtz.

Marc had to admit that, friends or not, Kurt's meteoric rise to power over the past few years *still* gave him the creeps. Somehow he felt all too glad to be in the company of someone like Kim—possibly the only girl on the base who could be as cynical as he could. *It just makes life easier,* he thought.

"I have an announcement," Kurt told the onlookers. "I've just received word that Terran forces are taking Tularis Prime. We can't risk this project being discovered, and after that last attack, we are unable to fold. We have to move now."

Marc shivered. *The StarKiller was never supposed to be used except as a proof of concept,* he thought, *or so they told me. Why are we moving? Please tell me it hasn't come to this. I'd rather destroy the Omega Dawn project than use it as a weapon.*

"I thought the StarKiller was never to be used except as a deterrent," Kim asked.

Marc relaxed a bit. *Wonderful. Someone else asked, so I don't have to.*

"The Tularis System has all but fallen," Kurt replied. "Terran forces have already shown a willingness to scorch the earth after they take control of a planet. At this point, you should assume that everyone on Tularis Prime is dead or soon will be."

Marc's heart sank. *My family....*

"We have decided to show the Terrans that we are willing to use the ultimate weapon—that we are even willing to make the ultimate sacrifice—to halt their advance on our territory," Kurt continued. "Today, we black out Tularis, our sun."

As a Commodore, Marc knew that he could technically pull rank and overrule him, but Kurt was in charge of this posting, and his orders came straight from Admiral Murrow, which made that a bad idea....

Almost as bad an idea as blowing up a star, he thought.

Marc closed his eyes, bit his lip, and sighed.

***

Erik Hanssen huddled under the heavy wooden table. Around him, the ground shook as wave after wave of missiles struck the barren desert, bringing pieces of brick and mortar down from the wall above his head. His granddaughter, Anna, huddled next to him.

"It's gonna be okay, hon," he said as she cried on his shoulder.

"I'm scared. Where's mommy?" Anna asked.

Erik cringed. *How do you explain death to a nine-year-old?*

"She's in a better place now, sweetie," he replied, fighting back tears. "She's with God."

“Will we see her soon?” she asked.

“I don’t know, honey. I don’t know.”

Another explosion shook the house, bringing bits of the ceiling down on their heads. Anna screamed at the top of her lungs.

As Erik held her tightly, his granddaughter’s terrified cry was drowned out by the sound of engines whining—*a fleet of landing craft settling to the ground outside, no doubt.* As the bright lights bathed their house, Erik and Anna covered their eyes and waited.

Any moment now, the troops would start firing, their pulse rifles obliterating anything and anyone in their paths.

As if on cue, the landing troops began firing at the oncoming soldiers—a deafening cacophony that left Anna’s ears crying in pain—and all the while, air raid sirens blared in the distance.

Suddenly, an even more violent explosion rocked the house, sending a ceiling beam falling onto the table above them, and along with it fell darkness. As the power failed across the city, the sirens stopped, and their world fell into an eerie stillness—dark, silent, and cold....

Part I:

Early Colonial Life

Spring, 2304

Chapter

About eighty-seven years earlier (2304)

When the doorbell rang at 10:30 in the evening, John Richards knew something was wrong. *Jane! Is she okay? Did something happen to Allison? Is Bobby hurt?*

The face at the door left him even more surprised, however.

"Mike? What brings you here at this hour?" he asked.

Mike Terrazzo was the headmaster at his children's school. *What could possibly be important enough to keep me awake this late at night?*

"I came with some bad news, John," he replied. "I wanted to tell you personally."

"What is it? Are my children okay?" John asked.

"Yes, yes, they're fine," he replied, then added, "Well, no, they're not fine. They aren't hurt, but fine would be... well, that's what I came here to talk to you about."

"Get to the point, please," John said curtly.

"It's about your son," he replied. "His Greenup test came back at only 25. There's simply no denying that your son may be... developmentally challenged."

"Don't you call my son a retard," John snapped. "He has more brains than you'll ever have."

"I didn't call him a retard," Mike calmly answered. "He simply has problems learning. John, you should really get him some help. I'm told there's an excellent school for mentally handicapped students on Mars Colony."

"We're not moving to Mars," John told him.

"You don't have to move," Mike explained, "but your son can't stay here. They have a boarding program there, and since you're financially strained, I'm sure he could get a full scholarship to cover all of his educational costs."

"He's staying here," John informed him matter-of-factly. "We aren't moving, and neither is my son. Our contract says that he is guaranteed perpetual education as long as we live here in Nashville."

"A technicality, but one that is easily remedied, John," he replied. "We can be very... persuasive."

"Out."

"What?"

"Get out of my house. Now. I don't ever want to see you here again."

As John shoved him through the open door, Mike turned to him for one final plea.

"At least think about it," Mike said. "Things really would be better for him—and for you—on Mars Colony."

And with that, John slammed the door in his face.

***

"Bobby," the young woman said gently, "what are you doing here? This isn't your class anymore."

To a twelve-year-old boy, Mrs. Binkley was a beautiful angel, her long brown hair flowing around her pearly thirty-four-year-old face....

And a body to die for, Bobby thought. *What does she mean, "This isn't your class anymore"?*

"You've been transferred to section 70," she continued.

Section 70? That's the handicapped class. There must be some mistake.

"Isn't section 70 the class for retards?" he asked.

"No, it's for people with trouble learning, just like you," she replied.

"Ha, ha! Bobby is a retard," one child chanted.

Soon, the entire class was chanting, "Bobby is a retard. Bobby is a retard," over and over and over.

Bobby was horrified, and ran from the room crying.

"Kids can be so cruel," Mike said gleefully.

"Can't they, though?" Mrs. Binkley replied, grinning from ear to ear.

***

"Hey, Bobby!" came a voice from across the playground.

Bobby turned. "Kate.... I suppose you're gonna call me a retard, too."

"Of course not!" she replied. "You know they didn't mean it.... Well, some of them did, but... you know what I mean."

"Thanks, Kate."

"I overheard Mrs. Binkley and Mr. Terrazzo talking," she said. "They said they want to ship you off to Mars, but your parents won't let them, and that's why they're putting you in the dumb class."

"They what!?" he exclaimed.

"Shh. Keep your voice down. I don't want them to know I heard them."

"Why not? It's not like you were doing anything wrong."

"I was kind-of sneaking around behind the school to make out with Matthew."

"Oh. I see," Bobby said.

"You know," she offered coyly, "you *could* get even.... You could make them pay."

"But how?" he asked.

Bobby could almost see the wheels turning in her head as she thought about this rare opportunity. Kate Hayward had always hated Mrs. Binkley—ever since she made her stay after school for putting gum in Pete Hillsdale's hair back in first grade—and this was just the sort of opportunity she longed for—the opportunity to get back at Mrs. Binkley in a way that couldn't be traced back to her.

And so it was with great anticipation that Bobby waited for her reply, and when it came, he was not disappointed.

"It's simple, really," she finally said, drawing a square on the dirt at the back of the playground as she spoke. "First, you wait until she is in the bathroom. Then, you sneak into Louis Belmont's lab and steal the freon canister and use it to freeze the door shut. Next, you...."

Chapter Two

Three days later

At precisely 1:35 P.M., Bobby watched as Mrs. Binkley entered the bathroom, setting the plan into motion.

Bobby froze the door shut. A few minutes later, Mrs. Binkley began trying to open the door, only to find the lock mechanism hopelessly jammed.

Bobby couldn't help but wonder what Kate meant when she said *"Make sure you don't use too much fertilizer. You just want to scare her."* He wasn't quite sure how much fertilizer was too much, so he only poured one bag into the wheelbarrow. As he sprayed the glycerine on top of it, it began to fizz.

Suddenly the door started to give way. Terrified, Bobby ran away. Bobby had already rounded the corner by the time his teacher slammed the bathroom door into the wheelbarrow and disturbed its rather unstable contents, but the resulting explosion nearly knocked him to his knees in spite of his distance.

"Jeez, Bobby, how much did you use!?!" Kate asked.

"Only one bag," he replied.

"Mrs. Binkley!" she screamed in horror as she ran into the burning building.

As the roof of the school collapsed, Bobby curled up into a ball and cried.

***

"I have some very bad news," Mike said, pushing his way into John's house as he did. "Your son blew up part of our school today. Thankfully, no one was killed, but six students and a teacher are in critical condition."

"I'm aware of what you claim he did," John replied curtly. "I'm also aware that you drove him to it by moving him into a class with severely retarded children in front of all of his friends."

"He locked a teacher in a bathroom and planted an explosive outside the door, John."

"He wouldn't know how to make nitroglycerine, and he's not smart enough to figure it out on his own. Someone must have tricked him into doing it."

"Regardless of your personal feelings in this matter, I feel—and the school board agrees—that your son is simply too dangerous, and cannot be allowed to continue attending our school."

"Are you breaching our contract?" John asked demandingly.

"Your contract was breached the moment your son committed an act of violence against a member of our staff," he replied. "Like it or not, your son is out. According to the law, your son will remain in the custody of the courts until he can be relocated to a boarding school on Mars Colony."

"You can't do this!"

"It's already done."

Chapter Three

Ten years later (2314)

THE sun rose like a tiny, golden disc over the Martian landscape, the rarified, terraformed atmosphere glowing a deep bluish color in response, but before the first ray of sunlight shone in the distance, Tim Hanssen was already on his way to the fields.

"Hey, Tim!"

"Hey, Jeff!"

Jeff Atherton was a burly man, about two decades older than Tim, a mere lad of 28. Jeff ran the "A6 Farm". This year, A6 was growing grain to replenish nutrients in the soil after last year's corn season.

Because of the thin atmosphere, crop-dusting aircraft were nearly impossible to fly, and even at a reduced dosage, aerosolized fertilizers and pesticides would be dangerous to the planet's inhabitants.

For tall crops like corn, they used crawlers—human-driven vehicles that had tall wheel stalks with long pipe sprayers in-between. In general, though, they had to spray most crops by hand.

Tim was stationed in A5, the fruit orchard, growing apple trees. Through the wonders of genetic engineering, they had created a breed of apple tree that could withstand the thin air, but even with all their advances, the cold Martian nights were too much for them to handle.

To keep the trees alive, Tim came in early every morning and opened the giant glass roof to keep the plants from overheating, then closed it in the late afternoon to trap the sun-warmed air for the long night ahead.

During the hot hours, he monitored the irrigation systems from a cool control room. Later in the afternoon, he drove the picker around the orchard, picking fruit and carefully spraying for any undesirable insects.

But today was different. Today, Tim was going to the city to interview for a construction job on the new skyscraper.

Tim carefully strapped a filter mask to his face before entering the border zone.

As Tim activated the giant doors, Angela walked up behind him.

"Oh, hey Angela," he said, slightly startled. "All you have to do is come in every hour and make sure the trees aren't getting flooded, and don't forget to push this red button at 3:3o."

"Relax, Tim," she replied. "I've got it. Your precious trees will be fine without you for a day."

Tim smiled. *Yeah, they're in good hands,* he thought. As he walked back outside into the harsh midmorning light, he wondered for a brief moment if the new job was worth losing what he was leaving behind, but he put it out of his mind as he stepped into his pod car and closed the hatch.

***

TIM had to squint at the bright sunlight as he stepped out of the pod car in New Paradise. Overhead, the monorail sped by, squealing like a pig on its way to the slaughterhouse.

Tim had barely taken his first step when a taxi pod shot by mere inches from his face. As it did, the taxi honked its horn. Tim could barely comprehend the shouting that followed; he thought the driver called him a forking Mormon, but he suspected he had misheard the man.

The city is beautiful, he thought—*the skyscrapers dotting the horizon, the deep blue sky; the orange-red dirt, the city lights.... I could really be at home here.*

And so he was in that state of mind when he entered the construction gate at fifty-first and Evelyn. The foreman met him and escorted him quickly into his office.

"Hey. Tim, right?" the foreman asked. He looked oddly out of place as he sat behind his mahogany desk.

"Yes," Tim replied.

The foreman got straight to the point. "I understand you were a network technician on Earth, and you want to run fiber for us," he said.

"That's right," he replied. "I shot the fiber for the Joswiak Center back in 'o3."

"Wow, that must have been some stunt. I understand they ran over a thousand miles of cable after the building was finished."

"Yeah, Joz wanted to make sure his network would always be the fastest, so he had us run it in conduit on the outside of the walls. Made the ceiling a bitch, though, 'cause he didn't leave holes in the concrete."

"Well, you're obviously qualified," the foreman replied. "The only real question is whether you're ready to change jobs."

"Yeah, that's the one thing I *am* sure about."

"In that case, I guess you should meet the architect. He's up in the terrace dome."

***

THE elevator door closed with a thud as Tim stepped into the ninety-second-floor hallway in the newly constructed Connelly Center. The interior walls were still bare steel studs, with the occasional outlet box, conduit, or bare water pipe attached here and there. Overhead, he could see a bunch of walkways, and above them, a giant glass dome through which you could see the stars even during the day.

Tim was awestruck as he stared out the window at the Martian landscape. After a few moments, he noticed the reflection of a tall man walking up behind him.

"It's beautiful, isn't it?" the man asked.

"Yes, truly," he replied. "Are you Mike Lawrence?"

"Yeah. You must be Tim Hanssen."

"That's me," he replied. "Say, this is a remarkable piece of work, but there's something I don't quite get."

"What's that?" Mike asked.

"We're on the ninety-second floor. Why are the walls so thick?"

"It's an air pressure issue. The atmosphere is so thin up here that we had to have thick walls and windows to withstand the pressure difference. That's why you aren't in a pressure suit right now."

"What if a window breaks?" Tim asked.

"There are oxygen shelters and airtight doors every hundred feet or so. We'll fill you in on all the details at the interior team orientation tomorrow."

"8:00 sharp," Tim replied. "I'll be there."

Chapter Four

A few weeks later

At five o'clock, the shift whistle blew, and Tim Hanssen carefully placed his tools at the side of the room so the replacement shift wouldn't trip over them in the near-darkness of the forty-fourth floor.

Much as he did every day, Francois cursed nearby, muttering that he just needed to install three more sets of mini-blinds to be finished with this room. And as always, he quit anyway, and all feigned amazement as the blinds man put down his hammer and saw.

With this strange custom in the back of his mind, Tim stepped out onto the streets of New Paradise, softly bathed in the orange glow of the slowly setting sun.

The sunlight glistened off the evening dew as the thunder rolled ever closer—the storm looming in the distance like an ever-present monument to the depth of human ingenuity—and with every passing moment, Tim marveled at the beauty of this place.

It truly did seem like paradise—the towering buildings along the glistening, tree-lined boulevards, the mountains in the distance, the birds overhead, and the puffy, white clouds silhouetted against the deep blue sky—but even in the presence of so much beauty, he still felt that something was missing.

Thus, as darkness fell and the rains fell and the dew fell, so too his heart fell, and Timothy Adam Hanssen found himself once again looking for his Eve in this city of paradise.

***

TIM shivered in the cool mist of the A5, the tall trees dripping mercilessly upon his head. As he walked towards the control center, he felt a gentle tap on his shoulder, turned, and found himself face-to-face with Jeff.

"Tim!" he exclaimed. "Jeez, I never thought I'd see you in here again."

"I'm looking for Angela," Tim replied. "Have you seen her?"

"She left early to run some errands," Jeff said. "Sorry you missed her."

"It happens.... Listen, when you see her again, tell her I stopped by."

"Will do, Tim. Will do."

***

ANGELA handed the driver a fifty as she stepped cautiously down from the taxi to the surface street below, the cold evening air burning her lungs like a bad novel thrown in a kiln.

Before her sprawled the Connelly Center—ninety-five floors of glass and steel—and, she hoped, her friend Tim.

As she approached, the foreman saw her and jogged in her direction.

"Ya lookin' for somebody?" he asked.

"Tim... Tim Hanssen," she replied nervously.

The foreman looked down at his watch. "You just missed him," he said. "He left about an hour ago... said something about turning in early. Sorry I can't be more helpful."

"No prob. Maybe I'll catch him another time."

***

"So, Tim, what'll it be?" the bartender asked.

Joe Kurtz, Jr. stood tall at six feet, four inches, with short brown hair and a neatly trimmed goatee. His height helped hide his rather rotund figure, but his beer gut looked oddly larger today, Tim noted.

"I'll have a Pulitzer, straight up," he replied. "How are the wife and kids?"

"They're good," Joe said. "Maria just has a couple more weeks before she finishes college. We're all really proud of her. And little James is an honors student in his third grade class this term. I even have the bumper sticker to prove it."

"And the rest of your family?"

"Well, my sister, Sara, is still on Earth. She's getting married next fall. My dad, Paul... well, he's getting up there, but he swears he's gonna make it to Mars to visit me before the wedding. I'll believe it when I see it. And of course, my brother Tom is working with you on the Connelly Center."

"Oh yeah?" Tim asked. "What's he working on?"

"He's a structural engineer working on the terrace dome," Joe replied. "You ought to go up and see him sometime. He follows all that Chelsea Cup stuff like it's rocket science or something."

"Umm... it's a shuttlecraft race. It... uh... actually *is* rocket science," Tim said questioningly.

"Oh. Good point," he replied. "Anyway, the point is, he's a real fan. He could probably tell you every bolt that goes into making one of those things. That's not saying anyone could actually *understand* anything he said, just that he'd make it *sound* fascinating."

Tim chuckled. "So where's that Pulitzer?"

"Let's see, Award malt liquor, a gold cup of strawberries from a well-formed plot, simile for blackberries, blend in some sugar for spice, bring it to a boil, then at the climax, add ice and cool things off to a cathartic denouement, and top it off with a prize cherry from grandma's garden.... Yup, one Pulitzer, coming right up."

"Thanks, Joe."

"Say, Tim, you okay?" Joe asked as the glass of ice suddenly sublimed in a puff of steam.

"Yeah, why?"

"You don't usually order something that stiff."

"I'm drowning my troubles," Tim replied.

"Trying to wash away the lonely?"

"Something like that. Oh, and make it to go. I don't want to drive home with that in my gut."

"Sure. Will do."

***

ANGELA stepped warily into Joe's Bar and Grille.

"Hello, Joe. Whaddaya know?" she asked jokingly.

Joe just grunted.

"Not much for talking today, eh?"

"Not much, Ma'am," he replied. "Say, your friend Tim was just in here a while back."

"Let me guess," she began, then was joined by Joe in saying, "you just missed him."

"One of those days, eh?" he quipped.

"One of those years."

Chapter Five

Two weeks later

THE heated air shimmered above the sidewalk as Tim ran towards the Connelly Center. He was already about ten minutes late and getting later by the minute.

"Stupid pod car," he muttered. "I should never have let those guys at Cheap Lube get their hands on it."

The sidewalk seemed to go on for miles ahead of him in a never-ending line towards an ever-elusive destination. When he finally reached the construction entrance, he checked his watch. *Twenty minutes. Not bad for a mile and a half on foot....*

Tim cringed. *Oooh, my feet.... Ouch. Next time I call a cab,* he thought as he rounded the corner. Suddenly, his feet were not the biggest source of pain. He rubbed his aching head, then rubbed his eyes. *Angela.*

"Angela?" he asked, staring at the girl with whom he had just butted heads. "What are you doing here?"

"Looking for you," she replied. "I heard you tried to catch me at work the other night."

"Yeah, about that," Tim began.

Angela interrupted him. "I have to get back to the farm before they miss me. Why don't we talk about it over dinner."

Tim stood in shock for a moment. "That... sounds nice," he replied. "Dinner it is. Seven o'clock? Terry's Steak House?"

"That's good for me. See you then."

"Yeah.... See you then."

As Angela left, Tim couldn't help wondering what just happened. *Did she just ask me out? And did I just want her to ask?*

***

THOMAS Kurtz watched longingly as the hostess seated a young couple from across the lobby. He managed to get a reservation at one of the nicest restaurants in town, and still he'd been waiting for nearly an hour.

Oh well, he thought, glancing briefly at Marcia. *At least I have good company.*

With that, he stood and walked over to the hostess.

"Excuse me, miss?" he asked. "Any idea what the wait time will be?"

"Probably about fifteen minutes," she replied.

"Tom?" a man asked from behind him.

Tom spun on his heel and ran headfirst into Tim, inadvertently knocking him into a chest-high planter.

"Tim!" he said, startled. "Good to see you."

"Would you like to join us?" Tim asked. "We're next on the list, I think."

"Are you sure?" Tom asked.

"Fine by me," Angela said. "I always like meeting Tim's friends."

"Honey?" Tom asked.

Marcia just smiled and nodded.

"Trish, could you make that a party of four?" Tim asked.

"Certainly," the hostess replied. "We should have something in just a minute."

A few moments later, they were seated at a small table in the front window. Above them, the space station Svoboda glowed like a small artificial moon in the night sky over New Paradise.

"It's hard to believe you're getting married, Tom," Tim said.

"Yeah. Who'd have thought?" Tom asked, smiling. "I finally met the perfect woman. Marcia's so beautiful, but she's not vain like a lot of girls."

"That's always a good thing," Tim replied.

With that, Marcia leaned over to Angela and struck up a conversation of her own.

"Have you seen my ring?" she asked, grinning ear to ear.

Angela smiled and nodded.

"She's always really sweet, too," Tom added.

"Hey, waiter! What's the holdup? Where's my escargot?" Marcia shouted.

"And she's smart, too."

"Jeez, you'd think that they had to catch the clams," she muttered.

"Isn't she incredible?" he asked.

Tim smiled a quirky smile and nodded.

"When's the wedding?" Angela asked, a look of disgust already beginning to creep across her features.

"It's this weekend," Marcia replied. "We're eloping."

"My parents said she wasn't good enough," Tom continued. "Shows you what they know."

Tim just sighed and shook his head.

Chapter Six

Ten years earlier (2304)

Samuel Jenkins jumped into his uniform to the sound of alarm klaxons screeching in his ear. By the time he reached the bridge a few moments later, the ship had shaken violently so many times that he had lost count.

"Ensign! Report!" he shouted as the bridge doors slid open.

"Captain on the bridge!" the ensign shouted back. "Sir! We're taking fire from an unknown enemy. The ships are not answering our hails."

"What's our status?"

"We've lost both engines and we're venting atmosphere," the ensign replied. "Life support has failed. We have at most twenty minutes of air."

"Sir!"

From the look on the navigation officer's face, Captain Jenkins could tell something was very wrong. *What the hell.... It's not like things could get much worse.*

"Yes, Lieutenant?" he replied.

"We have three more ships traveling at a high rate of speed towards our current location."

"Identify!"

"They match the signature of the Black Fleet sir," the Lieutenant replied.

My god, he thought. *The Black Fleet are the most notorious smugglers for three systems in any direction. What do they want?*

The sound of proton bombs ripping parts of the ship's outer hull answered that question. Then, as quickly as it had begun, the explosions stopped.

"Sir?" the Lieutenant interjected.

"Yes, Lieutenant?"

"Our attackers have engaged the Black Fleet."

"Ensign, prepare a directed EMP charge for launch. We'll blind their sensors and use the firefight as cover for our escape."

The ensign looked down at the ship status monitors and grimaced. "Our missile tubes are offline."

This sentiment was punctuated by another salvo of weapons fire.

"We just lost port thrusters," the ensign shouted. "We're dead in the water."

Captain Jenkins sighed.

"It gets worse," the lieutenant added. "Engineering reports that our aft core is losing coolant and could go unstable at any minute."

"So shut it down!"

"They can't. The feed valves are stuck."

I guess this is it, he thought. *It's a short run, so we don't have enough life pods for a tenth of our passengers.*

His reverie was quickly interrupted, however, by the lieutenant's shrill voice.

"What the *hell* is that?"

"Lieutenant?"

"We're receiving a hail," the ensign interrupted.

This is Captain Jonathan Forrester aboard the United Earth battleship Tritium. The transport ship C3X051 is under our protection. Disengage or we will open fire.

"Holy hydrogen, bat boy!" the ensign shouted.

"Whoa! Heavy!" the Lieutenant replied, smiling.

Commander Walker stepped onto the bridge from the lift and immediately chimed in.

"Don't you mean Bat..." he began.

"Only if you want to be sued," the ensign interrupted.

Captain Jenkins just stared.

***

Five minutes later

THE acrid air burned his lungs as Captain Jenkins stepped briefly back into the dying shell of his transport ship, C3X051, alongside Captain Forrester. He watched as dozens of people ran past them towards the relative safety of the Tritium.

"Everybody move!" Ensign Carlson shouted at the oncoming throng.

Jenkins turned to see the young ensign run past.

"The aft core is going!" the engineer shouted.

"What do we do, Rick?" Jenkins asked.

"It's your call, sir," the engineer replied.

"How long?" Forrester asked.

"A minute, two tops!"

Captain Jenkins froze. This was his worst nightmare... having to detach from a ship before he knew everyone was safely off. *It never gets easier*, he thought.

Captain Forrester obviously noticed his colleague's hesitation, and stepped forward.

"Jenkins? Jenkins!?" he prodded.

Captain Jenkins just stood there.

"Okay, seal it off!" Forrester ordered. "We're moving!"

Ensign Carlson pressed the red button on the wall and the door began to drop.

Mere moments after he said this, a young woman came running around the corner, dragging a 12-year-old boy and his big sister with her.

"Hold it!" she screamed.

Captain Jenkins watched in horror as the doors fell. By the time the woman reached the doors, they were almost to the floor. In those last few moments, the woman threw the boy under, then the girl, but the door was too low for her to get under herself.

"Get that door back open!" Forrester shouted.

"We can't, sir!" the engineer replied. "It's too late!"

The woman on the other side pressed herself against the door's glass window, and the young girl did likewise.

In that moment, Captain Jenkins stood frozen, thinking about how much the girl reminded him of his young grandson, Thomas—thinking about what it must be like to watch your family torn away at such a young age—wishing he had done something—wishing that he could have.

"Bobby! Allison!" the woman yelled. "I love you!"

Slowly, the warship moved away from the dying transport, the viewports moving farther apart, until they could barely see the woman beyond the empty space that lay between them. As the fire engulfed the corridor beyond the now-distant doors, the girl screamed.

"Mommy!"

With that, Captain Jenkins put his arm around the young girl and her brother and watched as their ship fell slowly towards the Martian atmosphere. A moment later, it exploded into a giant ball of fire.

"Mommy?"

Captain Jenkins hung his head.

"Mommy?"

Chapter Seven

Ten years later (2314)

TIM yawned groggily as his alarm clock screamed in his ear. A moment later, he reached out to turn it off, knocking it to the floor as he did.

"Damn it," he cursed as he got up, the alarm clock still beeping.

After he reached down and switched it off, he walked across the room to the computer terminal and began his morning routine.

First, he logged on to SolSlash, the geek news site.

> *In a scene right out of a bad movie, war has broken out on Anakis Three as armed paramilitary from the nearby Lenoran system stormed the government offices, killing the Prime Minister of Kent Province, Andrea Barristedt, and her three deputies.*
>
> *Similar forces have begun moving on neighboring provinces. The local governments have called for assistance*

> *from Earth, but at last word, no help was forthcoming.*

"Wow, sounds like a good book review. I'll have to read it later," he muttered as he turned the terminal off.

A few moments later, Tim was off for the city in his pod car. As he watched the sun peek slowly over the horizon, he reached for the radio.

> *Onlookers watched in horror as dozens of government officials threw themselves out of windows in a desperate attempt to save themselves from the flames. All in all, the death toll was estimated at more than five-hundred in this, the first day of fighting.*

"My god...."

Chapter

Eight

Seventy-seven years later (January 14, 2391)

A dark cloud bank rolled in from the coast as Erik Hanssen cooked breakfast.

"It's gonna be a wet one today, Papa," Anna said, a slight British accent in her voice.

Erik was visibly startled. He hadn't even heard her enter until she spoke.

"Are you ready for breakfast?" he asked.

"Yes, Papa," she replied.

Erik smiled as he flipped a pancake into the air, then stepped quickly back to avoid the hot oil that splattered everywhere when it landed.

"Papa," Anna asked, "where's Mama?"

"She's outside milking the cows," he replied. "Say, you want to give me a hand in a minute?"

"With what?"

"I've gotta bring the horses in. This storm's gonna be a bad one. I need some help hitchin' 'em up."

"Sure, Papa... after breakfast."

"Of course, hon. After breakfast."

***

KURT activated the viewscreen. They immediately saw a full screen graphic showing red X marks—bombing locations, presumably—along with a caption that read simply, "Attack on Kinji".

"What are they talking about?" Kurt asked. "Do those guys think we're stupid or something?"

> "You're tuned to TANN, the Terran Alliance News Network," the reporter said. "In regional news, Terran Alliance troops have just captured Kinji's capital city of Tyrano, and are moving on Bellany."

"Do you see any Terran troops?" Kurt asked.

"I doubt there are any Terran troops within a hundred miles of here," Marc replied. "I wonder if the Terrans know that their media is feeding them a load."

Marc Hanssen was a young man, about twenty-six years old, his pale face set off by short brown hair—the prototypical military brat except for the scruffy beard that he wore primarily to annoy the Admiralty.

"Your family doing okay?" Kurt asked.

"Yeah," Marc replied. "Tularis Prime is right in the crosshairs, but so far they've muddled through."

"Let's see what's *really* going on," Marc said, changing the channel.

> "...after securing the capital city of Tyrano. Our embedded reporter, Gilbert McIlhenry, is standing by in Tyrano. Gilbert?" the reporter announced.

"Yes, Annie," the man replied. "It looks like Tyrano was secured several hours ago, and Colonial Alliance troops are slowly pushing the aggressors back towards Worcestershire."

"Away from here," Marc noted. "That's why we don't see anything."

As he said this, air raid klaxons began to blare.

"This could get rough," Kurt said, sighing.

Overhead, the fighters flying cover created a rumbling sound that shook the stone walls. Kurt and Marc held their ears as the rumbling grew louder and louder. Silverware rattled on the countertop, bookshelves discarded their contents, and an antique picture frame fell from the end table, its glass pane shattering on the hard stone floor.

The rumbling slowly decreased and eventually subsided. Then, as quickly as they had begun, the sirens went silent.

"This is it," Marc said. "This is how it begins."

And silence still.

"Oh, yeah," he added. "It's January 14th. Happy thirty-eighth birthday, Kurt."

"Yeah. Whatever."

A few minutes passed in silence, and still they heard no signs of attack. When they walked down the hall and stepped out onto the balcony, they were greeted by a dark sky with no signs of any activity whatsoever except for the normal glow of the city lights in the distance.

"Where's the kaboom?" Marc joked. "There was supposed to be a Kinji-shattering kaboom."

Chapter Nine

Seventy-seven years earlier (2314)

DAWN rose slowly on Kinji. An orange glow bathed the horizon with light as purple clouds dotted the sky. Against that backdrop, a white ship sailed overhead, gliding slowly to the ground.

Thomas Woodrough, Jr. stepped up to the landing platform to greet the new inmates.

One-by-one, thirty new prisoners stepped down from the exit ramp and onto the waiting area.

"Welcome to Kinji," he said. "I am Thomas, the First Keeper. There are other Keepers around the planet watching you at all times. Make no mistake, this may look like paradise, but it is a prison."

"This prison has no walls," he continued, "no fences, and no guard dogs or barbed wire. Three things stand between you and escape. First, there are guards around the only landing platform. Second, there are defensive satellites in orbit. Third, you will each be tagged with subcutaneous trackers. Your children will be tagged, and your children's children."

The keeper pointed at a barely concealed camera on the side of a tree, then at three more cameras within the immediate vicinity as he said, "We will know where you are and what you are doing at all times. We will watch your every move, even when you sleep. The law here is simple. Any crime committed on Kinji will be punished by immediate death. You may interact as you please, but if you step out of line for even a moment, a bullet will be the last thing you see."

"If there are no questions," he concluded, "you are to proceed down those stairs to be fitted with control tags."

"I have a question," one prisoner asked.

"What is it?" Thomas snapped back.

"Why are we here?" the prisoner asked.

"What did you do on Barana?" he replied.

"I was a lawyer."

"Consider yourself lucky. They killed most of the lawyers."

"Sounds like a good start to me," one of the other prisoners remarked.

The lawyer's face contorted in anger at the laughter that ensued, and in a violent rage, he screamed and jumped at First Keeper Woodrough.

The First Keeper sidestepped the attack, and the prisoner lost his balance. Suddenly, from four directions, machine gun fire sent blood splattering everywhere. The prisoner was dead before his body hit the ground.

"Are there any more questions?"

***

"I'm gonna head home a few minutes early," Tim told the foreman as he hung up his hard hat beside the door. "I have a gig tonight. I'll come in early tomorrow and get caught up."

"Sure," he replied. "No prob. Have fun."

“You, too,” Tim shouted as the doors closed behind him. With that, Tim headed off across the parking lot.

The Martian winds tore at his skin as Tim climbed into his pod car. Suddenly, without warning, the ground shook violently. *Earthquake? Wow,* he thought. *That’s the first time I’ve felt one since I arrived on Mars.*

Then, the ground shook again. A chill ran up his spine as he turned around and saw two huge Earth ships hovering in the sky, with a steady stream of small objects trailing below them.

It was in that moment that he knew something had gone terribly wrong.... A moment later, a bright flash in the capital city of New London confirmed his worst fears.

Before he knew it, he was halfway across the desert. In his rear-view mirror, he watched as the Connelly Center exploded into flames, its glass tower reduced to rubble in mere seconds.... That’s when the bullets came.

Puffs of dust hit the windshield like bursts of rain in a hurricane, washing over it like nothing he’d seen before. The engine strained against the loose sand as he pressed it ever harder. Then, suddenly, it stopped just as he neared the capitol dome.

I made it, he thought... but the momentary respite was almost immediately broken by the whistling sound of an approaching projectile. He couldn’t turn to look at it, but he could tell from the noise that it was big... and close. With a sinking feeling in his gut, he covered his face with his hands.

Then, everything went black....

***

“In national news,” the reporter read, “warships from Earth have taken control of New London in retaliation for yesterday's attack on Anakis Three by paramilitary forces from the Lenoran system. The press secretary for the president of Earth read a prepared statement at a press conference a few moments ago."

The screen changed, and a burly man in a flannel shirt appeared. He looked briefly offstage, then looked back at the camera before speaking.

"Howdy," he drawled. The man hailed from the Alabama Province in the Protectorate of the United States, so this sort of beginning had become all too common.

"We wish to apologize to the galactic community for the speed of our response," he began. "A number of members of the Colonial Trade Alliance have recently fallen under the control of separatist factions. These terrorist elements have begun to take up roots in unaligned colonial worlds as well. According to our intelligence, one such group, the Colonial Liberation Front, has been conducting terrorist activities against colonial worlds using Mars as a base. I'm sure you can all understand that we could not allow such activity so close to the heart of Earth's government. In light of the evidence, we felt it was better to take preemptive action to ensure the safety of our citizens rather than simply waiting for the inevitable."

"Our deepest sympathy is extended to the families of those killed in the capitol dome," he continued. "A computer error mistakenly flagged it as a communications center. We will send personnel immediately to set up an interim government until such time as the people of Mars can elect more permanent leadership."

"We will bring you further announcements about our war on terror as more information becomes available," he muttered as he left the podium.

With that, the reporter reappeared and said, "Damage estimates and casualty reports are slow to arrive from outlying areas because of network disruptions. We hope to bring you more information soon. What we know so far is that at 4:02 p.m., the capitol building was bombed, killing about a thousand people, predominantly government officials and staff. At 4:11 p.m., the Connelly Center tower collapsed. Three hundred construction workers are believed trapped or dead. A few dozen other deaths have been reported from various communication centers throughout the area, and one local hospital experienced severe fire damage."

"A global communications blackout is in effect, enforced by a damping field. TANN will still be available via wired delivery."

Angela turned off the television, her face white with horror.

Four-eleven. Tim doesn't get off until five.

With that realization, her heart sank. Holding back the tears, she whispered, "I will find you. I promise."

***

TIM struggled to remain conscious—tried to watch the clock so he would know when he blacked out—but in the end, his resolve faltered and his world was bathed in blackness. That's when he saw the light—a bright tunnel with lights flashing as he went past, and then a bright light just in front of him. Slowly, out of the light, a face emerged.... *A girl? No, a woman—a beautiful woman.... An angel?*

As his eyes regained their focus, he shook his head. *No, not an angel.... An Angela.*

"Angela!" he screamed... or at least tried to scream through the drug-induced haze. It came out sounding more like "morphine", and the doctors promptly complied. Once again, everything went black.

A few minutes later, he came to again. This time, he decided against speaking, and simply smiled instead.

"Tim!" she exclaimed.

"Is this heaven?" he muttered through the drug-induced stupor.

"No. Valley Memorial," she replied.

"Valley? Why not New Paradise?"

"I'm afraid it was... umm... lost...."

"Milton would be proud," he muttered.

But Tim could tell from the tone of her voice that this wasn't just a poorly timed literary reference. *No,* he thought. *This is serious. Something happened—something terrible.*

"How..." he gasped.

Angela buried her face in his shoulder and cried. "It was a massacre," she whimpered. "They hit us from space. We... never saw it coming."

Out of the corner of his eye, Tim caught a glimpse of a man in a white coat stepping through the open door. Tim struggled with his prone position, desperately craning his neck for a better view, but after a few seconds, he decided that it was futile and let his head drop back to the pillow.

"Excuse me, miss," the man said gently. "I think he's had enough excitement for now. We should let him rest."

Angela nodded, smiled, turned, walked through the doorway, and closed the door behind her.

With that, Tim sighed, then hoarsely whispered, "I love you."

Chapter Ten

THE lights of the space station Svoboda glowed as brightly as the morning sun when Tom and Marcia stepped off the transport shuttle, arm in arm. The two newlyweds were quickly ushered to the honeymoon suite by a burly fellow who looked like he would be more at home as a truck driver or a bouncer at a bar rather than as the concierge at a resort hotel. *Even still, the service is excellent,* Tom thought.

The suite was beautiful—a luxurious living room with hand-carved wooden furniture and a fresco on the ceiling that was to die for. The chandelier made Marcia drool visibly. Oddly enough, Tom was turned on by this public display of salivation, but before he could say anything, Marcia turned to him and spoke.

"Honey?" Marcia began, "I'm going to go get a drink downstairs. I'll be back in a few minutes. Okay, honey?"

"Sure, hon. See you in a few."

"When I get back, I expect you to... be comfortable," she said, a lascivious look in her eye, then turned and walked out into the hallway.

As he entered the bedroom, Tom was rather surprised to find that the TV set was already turned on and tuned to MarsNews, the space station's news channel.

> "In an unprovoked attack," the anchorwoman's voice said as the screen cut away to images of the destruction on Mars, "the United Earth Provinces have declared Mars to be their latest target in their so-called war on terror, this despite strong support for the government of Earth from all of the Martian territories. This erratic behavior has left some questioning the motives of Earth's leaders."

The anchorwoman reappeared on the screen.

> "In an ironic twist, rumors of a colonial rebellion have surfaced. In our MarsNews/Colonial Journal poll, only about three percent of Mars residents would support such a rebellion, but forty percent said that they would support it if evidence showed that there were no terrorist training camps on Mars."
>
> "In a related story," she continued, "troops are reportedly massing on Barana in the Kinji system. The capital city of Mahi found itself surrounded by tens of thousands of heavily entrenched rebel troops intent on the overthrow of the provisional government in that system, claiming that the government shows too much favoritism towards Earth and its leaders."

"In other news, a new round of terror attacks rocked Earth stations on Triton today. Fifteen people were injured, three critically, as a suicide bomber ran into a crowded restaurant. Despite carrying enough explosives to level a city block, the incompetent would-be assassin apparently didn't know that plastic explosives don't generally explode when burned. In a panic, the man opened fire with an automatic weapon, injuring several customers and onlookers before being shot by a police sniper."

"My god," Tom said. "What have they done?"

***

As Tim groggily awoke in the cold, dark hospital room, he had two things on his mind—Angela and an unlocked window so he could get the hell out of there. As luck would have it, Angela, too, was sitting in a cold, dark room thinking of him, staring out an unlocked window, but that's not important right now.

Even a laptop would be nice, he thought, then decided to settle for the TV. As it slowly flickered to life, he saw the all-too-familiar glow of TANN's corporate logo filling the screen. Below it was a simple caption: *This station is temporarily unavailable. Tune to channel 42 for more information.*

With that, Tim changed to channel 5, the local news station. There, too, was the obnoxicon. Tim grunted and began flipping through channel after channel, only to be greeted by the same cryptic message. Even the usual TANN over-the-air station was down.

It's going to be that kind of week, eh, Tim thought as he finally reached channel 42. *Blech. More TANN news. Is that all that's on?* He kept flipping.... 43... 44... 45... 50... 100.... Eventually, it rolled back around to channel 1.

After exhausting all the options, he muttered, "I guess this is it. What's the expression? Better bad news than no news? I'm guessing that whoever said that never watched TANN."

> "You're watching TANN, the Terran Alliance News Network, with news updates every hour on the hour," the news reporter said.

Tim groaned, but watched anyway.

> "In Mars news, the Terran government has announced that they have taken control of the terrorist training base in the Connelly Center."

It quickly became obvious that he wasn't going to get any useful information this way.

"The Connelly Center wasn't even finished yet," he muttered, "and I watched it turn into a pile of rubble. So it's a terrorist stronghold now—a training base, even.... Must be somewhere between the pieces of concrete and the hole where they *buried my friends*."

The news report was about as accurate as a third grader doing your tax returns, but it was all he had, so he leaned back, turned off the TV, and smashed the remote against the bed rail until there was nothing left but the shards of the remote to match the shattered remains of his once-beautiful planet.

***

MARCIA slowly opened the door to the hotel room, wine bottle in hand. She hoped to surprise her husband. Of course, the wine was just the beginning. Quietly, she set the bottle on the counter, then went looking for matches to light the dozen or so complimentary red, scented candles that adorned the dining room table.

She was pleased to find a small book of matches in the desk drawer. Cautiously, she lit a match, then lit the candles one at a time. *That takes care of the atmosphere and the drinks,* she thought. *Now all that's left is the negligée.*

She had intentionally tucked her suitcase in the bathroom as she entered, hoping her husband wouldn't notice. As expected, he didn't. To get herself in the mood, she slowly, sensuously let her clothing slide off of her then-naked body to the living room floor, walked into the bathroom, and donned her black lace lingerie—Tom's favorite.

"Tom?" she whispered seductively in a raspy voice. "Oh Tom?"

There was no response. *That's odd.*

"Tom?" she whispered a bit louder, "Tom?" a bit louder still, and finally, "TOM!"

But still no motion. Concerned, she crept into the bedroom, hoping to entice him to join her in the front room... but she was not prepared for what she saw—Tom sitting at the edge of the bed, fully dressed, staring myopically at the TV.

"Tom?" she asked. "Is everything okay?"

He continued to stare. As she turned to face the TV, she saw it—Mars colony—or what was left of it.

She sat down beside her husband and put her arm around him, and for the rest of the evening, they stared at the screen together.

***

"Tim Hanssen?" a man's voice asked.

Tim opened his eyes, turned, and saw a man in a white lab coat standing at the door—possibly the same man he had seen a few hours earlier, but he couldn't be sure.

The slightly balding, quinquagenarian man spoke again. "I have some good news. You're free to go."

"Don't you need to make sure I'm okay first?" Tim asked.

"I'm afraid it's a bit more complicated than that," he explained. "Your insurance won't pay for extended care unless you've shown some indication of serious injury."

"And blacking out isn't a sign of serious injury?"

"I think it is, and you think it is, but they don't seem to think so," he replied. "Don't get me wrong, I don't like those cheap bastards any more than you do, but unless you can pay for additional tests out-of-pocket, I'm afraid there's not much we can do."

"I understand."

"A nurse will come by with a wheelchair to pick you up in a few minutes," the doctor said.

"Thanks, doc."

And with that, he quickly disappeared from the hospital room. A moment later, a nurse appeared with a wheelchair.

"I can walk, thanks."

"Hospital rules," the young man grumbled.

A few minutes of seemingly endless hallways later, Tim reached the entrance to the hospital. As the doors slid slowly open, Tim gazed in horror at the scene that unfolded before him.

Once-mighty skyscrapers lay in piles of rubble. Schools had been burned, and parks were laid to waste. The smog hung low like a dingy blanket over the dirt-covered streets, the walking dead wandering in agony around every corner, and through it all, he heard the din of suffering and saw the feeling of utter sorrow on every face, behind every smile, beneath every frown.

And so, as Angela helped him into the pod car, he looked upon the once glorious city, and with one last ounce of strength, he whispered, “I will avenge you. I will make you whole.”

Chapter Eleven

Two weeks later

THE air in the Lowered Bar Saloon in Adalia reeked of cigar smoke, its seedy, oft drunk inhabitants often choosing to kill themselves in multiple ways simultaneously. So it was with trepidation that Allison Richards made her way from the streets of the sleepy suburbs of Lenora Prime into this gritty underbelly of humanity.

The vibe she felt made her wonder for a moment if she'd found the right place, but a brief glimpse of one man changed all that.

Nate was the descendant of two former hippie wannabes who moved to Mars after the great California wildfires of 2182. Throughout his life, he found himself on the wrong side of the law, but never quite so much as now.

His given name was Ulrich Nathaniel Wanted on Twelve Planets Lawrence, but most people just called him "U.N. Wanted", and indeed, he generally wasn't. His face was legendary, his deeds somewhat dastardly, from bank robberies to political assassinations... but now, he had turned from a life of crime to a life of... well, crime really, but a more noble life of crime nonetheless.

Nate (as only his friends dared call him) was the leader of what he called the Colonial Revolutionary Army Platoon. He had chosen this name specifically for its acronym so that when foreign leaders saw him coming to overthrow them, they would simply say, "Oh, CRAP."

Much to his chagrin, the news media hadn't taken CRAP seriously, so he changed its name to a three-letter acronym, CRA, and suddenly everyone was terrified (though often the non-locals ask what CRA is, and upon being told, still often say, "Oh, CRAP," but that's another story.

Of course, taking over Lenora Prime certainly didn't detract from that terror, but Nate never forgave TANN for the problems they caused the CRA in its early days.

Allison, on the other hand, had always been the model student—sixteen years old, beautiful, kind, and loving—at least before the attack. All that had changed now.

"So what's your problem?" the bartender asked nonchalantly.

"Since the attack, I've been feeling a little bitter. It's exhausting taking care of me little brother, Bobby," she replied, putting on a deep Irish accent that she'd learned from her father. "Do you have any kids?"

"One," he answered. "Why?"

"But you aren't wearing a ring," she said questioningly.

"My wife passed away a few years ago."

"How long did ya stand there starin' at 'er after she died?"

"What kind of question is that?" he bellowed. "I *died* that day."

"I'm sorry. My mother died, too. She died because she stayed too long hovering over our father's body."

The bartender just stared.

"But it's all Captain Forrester's fault. He could have held the door open for two more seconds, and she'd be alive. And the government.... Why did they have to send us to that godforsaken planet in the first place?"

"It's a crying shame," he replied, then tried to go back to mixing drinks.

"So me Aunt Margo offers to take me brother in," she continued. "He isn't too bright. So, of course, I jumped at the chance to escape me burdens... and maybe exact revenge on the bureaucrats who ruined me life ten years ago, if you know what I mean...."

He stared again.

Across the table from Nate were two young men who looked to be in their late twenties or early thirties. They looked surprisingly sane for revolutionaries, so she thought she should get to know them—or at least warn them that Nate was a head case.

As she walked over towards them, the young men stood suddenly and walked towards her. She was totally unprepared for this, and for the first time in her life, she was at a loss for words.

She barely acknowledged their presence until they had already walked past her. Then, realizing her mistake, she turned around and followed them to the bar.

"H-h-hi," she stammered. "I-I'm Allison."

"Hi," the first man said, smiling. "I'm Tom. It's nice to meet you."

They stood there for a moment staring into each other's eyes, then suddenly Tom broke the gaze, shook his head, and regained his composure.

"Oh yeah, and that's Tim," he gushed.

"Nice to meet you both."

And the staring continued.

***

The room glowed red with the dim glow of dying embers from a fire long past, punctuated by the flickering candlelight emanating from the candle atop the table in the center of the room.

Thomas "Sandy" Morgan, so nicknamed for his hair, stood and addressed the five men who sat at his side.

"My friends and colleagues," he began, "today is a great day for all of us on Kinji. With our current cache of supplies, we are only a few missions away from being ready to attack. Soon, all of Kinji will be free from the tyrannical oppression of the United Earth Alliance. Cheers."

With that, he raised his glass in a toast.

"Cheers!" the others shouted, raising their glasses to his.

"As you all know," Sandy continued, "our final objective before the offensive begins is to steal plasma grenades from the storehouse at Tower 12."

"Sir?" one man interrupted.

Luke Kingston, he thought. *That guy makes* **me** *nervous.*

"What is it?"

"I think my team's time would be better spent doing recon on the landing platform."

"Noted. Luke's team will spend the day doing recon. Are there any other concerns?"

The room remained motionless until Sandy broke the stillness by handing out sheets of paper to each member of his executive team.

"In that case, here are your orders. We *ALL* meet at Matthew's Ridge at 0800 hours. Dismissed. Except for Michael. Michael, can I speak with you for a moment?"

Michael Morrison stepped meekly forward. "Yes, sir?"

"Follow Luke. Tomorrow morning, tell me of his every move."

"Is something wrong, sir?"

"I'm not sure. That's what I intend to find out."

***

The night sky over Lenora glowed a deep bluish green as Tom leaned against the glass doors of the Lowered Bar Saloon. The glass was fogged up beyond recognition, and he could see his breath in the air the moment he pushed the doors open.

"After you," he said, gesturing to Allison, who nodded and walked past him into the inky blackness.

"Ooh, a jewelry store," Allison said, pointing.

"Perfect," Tom exclaimed.

Allison crooked her head slightly as she and Tim stared blankly at their companion.

"Oh, sorry," Tom said, noticing their puzzled looks. "My niece, Maria, is graduating from college in a few weeks, and I wanted to get her a graduation present."

"Aww, that's sweet," Allison replied, smiling.

Tom grinned. "Let's see what we can find."

As they stepped into the warmth of the store, the only thing on Tom's mind was finding the perfect gift. *What would say "you've always been my favorite" without saying "your father has been a thorn in my side for fifteen years"? What would say "I love you" without saying "I'm sorry I never visit you, but I'd rather eat broken glass than have even a brief conversation with your mother"?*

The gruff voice of the shopkeeper broke his reverie. "Lemme guess... don't tell me... don't tell me.... Engagement ring? Or wedding ring, perhaps?"

"No, nothing like that," Tom replied. "Graduation present for my niece."

"So you're looking for something in earrings, perhaps? Or maybe a bracelet."

"I was thinking locket," Tom replied, smiling. "Something that says that she'll always be our little girl."

The shopkeeper thought for a moment, scratching his chin. "Ah. I've got it," he said, and walked into the back room.

A moment later, he emerged carrying a small cardboard box.

"She's a real beaut," the shopkeeper told him. "Solid 24 karat gold heart, inlaid with jade, with diamonds around the edge."

"How much?"

"Well, if I were on Earth, about ten thousand Lenoran Argents. Out here on the fringe, though, that sort of money is hard to come by, so I'll let it go for three."

"Three thousand... that seems fair. I'll take it."

As Tom handed him his identitoken, the man smiled and said, "We offer free inscriptions if you'd like."

"Sure. That sounds nice," Tom replied.

"How would you like it made out?" he asked.

Tom pondered this for a moment, then scratched something down on a piece of paper and handed it to the man.

The shopkeeper smiled and nodded.

***

THE near-absolute blackness of Kinji's moonless night was frequently disorienting. Many a man had wandered miles from his camp or had gotten completely lost in the dark just feet from his home.

A skilled tracker, Michael was careful to always keep Luke in sight. He knew that if he lost him, he would not be able to do any useful surveillance before daybreak. The light of Luke's headlamp made a fairly steady beacon, but every now and then, he would turn the wrong direction or walk behind a tree. At those moments, Michael could do nothing but stop and wait for the light to reappear.

Luke had just turned from the primary road onto a smaller path that led towards his shack. Luke's light flickered and died momentarily, then pointed suddenly towards him. Michael froze.

Are the trees thick enough? Does he know I'm here?

"Who's out there?" Luke shouted.

Carefully, Michael bent down in the shadows, grabbed a rock, and threw it high up in the trees.

"Stupid birds," Luke muttered as he turned back to the trail.

Michael breathed a sigh of relief. *Sometimes it pays to have done ten years in black-ops,* he thought.

As they rounded the final bend before Luke's shack, the light went black again. Luke watched and listened in silence. Slowly, the door creaked open, then closed.

Aww. He doesn't want to wake up his wife, Michael thought. *How quaint.*

Suddenly, the rustling of bushes behind him caught his attention. He quickly turned to see what was there. The sharp pain in the back of his head that followed told him that Luke also knew the value of rocks. As he lost consciousness, the last thing he remembered was a bright light shining directly into his eyes.

***

As they stepped out of the shop, the shimmering lights of the Adalia skyline glistened against the azure glow of the night sky.

"So where is this place?" Allison asked.

"About eight blocks due south of here," Tim replied, "through Moore's Park".

Allison shivered. *Moore's Park is littered with the belongings of unlucky souls who walked through it alone at night,* she thought.

"Don't people get killed in there?" she asked tentatively.

"We'll be fine. There are three of us," Tom replied.

As they cautiously approached the crypt at the center of the park, Allison felt her skin crawl. She couldn't tell if it was the cold night air or the dank, musty odor of the concrete tomb that carried with it thoughts of death, but now, more than ever, she wanted desperately to be anywhere but here.

The biggest problem with Moore's Park, she observed, *is that the only way out on the far side is through a dark, narrow alley that leads to the court square. I only hope the Adalian Slasher isn't....*

SNAP! A twig breaking behind them sent Allison two feet in the air as she screamed an earsplitting screech that would have broken glass if there had been any nearby.

"Wha... what was that?" she asked, trembling madly.

"Relax, 'A'. It was probably just a flying squirrel or something," Tom replied.

She paused for a moment, then countered, "but flying squirrels are extinct on Lenora. Have been for a decade. Stupid things kept flying into the path of transport ships."

"Well, maybe a raccoon then," he answered. "Look, I'm sure it's nothing to worry abo—abou—abouuuuut."

The look of terror on Tom's face was mirrored in Allison's, her complexion as ghostly pale as the winter's first snow, until he suddenly smiled a cheesy grin.

"Gotcha!" Tom shouted.

Allison hit him.

As Tom caressed his newly-injured shoulder, Allison's face turned pale again.

"What?" he asked.

She continued this expression, gesturing wildly with her hands, pointing behind him.

"Oh yeah, like I'm going to fall for tha..."

That's when he slumped over, unconscious.

Chapter Twelve

"Mister Morrison! Report!" Sandy shouted as Michael groggily wandered into the narrow clearing.

"There's not much to report, sir," he replied.

"So he didn't do anything suspicious?"

"Oh, I'm sure he did, I just couldn't tell you what exactly...."

"Excuse me?"

"I'm not sure what happened. He just disappeared," Michael said.

Michael could see the look of incredulity in Sandy's eyes as he said this, and braced himself for a tongue lashing....

"What do you mean, disappeared!?!" he asked. "People don't just vanish into thin air."

"He turned off his light, and I couldn't follow him after that," Michael replied.

Upon hearing this, a large vein in Sandy's forehead began to bulge involuntarily, along with his eyes. This, combined with his wild "morning hair", gave the young man an appearance strangely reminiscent of some sort of giant squid.

"You LOST HIM!?!"

"That's how it started. Then the next thing I knew, something hit me on the head... hard," he replied, rubbing his crown.

Sandy nodded and winced. "Don't let him see that you're hurt."

"Yes, sir," Michael replied.

With that, Sandy turned and walked away, pausing only long enough to add, "Everyone convenes in two hours. Put some ice on that. Dismissed."

***

THE morning fog loomed thick in the valley below as Sandy stared out across the grassy plain. Soon, ten dozen revolutionaries would stand here awaiting his command, but for the moment, he was alone.

So there he stood atop Matthew's Ridge, as it was called—little more than a couple of hills, really—and looked out as far as he could see in every direction. To his left were beautiful grassy plains that stretched as far as the eye could see. To his right lay a tree-filled valley, behind him, a desert, and in the distance ahead, a huge military complex controlled by the Keepers.

And so, as the fog rolled slowly out to sea, Sandy stood and watched the tiny specks deep in the forest grow slowly into fuzzy spots, which grew into little lines, which eventually grew into big blurs, and finally resolved themselves into something vaguely resembling people as they drew ever nearer.

One by one, they climbed the ridge from the forest floor below; one by one, they disappeared into the dense underbrush on the lower slope; one by one, they emerged into the clearing and made their way clumsily up to the peak where he awaited their arrival. So began another day, another campaign, another raid, and with luck, another victory over their oppressors... and all the while, Sandy watched... and waited....

And all the while, Sandy was being watched... and waited for....

A few minutes passed, and everyone was present and accounted for... except for Luke. *No matter,* Sandy thought. *Better to limit this mission to people I trust anyway.*

"Men!" he began, "We are about to witness the dawn of a new era—a rebirth of Kinji. No longer will we be prisoners here, but rather, we will be free—free to live our lives, free to fight our own wars or make our own peace, free to lead, free to follow...."

"What we do this day," he continued, "will go down in history as the first of many colonial revolutions. This the beginning of the end... and the end of the beginning. The moment of truth is upon us, my friends. It is up to you to seize the day—to seize the moment—and to take up your swords that one day we might be free. Onward to war! Onward to victory! Onward to freedom!"

The crowd uproariously applauded his rousing speech, then began to mobilize for their final attack on Tower 12.

"Team one," Sandy shouted, "you take the rear entrance. Team two, watch those defense cannons and take them out if they are activated. Team three, you take point. Team four, you're with me. Follow behind team three and help haul equipment after the area is cleared. Let's move!"

With that, team one took up defensive positions around the rear entrance, ready to fire upon anyone who attempted to sneak around behind the invasion force.

The second team carefully approached the first cannon. That's when things went terribly wrong. First, the cannon powered up as they approached and began to fire on their position.

They quickly fired back at the defense cannons, but were hopelessly outgunned and pinned.

A few moments later, the first team began to take fire from behind. Sandy watched in horror as thirty armed Keepers appeared and began firing on them. The first team was well entrenched, and picked off the first dozen or so Keepers with ease, but as they got closer, it became more and more difficult to evade their fire. First one revolutionary fell, then another, until in the end, none remained standing on either side.

That's when dozens more Keepers popped up in every window along the front side of the tower.

"Sir, I think we should retreat," Michael advised.

"Well put," Sandy replied. "Men! Advance in reverse!"

Michael groaned.

***

As he slowly regained consciousness, Tim rubbed his head.

"What the hell happened?" he asked.

Tom lay perfectly still, though his eyes fluttered a bit. The shuffling noise behind him told him that they weren't alone.

"Where are we?" he asked.

"You are safe," came the raspy, mafioso voice from across the room. "You hit your head on the way down. Terribly sorry about that. Otherwise, you're safe, and that's all you need to know."

That's when he got a better look at their surroundings. A single spotlight illuminated their position in what otherwise appeared to be an abandoned warehouse. One man stood a few feet away, presumably the source of the voice. He was backlit to some degree by moonlight streaming in from the solitary window behind him, but his features were indistinct.

Tom slowly stood beside Tim.

"I bet we could take him," he muttered to Tim, a bit too loudly.

The clicking of guns in every corner of the room quickly convinced him otherwise.

"Excuse me for being rude," the shadowed man said. "You can call me Mister X."

"At least it's not Mister E," Tim muttered.

"I heard that," the man replied in a cottony voice. The room immediately became so quiet you could here a neutrino whiz by.

A few moments passed, then the man started chuckling. "Heh. That's funny. Don't you think that's funny, Alberto? 'Cause I think it's funny, and if you don't think it's funny, well...."

"I think it's funny, boss," said a darker voice with a deep Brooklyn accent.

"Did I tell you to speak?" the raspy man interrupted. "If I want you to speak, I'll ask you to speak. Now go. Go get me some coffee. It's too early in the morning for me."

A scurrying sound followed.

"Now, as I was saying," he continued, "I believe you have already met my associate, Nathaniel. I apologize for our unusual manner of meeting, but we had to make sure you weren't being followed."

The sound of jaws hitting the floor echoed through the room.

"We have a... a little task for yous," he continued. "We need to you get some... information... to Kinji. Short story... some of our boys there are planning a little... eh... rebellion. Rocco over there will fill you in on the... er... ah... details...."

With that, a little nerdy guy, spindly and pencil-thin, stood and stepped into the light. His inch-thick, black-plastic-rimmed glasses glistened in the spotlight as he turned his head to look at each of them in a jerky, bird-like fashion.

"It's simple, really," he began. "You'll be delivering some weapons and ammo, as well as providing recon for the uprising. There's a bug in the sensor array over Kinji that causes it to go dark for one minute every 48 hours. If you time things just right and glide in without any extraneous energy emissions until you're close to the ground, you should be able to land safely without being detected."

"Once you're on the surface, you must carefully avoid the security cameras. If the Keepers notice you, they'll open fire, and you'll be little more than a stain on the ground. That said, since you don't have any subcutaneous tags, you'll be able to move around more freely than the natives as long as you avoid the cameras. That's why your involvement is crucial to the success of the uprising."

"Remember, you must do all of your recon and deliveries and get back within 48 hours. Your ship will leave on autopilot exactly 47 hours, 59 minutes after you land. If you aren't on it...."

Tim gulped.

Chapter Thirteen

"It's as if they knew we were coming," Michael spat.

"They did know we were coming," Weasel Willy replied.

Weasel, Sandy thought. *What an apt name. The man had such a mousy-looking face that even if he hadn't been spared the death penalty by ratting out his coworkers, he still could have easily gotten the nickname he bore. Hmm. Could he know something that I don't?*

"What do you know?" Sandy asked.

"Only what everyone else knows. More and more missions are... expected with each passing week. Somebody has to be feeding our plans to the enemy."

"I have a plan," Sandy said. "We're just shy of having enough explosives to complete our mission. We're going to do a little disinformation and use that to track down the leak. I'm going to give each of you your missions and you will pass on completely different fake missions to each of your men. After all is said and done, we'll go to each of the fake locations and look for footprints."

"And what if one of us is the mole?" Luke asked.

The first thought that came to Sandy's mind was *"You mean like yourself?"* but he resisted the urge to say it. It was better for them to believe that he had no backup plan.

"If one of us is the mole," Sandy replied, "we're pretty much screwed anyway, so I'm not gonna worry about it."

"But sir?" Michael interjected.

"But nothing, Michael. You have to trust someone. If you can't trust your closest friends, who can you trust? You'll all receive your orders as soon as I have drafted them. Let's just say that this phase will go for 'shock and awe' and leave it at that."

And with that, the matter was settled, at least for now. As the council left, Michael cornered Sandy.

"Please tell me you don't trust Luke," he asked.

"As surely as I would trust my own brother."

Michael thought for a moment before replying.

"Didn't your brother try to kill you?" he asked.

Sandy simply smiled and walked away.

***

"WE leave for Kinji *tomorrow*," Tim shouted. "How can you even *think* about flying to Mars?"

"There will be plenty of missions. My niece only has one college graduation," Tom replied.

"You do know that if you don't show up and they find you, they'll kill you...."

Tom sat pensively for a moment, glanced down at the package in his lap, then back at Tim, and paused a moment more before speaking.

"Then I guess I'll just have to get back in time."

***

Eight hours later

THE door to the cellar stood open as he approached. The house looked like little more than a slab with a few fractured wooden beams sticking up out of it. Could he be... could she be....

In a heartbeat, his question was answered. As Maria ran out of the stairwell towards him, his heart leapt with joy.

"Maria!" Tom shouted.

In the distance, Tom saw his brother, Joe, standing in the shadows.

"Joe," Tom muttered.

"Good to see you too, Tom," Joe shouted sarcastically.

Maria rolled her eyes.

"How are classes going?" Tom asked.

"They're in tents," she said.

"How hard can it be? It's your last quarter."

"Semester. Wait. What?"

Maria stared at him, puzzled.

"You said they're intense."

She groaned. "They're in *tents*. The buildings are... like... condemned?"

Tom chuckled. "If you tell me that your music classes are in juries, I might just have to shout in pain."

She stared at him again.

"Sorry. Bad joke," he muttered.

"So what brings you all the way out here, Uncle Tom?" she asked.

"I came to give you something," he replied.

As he held out his hands, she quickly reached inside and plucked the locket from them. Its chain seemed to almost instantaneously appear around her neck.

Slowly, with a smile, she read the inscription on the back.

For Maria. You'll always be my angel.

Maria smiled. Suddenly, she began pulling Tom towards the cellar doors.

Tom fought for a minute, then gave up. *What's the use?*

"Hey, Joe," Tom said.

"Hi, Tom," Joe replied.

"Look, I know we've had some... issues... in the past," Tom began. "For my part, I'm sorry. I hope we can let bygones be bygones."

"You're a pompous ass," Joe replied.

"That's fair. That's fair...."

"But for my daughter's sake," Joe interrupted, "I'll try. That kid really adores you, ya know."

"She's a real sweetheart," Tom replied. "If I ever have kids, I hope they're just like Maria."

***

MICHAEL carefully tore the seal on his orders and scanned them briefly.

> *All teams other than Michael and Willy are suspended for the duration of this exercise to minimize the amount of concurrent disinformation that must be tracked individually. The other groups will engage in disinformation exercises at a later date.*
>
> *Michael's team will attack Tower 12 to steal explosives. Willy's team will steal weapons from the cache in Tower 89. These missions will both begin at 1300 hours tomorrow.*
>
> *One of these missions may or may not be a decoy mission to distract the Keep-*

ers while the more important objective is completed.

***

WILLY quickly ripped his orders open, eager to get the disinformation underway.

> *All teams other than Willy and Terry are suspended for the duration of this exercise to minimize the amount of concurrent disinformation that must be tracked individually. The other groups will engage in disinformation exercises at a later date.*
>
> *Willy's team will steal weapons from the cache in Tower 89. Terry's team will plant and later detonate explosives under the cannons immediately adjacent to the launch platform. These missions will both begin at 1300 hours tomorrow.*
>
> *One of these missions may or may not be a decoy mission to distract the Keepers while the more important objective is completed.*

***

TERRY carefully peeled away his envelope, revealing his team's new orders.

> *All teams other than Terry and Adam are suspended for the duration of this exer-*

cise to minimize the amount of concurrent disinformation that must be tracked individually. The other groups will engage in disinformation exercises at a later date.

Terry's team will plant and later detonate explosives under the cannons immediately adjacent to the launch platform. Adam's team will steal weapons and trackers from the warehouse in the mountains between Towers 18 and 19. These missions will both begin at 1300 hours tomorrow.

One of these missions may or may not be a decoy mission to distract the Keepers while the more important objective is completed.

***

ADAM shredded the envelope containing his orders and nearly shredded the orders in the process. He had a feeling in his gut that he would have the opportunity to shoot the mole before too long. He just wished he had some idea who the mole was so he could save everyone the trouble....

All teams other than Adam and Luke are suspended for the duration of this exercise to minimize the amount of concurrent disinformation that must be tracked individually. The other groups will engage in disinformation exercises at a later date.

Adam's team will steal weapons from the warehouse in the mountains between Towers 18 and 19. Luke's team will steal the Bristol Diamond and the accompanying weapons-grade focusing lens from the old warehouse near tower 36. This is crucial for the final phase of our attack. These missions will both begin at 1300 hours tomorrow.

One of these missions may or may not be a decoy mission to distract the Keepers while the more important objective is completed.

***

LUKE staggered into his hut and grabbed the black envelope that had been slipped under the door. He halfway read it through the drunken haze before sending a digital photo of the page to the First Keeper.

All teams other than Luke and Michael are suspended for the duration of this exercise to minimize the amount of concurrent disinformation that must be tracked individually. The other groups will engage in disinformation exercises at a later date.

Luke's team will steal the Bristol Diamond and the accompanying weapons-grade focusing lens from the old warehouse near tower 36. This is crucial for the final phase of our attack. Michael's team will attack Tower 12 to steal explosives.

These missions will both begin at 1300 hours tomorrow.

One of these missions may or may not be a decoy mission to distract the Keepers while the more important objective is completed.

***

As Sandy delivered the final packet of orders, he smiled gleefully, positively giddy over his ingenuity. Now he had only to wait and watch.

Chapter Fourteen

My last stop, Tom thought as he stood shivering in the cold night air, but it was not the cold that made the hair on the back of his neck stand on end as he walked into Marcia's apartment. *Even if she didn't always leave the thermostat set on 68, I would probably still be shaking. Just the very* ***thought*** *of giving Marcia this news is enough to make anyone shiver.*

A few moments later, Marcia came in.

"Oh, hi, honey," she said. "Good trip?"

"Yeah, I guess. Listen, Marcia, you know how I said I was thinking of joining the rebellion?"

"Yeah, I remember, but why would you want to be a groupie for a rock band?" she asked, an impish grin decorating her dimpled face.

"Not that rebellion, Marcia," he replied. "I decided to join the resistance. I'm going on a mission and I doubt I'll be coming back."

"Of course you'll come back. You have to come back."

"And I don't think we should stay married."

"You... want a divorce?" she sobbed.

"It's a dangerous war, Marsh. I don't want you to be a war widow. I want you to be happy. I want you to find someone and marry him and live a long, happy life with him for the rest of your days."

"But I've *already* found someone who I want to live with for the rest of my days," she replied, sobbing.

"It's just... you have to trust me. It's just better this way."

"I... I don't understand," she said, clearly fighting back tears. "Is it something I said? Something I did? Did you meet someone else?"

"No, no, and no. I'm sorry, Marcia. It's not you, and it's not me, either."

"Then what is it?" she pleaded.

"Time and distance... change people," Tom replied. "We don't mean for it to happen, but it does. That's just the way life is, no matter how much we wish it weren't so."

"I love you," she whispered.

Tom's eyes grew distant and cold, a hollow look that cut through the room like a longsword through paper. Then he closed his eyes and sighed.

"I know, Marcia," he said. "I love you, too."

And with those words, he walked somberly from the room, knowing that, for better or worse, it was over.

***

As the sun began to set, the revolutionary council met once again, this time in the courtyard outside their usual meeting hall.

"Gentlemen, how were the raids?" Sandy asked.

"We were attacked," Michael said.

"So were we," Luke added, "but I don't think it was an ambush. I don't think they expected us. We didn't make it into the warehouse, though."

"They *did* expect us," Michael replied.

"Wait," Terry interrupted. "I thought you two were both mothballed for today."

"There's a bit more to it than that," Sandy replied. "Each of you only knew about two missions. Only two missions were attacked."

"So that means that it must have been someone on Michael's team," Luke suggested. "After all, no one on my team knew about Michael's mission."

"Fair enough. One member of my team *did* walk in on me while I was reading my orders," Michael admitted.

"Who?" Sandy asked.

"Mat Fisher, sir."

"Bring him here," Sandy ordered. "Prepare the firing squad!"

One by one, the firing squad wandered in, and Sandy handed them their orders.

A few minutes passed while Michael tried to find Mr. Fisher.

Mat, Sandy thought. *That's rich. He was away on a recon mission all day yesterday. Either Michael didn't notice one of his own officers was missing or he's playing Luke like a cheap tambourine....*

Finally, after what seemed like an eternity, Michael returned with Mat.

"Mat," Sandy began, "is it true that you saw Michael's orders yesterday?"

Michael looked at him and nodded slowly, as if to suggest the appropriate reply.

"Sir, yes, sir," Mat replied.

"Tambourine," Sandy muttered.

"What's that?" Mat asked.

"Never mind," Sandy replied. "And is it also true that you sent those orders to the Keepers?"

"What?"

"You have your orders," Sandy instructed the firing squad. "Who would like to do the honors?"

Luke quickly stood up. “It would be my pleasure to dispose of this... filth.”

As if on cue, the leader of the firing squad tossed Luke a sword in its sheath. A mere moment later, he drew the sword.

“Ready!” he shouted.

The firing squad snapped from parade rest to attention.

“Aim!” he shouted.

Remaining relatively relaxed in stance, the firing squad drew their weapons and pointed them in Mat’s general direction.

“Fire!” he shouted.

At that, the entire squad spun on their heels, snapped into ready with weapons aimed squarely at Luke, and fired.

Luke collapsed to the floor. With his last ounce of strength, he looked up at Adam.

“Help me, old friend,” he whispered.

Adam nodded silently, then put a bullet between Luke’s eyes.

Mat breathed a visible sign of relief. “You knew. You all knew.”

“You weren’t even in the valley,” Sandy replied. “You couldn’t have seen the orders. I’d be a lousy leader if I didn’t know everything that was going on in our company.”

The other leaders laughed.

“Man, Terry,” Sandy said. “You should have seen the look on Luke’s face when you said you thought he was mothballed.”

“How did you know it wasn’t Michael?” Adam asked.

“Simple,” Sandy replied. “Everyone knew about two missions and knew that one could be a decoy, but didn’t know which one. I already knew who the mole was. I just needed to make sure. I could narrow any attack down to two people easily, but the decoy ensured that I could narrow it down to only one in certain cases.”

"How?" Adam asked. "If they didn't know which mission was a decoy, why did that make any difference?"

"Because Luke was the decoy," Michael replied, interrupting.

Sandy turned and looked at him in surprise.

"Don't look so surprised," Michael continued. "I knew for certain as soon as Luke said he had been attacked, but hedged his bets. Last time I checked, that warehouse was empty and abandoned, although I suppose there could be *something* hidden there. There certainly wouldn't be much in terms of guards, though... unless it was an attack out of courtesy to take the heat off of the mole."

Sandy smiled. "You're gonna be a great strategist one day."

"Too late," Michael joked.

"You forgot one thing, though," Sandy said.

"What's that?"

"Those secret missions Mat has been going on for the past week."

"What about them?" Michael asked.

"Let's just say I'm quite certain that the warehouse was abandoned until last night...."

"You sneaky bastard," Michael replied, grinning.

"Now, on to our final piece of business," Sandy continued. "We need to find a replacement for Luke...."

***

"You made it," Tim said as he watched Tom climb into the shuttle cockpit through the lower docking ring.

"Yeah. I'm here," Tom replied

"So... how was Marcia?" Tim asked, smiling at what seemed totally obvious....

"I don't want to talk about it."

I guess that rules out the going away sex.... "That bad?" Tim asked.

"I asked her for a divorce," Tom replied.

As the metaphorical shoe dropped, Allison poked her head in.

"Hi, guys. How's it going?" she asked.

"I don't want to talk about it," they both replied in unison.

"Ooookay," she said as she gingerly pulled her head back out of the cabin, slinked off into the rear compartment, and shut the door behind her.

A moment later, her voice once again filled the cabin through the comm system. "Buckle up, guys. We lift off in ten... nine..."

"This is it," Tim said.

"six... five..."

"You ready?" Tom asked.

"I'm ready. Are you ready?"

"I'm ready."

"Two... one..."

"Oh, shiiiiiiiiit!" Tim shouted as the engines fired, shoving him hard into the seat. As he lost feeling in his feet, his only coherent thought was *"Why don't they make these chairs softer?"*

"Folding!" Allison shouted as they approached the Lenoran folding gate.

A moment later, they were sitting behind one of the outer gas planets just beyond Kinji.

A loud metallic thud told them that things were on schedule. As the docking port opened, eight CRA soldiers climbed up and into the cabin, filed calmly past them, and exited into the rear compartment, pausing only momentarily to allow Allison to slip back into the cockpit.

A moment later, a thud and a gentle clanging sound told them that they had separated from the other transport and were once again on their way.

"What are they for, again?" Tim asked.

"They're supposed to... how did they put it... cover our posteriors... or something," Tom replied, grinning.

"Great," Tim chided. "The Kinji forces will never spot three people doing recon if they're surrounded by eight soldiers wearing sand-colored fatigues in the middle of a *tropical rain forest....*"

"Oh, yeah," Tom replied. "Who wants to bet we end up covering them?"

Allison and Tim chuckled.

"Can we get a status check?" a voice shouted over the comm.

Allison stared at the guidance computer. "We'll be over Kinji in about twenty seconds. Hold on to your lunch."

"Engaging radar jamming," Tim added.

With that, an odd hum filled the ship, followed by a clunk. Finally, the hum diminished somewhat.

"Active scattering field engaged," Tim noted. "Sensor nets should go down any time now."

"Time until satellite network shutdown," Allison said, then paused before adding, "about 20 seconds."

A few moments passed as they crept towards the planet. As they watched, the defense satellites' interior lights blinked, indicating that they were in diagnostic mode.

"Satellites are now in diagnostic mode," Tom said, almost cheering. "Atmospheric insertion in five... four... three... two...."

As his count reached one, the nose of the shuttle began to glow a dim, reddish color. The din from the air rushing past the ship's underbelly quickly grew from a whisper to an almost deafening roar as they plummeted through the atmosphere.

"We're coming in hot," Tim said, straining to be heard over the noise. "This ship wasn't designed for these sorts of aerobatics."

"She'll hold," Tom replied. "I once did the Kessel run in under 50 parsecs."

"Oh, man! I loved that movie," Tim shouted. "But isn't a parsec a measure of distance?"

"It's a chase," Tom replied. "I started with a lead of under 50 parsecs and didn't get caught."

"Oh," Tim said, chuckling. "Now, it makes sense. So... wait... you mean somebody made up an *actual* space race just so that a line from a movie would make sense?"

"Yeah," Tom replied. "I swear some people just have way too much free time."

"Planetary impact in fifteen seconds," Allison said.

"Damn, I wish you wouldn't put it that way," Tim scolded.

"Sorry. Planetary *contact* in ten... nine... eight... seven... six...."

"Port engine failure!" Tom shouted.

Tim looked at Tom for a moment, then both shouted, "Oh, shiiiiiiiiiiiiiit!"

Chapter Fifteen

THE unmistakable odor of bleach filled the air as Marcia stepped into the lobby of Valley Memorial. When she reached the information window, a young girl greeted her with a smile.

Probably barely out of high school, she thought.

"I have an appointment with Dr. Alfonse," Marcia said.

"Yes, Marcia, right?" the girl replied, brushing her long red hair slowly out of her eyes.

She nodded.

"Step right through those doors," she said, pointing to a distant pair of double doors. "He's expecting you."

Marcia cautiously stepped away from the window and stared at the double doors at the end of the hall. Their mottled finish gave them a dated look, their puke-green color, doubly so. In short, she thought they looked as though they had been on Mars when the Berlin Wall fell.

Sighing, she trudged through the creaking doors and over to the nurses' station. A few moments later, the doctor entered from one of the examining rooms to her left.

"Ah, Marcia, how good to see you. We have much to talk about," he said, gesturing for her to enter examining room 3.

"So what's the call? Endometriosis?"

"No, no, nothing like that."

"So, what is it, doc?"

"Marcia, Marcia, Marcia.... I don't quite know how to tell you this...."

"How about the short version?"

"You're pregnant."

Marcia's eyes bulged and her jaw fell agape.

"How about the long version?"

"You're six weeks pregnant... with twins."

With that, she simply stood there staring into space.

"Marcia? Marcia?"

***

As the port engine sprang to life, the shuttle screamed a metallic shriek, then lurched suddenly a couple of times, coming to rest with a loud thud. As the engines shut down, the hull let out one final low-pitched growl, then spoke no more.

"Tim?" Tom asked.

"Yes?" Tim replied.

"Is this heaven?"

"If it is, I'd hate to see hell," Allison said, interrupting. "Listen, guys, I'd love to stay and chat, but we're gonna have Keepers on our backs in about five minutes if we don't high-tail it out of here."

"She's right," Tim said.

"You would take her side," Tom replied.

With that, Tom swung the hatch open and proceeded to fall headfirst into a thicket.

"Ow," Allison whispered, snickering, as she carefully lowered the ladder.

In the distance, she watched as the CRA soldiers headed off into the surrounding forest. Just as the soldiers were about to disappear from sight, one turned and addressed them.

"You guys coming?" he shouted.

"What's your name, soldier?" she quipped.

"I'm Kirk, ma'am," he replied tentatively.

"Well, Kirk," Allison shouted, "I'll come when I'm good and ready."

"Not unless you want me dropping on top of you," Tim countered.

"Yeah, yeah, yeah," she replied, stepping down to the ground.

As Tim dropped to the ground behind her, the ship shimmered and faded. Then, the trio scurried off into the forest after their CRA companions.

***

The sky was dark over New Paradise. *It's going to rain tonight,* she thought. *If ever there were a good day to not be on the surface, it would be today.*

The rarified, highly sulfuric Martian atmosphere made Earth's so-called acid rain seem like a light vinaigrette by comparison. When it rained, life basically stopped. You couldn't go outside unless you wore a hazmat suit, so you couldn't easily go home if you were at work or go to work if you were at home. People lucky enough to live near the subrail could often take a covered walkway home. For everybody else, it was a living nightmare. Fortunately, it only rained about three or four times a year, and usually only for a few hours.

Today, though, was different. The dust from the attacks was playing games with the weather. Forecasters predicted three days of hard rain in a row without stopping.

*Yeah. It's a good day to be somewhere else. Or more like a good **week** to be somewhere else....*

Thus, Angela was particularly happy to be leaving when she stepped aboard the T.S. Pacifica, bound for Svoboda Station. As she stepped through the doorway, the Captain got on the P.A. system.

"May I have your attention?" he began. "I've just received word that this shuttleport is closed for security reasons. They're letting us leave, but only if we leave right now. If you're already on board, great. If not, I extend our sincerest apologies, and we will make every attempt to reschedule your flight at your earliest convenience."

Angela sat calmly down in her seat and buckled her seatbelt, a cold chill running up her spine. Slowly, the ship lifted off the pad and began its ascent. That's when she saw them....

***

ALLISON turned as they approached the clearing.

"Did you hear something?" she asked Tim.

Tim slowed his pace for a moment and stared at her.

"I thought I heard leaves rustling," she explained.

"You mean like this?" he asked, stomping on the leafy path beneath his feet.

Allison chuckled for a moment, then backhanded his chest.

"Smartass," she said.

Her sentence was punctuated by an odd whining noise.

"What the..." Tim shouted.

Suddenly, the clearing was filled with a bright flash of light as a flash grenade exploded nearby, its purveyor nowhere to be seen.

A moment later, the sound of gunfire filled the air. In the distance, four Keepers stood behind a tree diagonally across the clearing from their position, their white body armor glistening in the light that filtered through the trees.

Tim immediately jumped for cover behind a nearby tree, followed by Tom. Allison hit the ground. *Hard.* About thirty feet ahead of her, three CRA soldiers crouched behind a tree stump, pinned down by gunfire, unable to move.

One soldier pulled his rifle from his shoulder and stood to take aim. As his commanding officer tried to yank him back to the ground, his chest turned black, a phase pistol blast charring him fatally. He fell to the ground in a slump.

"Shit!" his CO yelled, then turned and looked behind him.

At that moment, Allison looked into his eyes and saw something she never expected to see.... *Fear?* She wondered... *or was it something else?*

"Hey, you! Can you see to throw a grenade?" he shouted.

After a moment of confusion, Allison realized that although she could clearly make out the erect Keepers through the trees from her vantage point, they might not yet have noticed her around the corner.

"I think so," she shouted.

Suddenly, she found herself staring at a plasma grenade from about six inches away.

"Eeek!" she squealed. "What do I do with this?"

"Pull the pin and throw it!" the man shouted. "Fast!"

She did so. A moment later, the bright explosion told them it was over... for now....

***

ANGELA stared blankly out the window of the shuttle. She found it odd that in an era when one could level entire continents from space, the Terran forces still found it necessary to send aerial assault craft to reinforce their total subjugation of the indigenous people.

They came slowly at first—one, then two, then ten, then a hundred. Entire blocks were leveled before the first shots were fired in response.

The shuttle slowly crept through the ionosphere, the sky turning from a deep blue to black, then suddenly red. Where her home town once stood, a giant fireball arose. The explosions quickly engulfed her home, followed by the farms, then the city, then the spaceport that she just left—now little more than a giant scorch mark on the ruddy Martian surface.

A moment later, the thunk of metal clamps latching on to the ship's airlock told her that they had docked.

"Please remain in your seats," the pilot announced. "For security reasons, all passengers are being thoroughly screened at the gate, so it's going to take a little longer than usual to disembark."

This should be interesting, she thought.

"At this time, the first three rows may proceed to the exit," the announcement continued.

Angela stood cautiously, grabbed her bags, and walked through the jetway.

I wonder what they're looking for, she thought. *Do they really think there are terrorists on Mars? Smugglers? Are they looking for a scapegoat? What's with the armed guards?*

As she neared the door, a struggle broken her silent reverie. A man, probably in his twenties, broke away from the crowd and started running. A split second later, a guard reached out and grabbed his arm.

"I'm innocent!" the young man shouted as the guard slammed him face-first into an artificial concrete pillar.

"Yeah, sure ya are," the guard muttered. "Tell it to the judge."

A chill ran up her spine....

Chapter Sixteen

A scuffle outside had Sandy on his guard faster than a gunshot in Beverly Hills. As he peered out the window, a phase pistol blast shattered the glass over his head.

Sandy uttered a few obscenities and ducked. When he again peered out, he saw a Keeper standing outside the window with the phase pistol pointed directly in his direction.

Sandy and the Keeper just stood there, transfixed, pistols aimed in each other's direction, looking into each other's eyes and seeing fear.

The next thing Sandy saw was the young man's body slumping to the ground, revealing....

Who the hell is that?

"Friend or foe?" Sandy shouted through the now-broken window.

"Would I admit it if I were the latter?" Tim replied, entirely straight-faced.

Sandy laughed.

***

Angela stumbled, exhausted, into the vidlink booth. As she keyed in Tim's secure portable number, she wondered how secure it was.

Oh well. No point worrying about it now.

"Tim?" she asked out of habit.

"Do I look like Tim?" Tom replied.

"Where's Tim?"

"He's... busy," Tom replied, glancing cautiously in the general direction of Sandy's shack.

"If you could give him a message, I'd really appreciate it. Tell him I'm okay. I got out before the attack."

"Attack?" Tom asked incredulously.

"You... didn't hear?" Angela replied. "No, of course not. You're off in the middle of nowhere doing who knows what. Earth just tightened the reins on Mars. It was brutal."

Tom stared at the screen in silence for a moment, then asked, "Where are you now?"

"Svoboda Station," she replied. "I'm trying to get the hell out of here."

"Good plan."

"Tell Tim that I love him," Angela said. "Gotta run. My transport is about to leave. I'll meet him on the Moon in New Albany."

"I will. You take care of yourself," Tom replied.

With that, she closed the vidlink channel and started jogging to her gate.

***

Sandy stood at the front of the battered shack and prepared to address the team leaders.

"Thanks for the intel, Tom, Tim," he said as he shuffled the stack of papers on the podium. "The aerial force will arrive within sensor range in three hours. We have to be ready to blow the sensor grid so they can land. The one-minute blackout window isn't enough to get them all on the ground."

"Are we done here?" Tim asked.

"Go," Sandy replied. "Be safe."

With that, Sandy shuffled his papers again and whistled to get everyone's attention. The room grew quiet, and he stepped up to the podium.

"This is how it's going to go down," he began. "Our target is the Keepers' main base of operations. Terry, your team is red team. There are three communications arrays. We've already planted explosives at both of the remote arrays. The third one is located on top of the main keep."

Sandy pulled out a laser pointer and aimed it at a crudely drawn map hanging on the wall behind him.

"Your job," he continued, "is to take out the array with a shoulder-fired rocket. We have teams standing by at the other arrays to blow them at the same time. Once you have taken out the main array, wait on the roof to help green team, then move in on your secondary target—the shuttle launch area."

"For those of you who don't know," he said, training the laser pointer on a sketch of the shuttle pad, "thanks to Terry's team, we have explosives planted under the pad, but we need to make sure all of the shuttles are completely disabled, pad or no pad. Once you're at the pad, I want you to set off the explosives. Light it up, then use missiles to finish the job."

Terry nodded his understanding.

"Willy," Sandy continued, "your team is blue team. Once communications are down, you're going to come in from the front. Expect heavy resistance."

Willy nodded. "I'm an electrical engineer. I live for resistance."

Everyone laughed.

"Michael," Sandy said, "you're leading the green team. As soon as communications are cut, it will be safe to enter the utility shack around back. Once you get in there, pull the master breakers. Then join the red team on the roof. They'll help you drop in through the ventilation system before they head to the launch pads."

"Lock and load," Michael replied.

"Adam, your team is black team. You'll be the follow-up team. Once the facility is secured, your job is to take control of the planetary security grid, then use it to take out the remaining Keepers and take over the other stations."

Adam nodded.

"Are there any questions?" Michael asked.

"What if they surrender?" Terry asked.

"Tag them with trackers," Sandy replied. "We don't want them alerting Earth. Any other questions?"

"When do we leave?" Michael asked.

Everyone chuckled.

***

TIM jogged along beside Tom and Allison.

"How long before the launch window?" he shouted.

"Eight minutes!" Allison replied.

As they stepped into the clearing where the shuttle lay, a crackling sound put them on their guard. No sooner had the shuttle disabled its holographic cloak than the air erupted with the whine of phase pistol fire.

Tom knocked Allison to the ground as Tim dove behind the now extended entry ladder. It afforded him little protection, however, and a moment later, a phase pistol shot grazed his left arm.

"Jeez!" he shouted as he drew his phase pistol to return fire.

As Tim fired a few shots into the thicket, Tom dashed across the clearing under the shuttle and ducked behind a landing strut.

That's when they saw it—not one Keeper, but twelve Keepers, armed to the teeth.

"Get Allison inside," Tom shouted, blindly firing shots to draw the Keeper's fire away from his companions. One of those shots hit its mark as a Keeper fell with a thud.

Tim quickly grabbed Allison by the waist and hoisted her halfway up the ladder. She scrambled up into the shuttle's underbelly and Tim followed.

"Come on, Tom!" Tim shouted, sticking his head out only briefly.

Tom looked briefly at the Keepers, then at the ladder, then back at the Keepers, and finally back to the ladder again. He decided to make a run for it.

His feet padded quickly across the open ground. *Just a few feet farther*, he thought. He could almost touch the ladder. As his hands made contact, an odd sensation washed over him.

Tom looked down. The charred remains of his uniform looked like a tree after a lightning strike. "Oh, my," he said in confusion as he slumped to the ground.

Chapter Seventeen

ANGELA collapsed into her seat just as the stewardess made the announcement that they had been cleared for departure.

The stewardess caught her eye. Something about her seemed familiar. *Could it be? From the last flight?*

"Excuse me, miss?" she asked. "Were you the stewardess on flight 983 from the surface?"

The stewardess laughed. "No, that's my twin sister. I get that a lot."

She paused for a moment, apparently deep in thought.

"Wait," she continued. "Were you on that flight?"

"Yes. Why?" Angela asked.

"You're really lucky," she replied. "It almost didn't get off the ground. The head of the Martian government was on that flight, so they let him leave under diplomatic immunity rules."

"They knew?"

"Knew what?" the stewardess asked.

"Are you saying the Martian government knew about the attack and didn't warn anyone?"

"That's not the worst part."

"How much worse can it get?" Angela asked.
The stewardess just grimaced in reply.

***

"TOM!" Allison shouted.

Tim tried to hold her back, but she was already falling head first through the opening. Tim watched, jaw agape as she spun in midair, pulled out two phase pistols, and fired eight shots into the crowd of Keepers. Five Keepers fell.

She hit the ground with a thud and continued to fire. Keeper after Keeper collapsed in a heap until none were left.

"Holy shit!" Tim shouted. *Remind me not to get on **her** bad side....*

A few moments later, she was hauling Tom's unconscious figure into the shuttle.

***

TERRY kept his head down. His team waited in the underbrush while he slipped stealthily into the clearing that surrounded the main Keeper base.

The communications dish was jet black, which would have made it almost invisible against the night sky were it not for the night vision goggles he was wearing. They lit up the wrought iron structure like a deer in headlights.

Pressing the base of the tripod-mounted missile launcher against the ground with one arm, he lay face down and cautiously trained the laser sight on his target.

Just a little lower, he thought. *I need to hit the mounting plate at the base. If I aim too high, the explosive round might rip through the thin skin of the dish and keep going. They could probably still get a signal out then. If I aim too low, it might clip the edge of the building and detonate before it even reaches the dish. Right... about... there....*

With that, he pulled the trigger. He quickly covered his ears as a missile shot out from the launcher, following the laser beam to its destination.

The explosion shook the ground. As soon as it subsided, Terry pulled out three flares and shot them into the air to signal that their task was done. By the light of the flares, he could see that the satellite dish lay in a molten heap.

"Okay, people!" he snapped. "To the roof! Let's moooooove!"

***

THE radio blared. *Michael, you have a go.*

With that, Michael ran so hard that he thought his lungs would collapse as his team scrambled across the clearing towards the utility shack.

As they slammed the door open, an alarm started blaring.

"Shit!" he shouted. "The door has an alarm!"

His men quickly began pulling the master power breakers in each breaker box.

When they reached the fifth and final box, as they pulled the breaker, the alarm klaxon stopped its cacophonous wail, the eerie silence rushing over them like nausea after eating bad shellfish.

"That's it. To the roof!" he shouted.

***

THE red team stood patiently on the roof waiting for their cargo.

Terry watched as Michael's team climbed the ladder that ran up the side of the building. Suddenly and without warning, gunfire erupted nearby. The side of the building began to spray shards of concrete as bullets ricocheted off its pockmarked facade.

Off in the distance, a Keeper stood, dressed in black, barely visible against the surrounding landscape. Of course, with the Keeper's night vision gear, he looked more like a small lighthouse than a person, the bright green "light" blinking and flashing in the distance as he turned his head.

"Optics off!" Terry shouted to Michael's green team.

No sooner had he said this than one of the bullets connected with its target, and one of Michael's men screamed in pain and fell backwards, knocking three more to the ground. Michael quickly dove over the top ledge, collapsing in a heap on the other side.

After Terry helped Michael's remaining team member up to the roof, he dropped to lie prone on the rooftop, plasma rifle firmly in hand. Slowly, cautiously, he lined up his sights on the Keeper. He pulled the trigger slowly, carefully, to avoid throwing off his aim.

The plasma rifle erupted with a red flash. A moment later, it became obvious that it had done its job. When the wash faded from Terry's night vision optics, he could plainly make out the Keeper's night vision optics resting several feet from the Keeper's body, his head neatly severed from his torso.

"Bring 'em up," Terry shouted.

"Hey, Will," Michael added, "take Katie and get her some help. The rest of you, come on up here."

One man shouted back, "Sir, I twisted my ankle in the fall."

"Okay, then, Ralph," Michael answered, "*You* limp with Katie for help. Will, Joey, you're with me."

While the two men scurried up the ladder and onto the roof, Terry kicked in a skylight and anchored himself to help lower Michael's team through it. The rest of his team planted their feet similarly.

Just to be safe, Terry lowered a small video camera into the opening and panned it around. Seeing no signs of Keeper activity, he waved Michael's team on.

Within moments, Michael, Will, and Joey had clamped cords to their safety harnesses and had climbed cautiously through the broken out skylight.

Terry and his team slowly worked the ropes until they went slack.

"They're clear," he said to his team. "Let's go get that platform."

***

MICHAEL's feet hit the floor with a thud. As he looked around, the dull glow of emergency lighting revealed what appeared to be a shower facility. A sign on the wall of the nearest stall read, "Swipe water ration card here." He shuddered to think about it. *Compared to this, living by the stream doesn't seem so bad,* he thought.

As they neared the door, a shadow caught his eye. *Someone is about to take a shower,* he thought.

"Hide!" he shout-whispered hoarsely.

The troops all scattered in different directions. As the door opened, Michael could barely make out the figure of a young woman—*probably in her twenties or so,* he thought—walking across to one of the stalls. She began to undress. Slowly, almost seductively, she unbuttoned her blouse and jeans. They fell to the floor like a feather wafting through the air. As she reached behind her to unhook her bra... she suddenly paused.

"I wonder if this works," the girl said to no one in particular as she reached down to the ground and picked up her shirt.

She reached into her shirt pocket and pulled out a small identitoken. Cautiously, the girl swiped it through the reader, but the reader remained dark.

"Damn," she whispered to herself.

"Damn," Michael whispered.

The girl froze.

Chapter Eighteen

TERRY stumbled. He hadn't expected to trip over anything in the open field on his way to the launch platform, but there it was.... *But what is it?*

As he stooped down to examine it, he had a bad feeling in his gut. He wasn't sure why it wasn't buried, but the object's significance could not be overlooked.

"Plasma mines!" he shouted. Keep your eyes out.

Cautiously, they crept across the open field, watching for any indentations in the surface that might indicate a buried incendiary device. As they neared the pad, about forty feet away from the first support post, they reached a point at which they could walk no farther—a ring all the way around the platform, several feet wide.

This wasn't here before, Terry thought.

"This is it," Terry said. "End of the line. Can somebody scan for our explosives and see if they're still under the platform?"

A young man in his thirties stepped forward. "Yes, sir," Kirk replied, pulling a laptop out of his knapsack.

"Are we ready to blow this thing?" Terry asked.

"You have a go. The explosives are right where we left them," Kirk answered.

The click was gratifying as Terry pushed the button... then... nothing....

"Are you sure they're there?" Terry asked.

Kirk checked his readings. "The bombs tell me that they've detonated. I'm not sure what's going on, sir."

Terry reached into his knapsack and pulled out a pair of binoculars. With them, he could just make out the plastic explosive packs that should have been engulfed in flames by now. He could also see the detonators blinking. Last, but not least, he could see the trigger wires hanging limply beside the detonators, no longer attached to the blasting caps....

"They disabled them. They knew we were coming," Terry asked.

"Now what?" Kirk asked.

Cautiously, Terry took a bag of stolen trackers from his backpack and began taping several of them inside a pair of magnetic boots.

"Now, we wait."

***

WILLY crouched at the base of the tree while his team members crouched behind nearby trees and rocks. The main base entrance lay just ahead.

"What's the time?" Willy asked.

"Any minute now," a girl whispered from nearby.

"What do you mean, any minute?" he whispered back.

"Well, the air strike should have been here about three minutes ago," she replied.

"They're late?" he whispered angrily.

Willy shifted uncomfortably. *They aren't coming,* he thought. *What do we do now?*

"Sir?" she asked.

Is it over? Are we alone? Can we do this without them?

"Sir?" she asked again.

"Yes, Joanna?" he asked, staring blankly into the distance.

"I think we should move," she said. "The power has been cut. If we wait too long, they'll have it fixed and we won't get anywhere."

She's right, but without the air strike to take out the gun towers, we'll be helpless.

"Sir?" she asked. "Sir?"

***

As the rear doors shut, the shuttle shook violently.

"What was that?" Allison asked.

Tim looked out the window and saw his biggest fear: ten rail guns pointed directly at the shuttle.

"We're under fire, and it's gonna hurt," Tim replied. "We have to leave. NOW."

"We can't take off now!" Allison replied. "The defense satellite blackout doesn't begin for another forty-two seconds."

"We can probably avoid the satellites if we stay close to the ground," Tim said as he pressed the button to retract the landing struts.

The shuttle hovered at ground level, then spun around and shot apart one of the rail guns. Moments later, they were flying at about fifty feet off the ground, just above the treetops.

"Ten seconds," Allison shouted.

That's when they saw it. They were in a valley. More to the point, the valley had an end. The waterfall ahead of them would have been very beautiful had they been enjoying it safely from the ground. However, hurtling towards it at 600 miles per hour, the waterfall seemed far less pleasant.

"Five seconds," she shouted.

The sheer cliffs loomed larger in their windows.

"Four!"

Tim began twitching nervously. The walls of the valley were growing narrow, and the waterfall seemed to jump out at him like a jack-in-the-box, though he knew it was an illusion. Slightly more terrifying were the two low-altitude security hovercraft heading in their direction from both sides of the canyon.

"Three!"

The waterfall was closer now. He could barely make out what appeared to be a barrel floating near the edge.

"Two!"

Tim realized that, much to his horror, he could not only make out the barrel clearly, but also the idiot riding inside it.

"One!"

Suddenly, Tim pulled the controls back as hard as he could.

"Zero!"

The shuttle screamed as metal stretched in ways that it was never intended to stretch, while Tim fought to remain conscious in spite of the G-forces that tugged at him.

Slowly, the shuttle's inertial dampening kicked in and things stabilized a bit.

Over his shoulder, Tom stirred.

***

"HERE's the plan," Terry said.

Cautiously, he picked up his bag of what were now magnetic tracker boots.

"There's an access tunnel from the roof to a service catwalk above the shuttle launch pads," he continued. "All we have to do is get close enough, and these magnets should stick to the hull."

"I don't understand," Kirk replied. "Aren't we shutting *down* the satellite defense system?"

Terry simply smiled.

Not yet.

***

"LET'S move," Willy finally shouted.

No sooner had they stepped out into the open clearing than he came to regret that decision.

The guard towers sprang immediately to life. Rail gun rounds showered them with dirt as they struck the ground just inches away.

"Fall back!" he shouted as they scrambled for cover.

As they cowered behind a boulder, Joanna slowly stood, aiming a shoulder-fired missile launcher over the top, pointed it in the general direction of the guard tower, and fired.

Suddenly, the ground shook beneath them.

"Did I do that?" she asked.

"I don't think so," Willy replied. "Too big!"

That's when they heard five more distant booms as six supersonic gliders crossed overhead.

"Looks like somebody called in the cavalry after all!" Joanna screamed.

As she said this, the two nearest guard towers simultaneously shattered in a shower of concrete shards. Moments later, the two remaining towers flared up in a giant fireball. The barracks were next, flashing brightly as explosions rocked the area.

"I think that's our cue," Willy said, smiling.

The radio crackled to life a moment later.

"Sorry about the delay, guys," the disembodied voice said. "We missed the last satellite glitch window, so we had to wait for the next one."

Willy rolled his eyes. "Well, your timing couldn't be better."

***

MICHAEL jumped as the explosions rocked their location. The first salvo shook them up a bit, the second slightly less. The third round, however, brought down little bits of plaster from the ceiling.

"Eee!" the girl screamed.

Michael stepped forward, weapon at ready.

"Please!" she pleaded. "Don't hurt me. I'm just an IT director."

Should I shoot her? I've always wanted to shoot an IT director, Michael thought. *Nah. Too much paperwork.*

"Come on. You're going to help us." he said forcefully.

"Why should I help you? You're all criminals!"

"No more than you," Michael replied, smiling gently.

She stared at him in silence for a moment, looked at him with a puzzled look, then said, "I believe you. I don't know why."

Michael sighed, stared deeply into her eyes, and said, "I'm sorry."

"What do you mean?" she asked as the tranquilizer dart stuck into her belly.

As she slumped to the floor, Michael lowered his weapon, reached over, picked up her shirt, and covered her with it, pausing only briefly to grab the identitoken from the ground beside her.

Chapter Nineteen

As they crawled onto the catwalks overlooking the launch pad, Terry took one of the magnetic tracker boots out of his bag. Taking it carefully in his hand, he gently dropped it in the general direction of the shuttle's nose cone.

It bounced harmlessly to the ground.

"They're not sticking," Terry said. "What's wrong with these things?"

"They will," Kirk replied. "These aren't permanent magnets. They're mag boots. They weren't designed to lock on when dealt a glancing blow. We just have to get them close enough...."

"How are we going to do that?" Terry asked.

Kirk smiled and pulled a rope out of his bag.

I had to ask.

***

As Willy entered the main doors of the keep, he braced himself for a firefight, but found no one.

"Where is everyone?" he asked.

The room was dark except for a small, lighted exit sign nearby.

"I'm guessing they went that way," Joanna suggested.

"Worth a shot," Willy replied.

They jogged through the doorway. On the other side, they found a long hallway that led to a single door. Through the windows, they could see a long tube, made mostly of glass, its shattered remains blowing listlessly in the breeze.

"If they went this way, we can't follow them," Joanna said.

"I guess it's up to Terry now."

***

How are we going to do that? Terry *really* wished he hadn't asked now. As he dangled by a rope some thirty feet below the catwalk that overlooked the launch pad, he suddenly felt like his stomach was about to leap forth through his mouth.

Fighting back the urge to lose consciousness, he cautiously placed the boot on the roof of the shuttle. *It stuck! Son-of-a....*

"It stuck!" he shouted. "Swing me to the next one."

One down, two to go.

As they carefully slid his rope towards the second shuttle, a feeling of dizziness set in. The rope creaked uncomfortably under his weight, and the sharp edges of the catwalk did nothing to boost his confidence in its ability to support him.

Not happy, he thought. *Not happy at all.*

"Okay!" Kirk shouted from overhead. "Plant it and go. We have one more left."

Terry slammed this one a bit harder into the underbelly of the shuttle. It slid slightly, but then stuck firmly in place.

“That was a bit too close!” Kirk shouted. “We don’t have any spare mag boots, so you’d better not drop any!”

That’s right, he thought. *The only spare is on the ground below.*

“Swing me around,” Terry shouted.

As the rope neared the third shuttle, one strand popped suddenly.

“Uh, Houston, we have a problem,” Kirk shouted. “Your rope isn’t doing so well. We’re going to reel you in.”

As he said this, the doors below opened, and several keepers ran towards the shuttle’s doors, oblivious to their presence.

“That’s a negative. We only have one shot at this now,” Terry shouted back. “Swing me over!”

The second strand of rope popped.

“Shit!” Terry shouted as he dropped several inches.

He watched helplessly as he saw the third and final strand begin to unravel.

Only one shot, he thought, and began swinging his body in an arc to get himself closer to the shuttle. One swing, two swings, three swings.... *Almost there,* he thought.

His hand hovered just inches from the shuttle when he felt himself falling, out of control. As he twisted his body around to face the side of the shuttle, he swung his arm out, and....

Slam! The mag boot stuck to the side of the shuttle, nearly ripping it out of his hands as it tried to slow his descent down the side of the ship. Sparks flew in every direction as it gouged a deep scar through the paint job and into the metal skin beneath.

Just a little farther, he thought as he neared the wing. *If I let go now, I’ll lose consciousness when I hit the ground and those engines will burn me alive.* Slowly, the mag boot began to gain some control over the situation, and his descent was reduced to a slightly more comfortable “oh crap” feeling as he neared the bottom of the shuttle’s side panel.

That's my stop, he thought, letting go suddenly. He hit the ground with a thud, then everything went black.

Chapter Twenty

"MAN down!" came the screaming voice from the radio. Michael immediately recognized it as Kirk.

"Where are you?" he shouted back into the radio.

"He's on the launch platform!" the voice replied.

"How do we get there?" he shouted again.

The pause at the other end told him all he needed to know. Michael reached into his bag and pulled out a syringe. As he pulled the safety cap off, one of his team members grabbed his arm.

"Are you sure you want to do that?" he asked.

"Do we have a choice?" Michael asked as he stuck the needle into the girl's thigh.

A few moments later, she groggily opened her eyes.

"Wh.. where... where... am... I?" she stammered.

"You're in the keep," Michael replied. "There's been an accident. I don't have time to explain. We need to know how to get to the launch pad."

"You," she muttered. "You're the one who knocked me out."

"Yes, I'm really sorry about that," he replied. "Look, one of our friends is about to become a crispy victual in about a minute if we don't get him off that pad."

"Take a right, then the third right, then the second left," she murmured. "You can't miss it. Big sign, ugly neon...."

They started running.

***

KIRK watched in horror as he heard the first ship powering up its engines in preparation for launch.

Suddenly, the metal deck plating began to shake under their feet.

"Get back!" Kirk shouted. "This catwalk isn't stable!"

The remaining members of the team quickly scrambled to safety, but Kirk remained behind, just beyond the edge of the roof.

"Where are you?" he shouted into the radio.

"We're almost there," Michael's voice replied between gasps for breath as he ran through the double doors out onto the platform below them.

Kirk watched Michael grab Terry's leg and drag his unconscious figure across the pad. As the door slammed shut behind them, the pad turned suddenly red with flame from the primitive engines, their fiery exhaust causing the entire building to tremble.

With that trembling came the sound of screeching metal. As the third ship began to launch, its locking clamps failed to disengage, turning the end of the catwalk where they had been standing into a curled up heap of new age metal artwork.

The catwalk is crumpling faster than a politician takes a bribe, Kirk thought.

Suddenly, the section on which he was standing began to tear away from its moorings.

Campaign contribution, he corrected himself as he felt the platform dislodge itself beneath his feet. Thus, he did the only thing he could think of.... He jumped.

The feeling of free fall isn't all it's cracked up to be, he thought as he flew through the air. The previously solid catwalk now was several feet beneath him, and the ground seemed dizzyingly far beyond that.

Kirk felt his hand graze the edge of the roof, but there was nothing to grab—no handhold to latch on to.

I'm going to die, he thought. *This is really it. I'm going to die.* He almost wanted to laugh at the irony of being so close, yet losing it all because he stood out there on a lousy metal railing.

That's when he felt a hand grab his arm.

As he dangled from the precipice, his team slowly pulled him over the edge and onto the roof. That's when he noticed the face behind the hand that grabbed him—a young woman in her early twenties.

"It's good to see you again, Ashley," Kirk said.

Michael stared at him.

"You know her?" he asked.

"How do you think we got the trackers?" Terry replied, smiling.

And so, they stood there on the roof and watched as the Keeper ships flew steadily skyward. The satellite defense network, long since recovered from its diagnostic cycle, sprang to life.

The radio crackled. "Unknown craft, you are traveling in a restricted area with prisoners aboard. Land immediately or you will be destroyed."

The shuttles continued their preprogrammed ascent, but after a few moments, beams of bright yellow light streamed forth from several of the satellites, converging on the three shuttles. A momentary flash of light later, all that remained were a few scattered bits of metal fluttering in the breeze.

"Adam?" Michael asked into the radio.

"Yes?" came the response.

"I take it you programmed those shuttles?"

"Maybe," the voice replied coyly.

"Do you have control over the defense satellites yet?"

"Uh... just now, sir," the voice said.

"Very good," Michael replied. "Carry on."

***

THE blue sky faded slowly to black as they left the mesosphere.

"How's our patient?" Tim asked.

"Not good," Allison replied. "Honestly, I think we should wake him—give him a chance to say goodbye."

"Wow," Tim replied, shaking his head.

Tim pressed a few buttons to his left, and the viewscreen sprang to life.

"Marcia?" Tim asked.

"Yes?" she replied.

"I'm afraid I have some bad news. It's Tom."

"Wh-what... what happened?" she stammered.

"He's been shot," Tim replied bluntly. "There's... nothing we can do. We thought we should wake him so you could say goodbye."

Marcia stared at him in stony silence.

Tim nodded towards Allison, and she injected him with a stimulant. A few moments later, Tom began to stir, showing some semblance of consciousness.

***

ANGELA sat there for a moment wondering what to make of the news.

What was his name? Chuck Graham? A known Terran terrorist working in the Mars government? A twenty-year-old kid? Released for lack of evidence?

"Are you certain?" she asked.

"It's all over the news," the stewardess replied... or at least the underground news.

Why do I have a feeling there's a whole lot more to this story than we've been told?

Angela shivered.

***

Tom tried to clear his head. *What's going on? Where am I? Is this Heaven?*

"We have someone on the link to talk to you," Tim said.

As he felt Allison's hand take his under the table, Tom nodded his understanding. *No, it's a farewell party, and everyone was invited. Great.*

"Marcia," Tom began, "I always knew something like this might happen, but I had hoped it wouldn't end like this."

Tears welled up in Marcia's eyes as she looked at him, his mortal injuries consuming him. She tried hard to hold back the tears, rubbing her eyes and squinting, but Tom could see that a part of her was dying with him.

"Tom, I have some good news," Marcia began, clearly struggling to sound happy through the tears. "I'm pregnant. We're having twins. You have to get better, Tom. You're going to be a father."

Tom shook his head. "I'm already a father, Marcia. Even when I'm gone, I'll still be with you and our kids."

"No, Tom!" she wailed.

Tom smiled painfully. "I want you to promise me something."

"Anything."

"I'm not gonna be able to be there for you, Marcia, but you need family," Tom said. "I want you to go live with my brother, Joe. His family will help take care of you and our children."

Marcia's eyes were overcome with tears. "I will. I promise," she replied. "I love you, Tom."

"I love you, too, Marcia," Tom replied.

And I always will. And with that thought, the darkness overcame him once again.

Part II:

A New Nation

Forty-five years later

Chapter Twenty-one

Forty-five years later (October 3, 2359)

EFFUSIVE applause permeated the hall as thirty thousand onlookers welcomed their newly-elected President. Out of the corner of his eye, President Johnson could see his chief aide, Sheila Zarzycki, just offstage, motioning for him to start, so he motioned for the crowd to let him speak. Predictably, they continued cheering, so he decided that perhaps he should just cut in....

"Citizens of Kinji," he began, pausing a moment for a break in the din. "Citizens of Kinji," he repeated, "today is a historic day in our planet's history."

The crowds began cheering again. President Johnson smiled and waved for them to stop, which only seemed to provoke them further. Sensing the futility of his efforts, he buried his face in his hands and shook his head.

"My fellow Kinjans, today marks the first time in our planet's short history that a democratically-elected government has taken power."

He paused for a moment to take a sip of water before continuing. "It seems like only yesterday that Kinji was a planet of political prisoners, held captive under the dictatorial rule of tyrants. Now, as we enter this sixth age of mankind, we are a bright light in the moribund sea of mediocrity that the human race has long become.

"We stand as one people, democratically ruled—a thriving powerhouse of freedom and economic prosperity—while many planets toil under threat of war. In a time when some have seen democracy and freedom as a liability, we have seen it as a challenge.

"My friends, I am standing here today as proof that we have met that challenge.... We have met that challenge in the fields of battle. We have met it at the table of peace. We have met it in the voting booths and in the streets. We have challenged the unseen enemies of peace—the brokers of fear, of tyranny, of oppression, of terror—and we have won.

"From this day forward, no longer will this great planet be seen as a den of criminals, but as a shining example of the good in humanity. Together, we have changed this planet from one of wanton destruction to one of peace, of freedom, of democracy. Today, we have changed the world. Tomorrow, we will change the universe.

"I look forward to the next six years as your President, and to serving you, the people of Kinji, without whom none of this would have been possible."

"Thank you, and good evening," he concluded, then turned, smiled, and left the stage. The moment the stage door closed, President Johnson clutched his stomach, then his throat.

"Mr. President!" Sheila yelled, running to his side.

"Water," he hoarsely whispered. With that word, his eyes grew dim, and he collapsed in a heap.

"We have a medical emergency!" she shouted. "Somebody call an ambulance!"

***

Sunlight slowly crested the hills on the horizon as day crept over Mikarta, Kinji's capital city. In the courtyard of Crestview Medical Center, Dr. Paul Murphy sat for a moment of quiet reflection. As he stood to leave, a young resident appeared seemingly out of nowhere.

"Dr. Murphy! Dr. Murphy! We have an emergency."

He gritted his teeth. *Never a break,* he thought. "I'm off-duty this hour. Can't someone else handle it?"

"Sir, it's the President," he replied.

The look of shock on the young man's face told him immediately that he was serious. Without skipping a beat, he replied, "No rest for the weary, eh," then broke into a run.

As the emergency room lobby doors swung open, the doctor shivered. A beautiful, young EMT wheeled the patient quickly through the doors.

"Whaddawegot?" the doctor asked as they walked furiously down the hall to the operating theatre.

"Poisoning," Holly replied. "The field lab showed traces of cyanide and arsenic on his water bottle."

"Have you administered sodium thiosulfate?"

"Yes, on the way. We also pumped his stomach."

When the operating room doors opened, a nurse stood waiting.

"Nurse, let's get him on dialysis, prop his feet up, and lower his head. You!", he shouted at the EMT, "get me a saline drip with dimercaptosuccinic acid and a milligram of epi."

A sudden whine tore their attention away. "Doctor!" the nurse shouted. "He's coding!"

"Paddles!" he replied. "Charge to 200 joules, and add 600 milligrams of brilliant blue G-250 to that IV mixture."

As the lab tech adjusted the IV dose, Holly grabbed the defibrillator paddles, slathered them with conductive jelly, rubbed them together, and placed them against his chest.

"Clear!" she shouted, and pressed the red button. The President's body jerked and shivered, his heart beating for a moment, then returning to a stopped state.

"300 Joules. Again!"

"Clear!"

He shook again. The EEG registered a slight blip, then nothing.

"360!"

"Clear!"

The President shook, this time much more violently. Again, the EEG chimed its incessant beep.

"Okay, that's it," the doctor said. "Get me a flow pump."

The nurse quickly ran from the room as the doctor grabbed a surgical scalpel. With a swift incision, he cut his way into the man's chest cavity.

"Bone saw and rib spreader?" he asked

Holly stood, dazed and in shock. The doctor looked at her, quickly shook his head, and reached across the room, bringing a small bone saw to cut the sternum and a rib spreader to hold the rib cage open.

Within seconds, the nurse reentered the room, carrying a small pump. The doctor quickly took its four tubes and forced their sharp ends through the walls of the aorta and other key blood vessels attached to the heart. A moment later, it began pumping blood through his veins.

As Holly hooked the President up to a ventilator, the doctor quickly wired his ribs shut and sutured the opening as much as possible, leaving room for the tubes to run to the pump that sat on his chest.

The doctor then carefully cauterized the remaining blood vessels around the gaping hole.

"Time?" the doctor asked.

"Five-twenty-six, the nurse replied."

Less than six minutes had elapsed since the onset of cardiac arrest. *Amazing,* he thought.

"Now what?" Holly asked.

"Now, we wait," the doctor replied.

***

SHEILA Zarzycki made her way into the President's office.

"You're late," Diego chided sarcastically.

"*You* try waiting on hold with the hospital for ten hours and see if *you* make it to the daily staff meeting on time...."

As the acting President, Vice-President Diego Sanchez wasn't the brightest bulb in the string—*he's certainly no President Johnson,* Sheila mused—but he made up for it with his ebullient personality.

Sheila, however, was anything but joyous. Her sleep-deprived facial features were surpassed only by her bad-hair-day plumage, no doubt owing to the same root cause. Indeed, this had been the sort of day that they made movies about—really bad, B-rate movies with cheesy special effects and an alien popping out of the President's forehead.

And so, in that spirit, Sheila groggily pulled an inch-thick folder of information out of her briefcase and dropped it flamboyantly on the table. It hit with a thud, and the enclosed papers spread themselves out like cards in a game of solitaire.

"What's this?" Diego asked.

"It's the lab report on President Johnson," she replied. "I think you should all take a look at it."

Secretary of State Tim Luthier reached out and grabbed a copy. The other five cabinet members sat there and waited.

"Well, go on," she said insistently.

"Aren't there privacy laws designed to prevent exactly what we're doing here?" Diego quipped.

The room erupted in chuckles as everyone grabbed a copy.

Donna Atkins, the Secretary of the Treasury, made an effort, but her eyes glazed over quickly. Secretary of Defense Mike Torledo merely cringed. The others showed outward signs of sheer exasperation.

"Dear God," Diego whispered, his eyes growing ever wider.

"We have reason to suspect that this was an inside job," Sheila said. "I have asked the police to stay out of this and allow us the time we need for our own internal investigation."

"Is that wise?" Tim asked.

"As far as the news media is concerned, President Johnson is in the hospital recovering after a near-fatal heart attack," Sheila replied. "Under no circumstances are they to find out otherwise until after the investigation. We should try to avoid tipping our hand too early."

"Agreed," Diego replied. "We have to act quickly and quietly. If the guilty party suspects that we are on to him or her, critical evidence may be destroyed."

"Where do we begin?" Donna asked.

"I trust everyone in this room, so I trust anyone you trust. Call upon your most trusted staffers to search every inch of Mitnik Stadium and the offices here. There is an assassin somewhere in our midst, and I need every one of you to work together to rout him out."

Everyone in the room nodded their assent, and with that, the acting President shouted, "Dismissed!"

***

HOLLY walked cautiously into the waiting room from the operating theatre. Six men in crisp, black business suits stood between her and the exit, wearing dark sunglasses and sporting an unusual bulge under their jackets.

"Miss Tyler?" one asked in a deep growl.

"Y...y...yes?" she replied.

"Let's be clear. You heard nothing, you saw nothing."

What are they talking about?

"Uh... okay?"

"The President had a mild heart attack and is recovering nicely."

"But..." she protested. "Oh. I see."

"For national security reasons," he continued, "you are under strict non-disclosure until such time as an official announcement is made regarding the true nature of his ailment."

"Doctor-patient confidentiality would prevent me from saying anything anyway," she replied.

"But doctor-patient confidentiality laws don't carry possible sentences of fifty to life."

Holly felt a lump rising in her throat. *Hey, doctor, could we get these guys some Chlorpromazine?*

"Okay. I get the idea...."

Chapter Twenty-two

Terésa Gonzales groaned. *Where am I? And what's that damned ringing? Oh. The telephone. Call back later.*

The ringing continued unabated for what seemed like hours. As she buried her head in a pillow, she heard a knock at the door.

"Terésa! I know you're in there," a man shouted from outside.

Chuck. Shit. It's work.

Slowly, cautiously, she pulled herself to her feet and trudged to the door.

As she opened the door, Chuck Graham shouted, "What's going on? I've been calling you for twenty minutes!"

"I just got in at two this morning from Mikarta," she replied. "You should know. You sent me there."

"Well, you're going back," he interrupted.

This has to be a bad nightmare.

"The mission failed," he continued. "President Johnson is still alive."

***

The laser light stung her eyes as Carlie Sinclair stepped into the entryway of the Earth Central Intelligence Agency headquarters. Beside her, two doors slid open. As she entered Command Central, she saw her partner, Jack.

"Hi, Jack!" she shouted. "Taken control of any planes lately?"

About a dozen agents chuckled at the obvious pun.

"That is *so* not funny," he replied.

Their laughter was interrupted, however, as the door to Chairman Byrd's office opened and three tall men in impossibly neat black business suits stepped out into the room, silently walked to the exit, and left as quickly as they had entered.

Jack looked at her quizzically. "You seem to keep up with all the black-ops around here. Care to enlighten me?"

Carlie just turned, smiled, and sat down at her desk.

"You don't have a clue, do you?" he asked.

She didn't, of course, but she wasn't about to let on.

"Wouldn't you like to know?" she joked.

So he doesn't know, either, she thought. *What's going on?*

Carlie hurriedly flipped through the piles of paper on her desk, desperately looking to see if she had missed a memo somewhere. *No, nothing here. I'd better check my email.*

As soon as she logged in, she saw it—the most horrible thing anyone can see—*five thousand messages... all marked urgent. It's going to be that kind of day.*

Fifteen minutes later, she reached the bottom of the pile. Nothing. Not one single email message that could explain the men dressed in black.... She slammed her hands down on the desk in disgust.

"Damn," she cursed.

"Wow," Jack said with a smile. "You really *don't* have any idea, do you?"

"No, she doesn't," Chairman Byrd replied. "Both of you... my office... five minutes."

In the confusion of the last few moments, she hadn't even noticed his stealthy entrance. Chairman Byrd was a tall man with dark skin, long, black hair, and a manner of dress that totally belied his middle eastern heritage—for some reason, he had a thing for kilts—but his features gave him away.

She quickly shook off her surprised stare and managed to get off a sharp "yes, sir" before he noticed, much to her relief. As he left the room, Carlie muttered her feelings on the matter.

"Man, someone should hang a bell around that guy's neck."

Jack just chuckled and smiled.

***

THE fog rolled in from the coast like a juggernaut, swallowing everything in its path as the bullet train sped into the station at 4th and King in New San Francisco (built on the ruins of "Old" San Francisco, which was obliterated in the great quake of 2137).

Alfonse DiRoma sat waiting for the train to reach Sacramento station, never knowing that his archnemesis, Jonathan Park, was riding only three cars back.

As the train pulled into its final station in Sacramento, Alfonse stepped off, turned left, and walked out of the station. Had he turned around, he might have just been able to see Jonathan in the distance, but something shiny caught his eye at a street vendor. As his eyes focused, he realized it was just a Roullexxx watch—*stupid knock-offs*—and kept walking.

A moment later, he turned a corner and approached a coffee machine. He selected a non-fat mocha and inserted his identitoken. But this was no ordinary coffee machine. After checking his identity, the front face of the machine slid sideways, revealing a hole in the floor with a ladder inside.

Slowly, cautiously, he climbed down the ladder. As his head cleared the top of the hole, the vending machine closed.

A mere split second later, Jonathan Park approached the same machine. With a light British accent, he ordered a non-fat mocha and inserted his identitoken.

A few seconds later, Jonathan wandered off contentedly, drinking his coffee.

***

THEIR fear was palpable as Carlie and Jack stepped into Chairman Byrd's office.

"Randy," Jack began.

"Jack," Chairman Byrd interrupted. "We have a bit of a situation. Those were operatives from the Terror Information Network."

"What do those losers want?" Carlie asked.

"It's Kinji. Apparently, rogue elements are trying to destabilize the government there," he replied.

"That's good, right?" she asked. "I mean, they're already a rogue prison planet. We could just let things self-destruct naturally and regain control."

"I'm afraid it's not that simple," he replied, pausing for a moment to sip his non-fat mocha. "Kinji is a hotbed of political dissidence. It's bad enough that they have formed a new government there. The last thing we need is for it to turn into a factionalized mess with fundamentalist terrorist cells and leftist loonies."

Carlie seemed to ponder this for a moment, scratched her head, and stared at him with a puzzled look.

"It's politics, Car. I don't like the way Kinji was handled any more than you do, but I have my orders... and now you have yours."

"We do?" Jack asked.

"Your mission is to infiltrate Mikarta Central Intelligence and find out everything they know. We still have satellites in orbit around Kinji. If we know the precise location of the threat, we can obliterate it from orbit."

Carlie shivered. These were the moments that made her uneasy. *Any error could mean vaporizing a hospital... or a junior high school. I mean sure, teenagers can be annoying, but....*

Her sarcastic musings were brusquely interrupted by Chairman Byrd.

"Dismissed," he snapped.

By the time she realized what was happening, she was sitting on a train to the spaceport in Redmond.

Oh well, she thought. *At least I can sleep on the shuttle....*

***

TERÉSA Gonzales staggered into Dimpled Chad's Bar & Grille in downtown Mikarta.

"What'll it be, T?" the bartender asked.

"Hey, John," she slurred. "Gimme a Dhhhry Martiniiiii... on the rahhhcks."

"Whoa, slow down there," he replied. "I think you've had enough."

"I can ha-hand-handle it. Bring it on."

"Okay," he replied, "but I don't have any olives up here. I'll have to go in back and get them. I'll make it for you in a moment."

With that, she smiled as he walked back through the swinging doors into the kitchen.

Once he was safely out of range, he pulled his cell phone from his pocket and dialed a number that he had dialed many times.

"Diego, my friend.... It's your girlfriend. She's here again.... Yes, I'll keep her here until you get here.... Hot sauce and Coke. Yes. Sure. I'll see you in a few minutes. Bye."

***

VICE President Sanchez stepped out of the President's office and into the reception area.

Dammit, Terésa, he thought. *Why did you have to pick tonight?*

"Martha, could you be a dear and hold my calls?"

"Sure," she said. "And if your wife calls?"

As he walked out into the darkness of the Kinji evening, he replied, "Tell her I'm poling my constituents."

***

A short, rotund man with long hair and baggy clothes sat on a ragged green couch, turning his head briefly and staring for a moment as Alfonse DiRoma entered the bunker.

Miklaus Wunderkind was the prodigal son of the Colonial Liberation Front. Around the office (behind his back, of course), his nickname was troll, not because of his personality, but because that was the best way to describe his overall appearance.

"Hey, Mik," Alfonse said.

"Eh, Alf," he replied, then turned his head back around and reglued his eyes to the TV in front of him.

"What's happening in the world?" Alfonse asked.

"You know, it's weird," he muttered, half to Alfonse, half to himself. "Last week, *we* were the ones blowing things up on Kinji. This week, it wasn't our guys. I don't know what's happening. Sometimes I think the world's gone mad. Ya know what I mean?"

"Yeah," Alfonse replied. "Wait, what?"

Chapter Twenty-three

THE shuttle Terra Firma III sped towards the folding gate at Mars. Carlie was sleeping peacefully in seat 13A, when she was abruptly awakened by a shudder.

"Wha... what was that?" she asked hurriedly.

Jack simply sat there slack-jawed.

"Jack? Jack? What was that?"

Jack managed to regain enough composure to point. That's when she saw it. The docking port door was open, and a small escape pod was firmly attached to their hull.

She could see the folding gate in the distance as she watched the attacking ship in horror.

If we could only close the docking port and somehow break free, she thought.

No sooner had she thought this than three people wearing ski masks entered.

"Do not be afraid," one man said. "We have a bomb, but we will not use it if our demands are met."

The man spoke in an accent she had never heard before. *Intriguing,* she thought. *I wonder who they are.*

A moment later, her data pad sprang to life with a news feed from Command Central. It read:

Kinji terrorists hijacking shuttles; flying into space stations, folding gates. Use extreme measures.

With that, Carlie pressed a few keys on the data pad and the shuttle ground to a halt.

"What is this going on?" the crazed man shouted.

"I'm what's going on. The Earth Central Intelligence Agency has taken control of this vessel. Your attempt to crash it into the folding gate cannot be allowed. This vessel isn't moving until you are safely back on your ship."

"I have a bomb! I *will* use it!"

"Go ahead," Carlie replied. "If you do, we all die. If I let you take control of this shuttle, we all die, and the explosion wipes out half of Mars. Take your little turf war elsewhere, boys. There isn't enough room in the Sol system for your kind."

The entire room was so silent you could hear ions bonding. The hijackers just stood there, while Carlie sat staring at them.

Do you suppose he bought it? Carlie thought. *If he breaks into the cockpit, he'll find the pilot pulling back on the yoke—a neat trick of text messaging, but a trick nonetheless.*

And what happens if he doesn't? Do I try to shoot them in this tiny, pressurized tin can?

So she did what anyone would do in such a situation. She froze. Everyone remained motionless for a good fifteen seconds. Just when she thought she was about to crack, one of the terrorists broke the silence.

"Kinji Libre!" he shouted.

"Kinji Libre!" the others echoed.

With that, they excitedly walked out the docking port. A moment later, it closed behind them, the ships separated, and the tiny pod craft flew through the folding gate and disappeared.

"Wow," Carlie said. "That was... interesting."

Jack just sat there, motionless.

***

Sheila walked down the hall towards her apartment. As she put the key in the lock, she heard motion behind her.

"Eeep!" she screamed. She turned towards the sound, then realized it was just David, her neighbor, and relaxed.

"Whoa," he said. "Sorry to scare you. That kind of a week?"

"You could say that," she said, chuckling.

She could feel her palms beginning to sweat, her breathing becoming more shallow, her eyes growing wider, but something inside her said she shouldn't feel this way.

He's... he's a geek and... and I ***can't*** *be falling for him. I just* ***can't*** *be,* she thought, but the feeling wouldn't subside.

Maybe he'll ask me out... please, oh please... no, please don't! What am I saying? I have a ***boyfriend****! I can't do this. This is driving me* ***crazy****! Doesn't he know* ***I love him****!?!*

"Listen, I was about to make brownies and... well, my cake pan must have gotten put in the wrong box, and I don't want to try to finish unpacking the entire house before I start cooking... so I was wondering...."

Suddenly, she felt as though a great deal of pressure had been released. *If that had been geological pressure, the earthquake would have leveled half the planet,* she thought, and began laughing uncontrollably.

"Was it something I said?" he asked.

"You want to borrow a pan," she said, shaking her head and laughing.

"Yeeeeaaah..." he drawled, a look of sheer confusion on his face.

"Sure. I'll go get it," she replied, smiling.

With that, she disappeared into her apartment and returned a moment later with the cake pan.

"Thanks," he said. "I'll bring you some later if you'd like."

"Sure," she replied. "That would be great."

She eyed him intently as he walked down the hall and stepped into his apartment before relaxing with a sigh befitting a lovesick puppy.

Dejectedly, she slipped into her apartment and headed for her room. *What a day,* she thought.

Sheila collapsed on her bed, utterly exhausted, the moonlight cascading down upon her through the sheer curtains like a wispy fog by a mountain stream.

The room was filled with an eerie stillness, like the eye of a hurricane or the calm before a thunderstorm. The only thing changing was a red glow across the room, throbbing methodically as though marching in time to a drum cadence from an invisible band.

And so, groggily, she slogged her tired form across the room and pressed the "play" button on her answering machine.

> *Sheila, it's Ron. Look, this just isn't working out. The past couple of weeks, you've been... how do I put this gently... nuts. Whoops, guess that didn't quite work. The point is, you've changed. You're not the calm, easy-going girl that I fell in love with.*
>
> *All of a sudden, you're out late every night doing God knows what, and you're defensive every time I bring it up. I mean, what am I* **supposed** *to think? Even if you're not cheating on me, that's not the point, and I* **do** *believe you. What hurts is that you don't trust me enough to tell me what's going on in your life, and I just don't know how to deal with that.*

So it boils down to this: it's over. I can't see you anymore. I can't be your knight in shining armor who keeps shouldering your burdens. I have enough burdens of my own without that. I need someone I can trust—someone who trusts me—someone who... someone who isn't you. I'm sorry. Goodbye, Sheila.

The message was punctuated by a shrill beep, which shook her to her senses, and with that, she burst into tears....

***

LIKE an eagle gracefully swooping down to capture its prey, the shuttle Terra Firma III glided to a halt just outside Mikarta. No sooner had their landing struts touched the dusty surface of Kinji than a herd of men dressed in black arrived to escort them....

As the door opened, a young man entered. Carlie thought he looked oddly familiar, but shook it off.

The man rubbed his eyes, then looked around the cabin, meticulously studying every passenger.

"Jonathan Park, Mikarta Central Intelligence," he said, a slight British accent betraying his Earth heritage, despite his otherwise very Mikartan attire. "Please remain seated. We have reason to believe that there may be criminal elements on board."

Suddenly, a man jumped up and ran towards the rear exit. Less than a second later, he was lying face down on the ground, having taken a bullet to the brain.

"Anyone else?" Jonathan asked.

***

The water gurgled gently around her as Sheila sat in her tub. The cold, sanitary, white walls made her suddenly feel even smaller than she already did, but she pressed on, her pen strokes periodically interrupted by teardrops as they ran off her nose and dripped onto the page.

She read the note back to herself once again, just to make sure that she hadn't made any mistakes... but deep down inside, she knew it was too late to change things even if she had....

Dearest love,

I can bear this pain no longer. I can never forgive myself for what I did to you. You were the best thing that ever happened to me. You were always there smiling when I needed to laugh. You wiped away my tears whenever I cried. I love you more than life itself. But now you're gone, and I can never bring you back. I miss you so much.

If this is my lot, let me live no more to hurt those I care about... and know that I am truly, truly sorry.

As she put the pen down, she took a deep breath. Slowly, methodically, she pulled the razor blade lengthwise down a vein in her other wrist, squinting at the pain. With an agonizing sigh, she breathed one last breath as she slid slowly down into the bathtub, already red with her blood.

***

As they entered the dimly-lit office, Diego smiled at the way her flesh glistened in the moonlight like the soft glow of sunset on a misty spring eve. The moment he shut the door, Terésa climbed atop his desk. Then, she purred as Diego slowly slid the strap of her dress from her shoulder.

"Diego," she said in a sexy rasp, "would you mind if I... go to the restroom and slip into something more... comfortable?"

"Sure, hon. It's down the hall to your left," he said, smiling an impish grin.

Terésa walked out of his office and quickly turned down the main corridor. A night of sex in the office—it was the perfect cover, but she had to finish quickly so he wouldn't notice her absence.

Let's see.... I think it was the third door on the right, she thought as she turned the corner into the executive corridor.

With the skill of an expert locksmith, Terésa picked the lock. Moments later, she was standing in front of a desk. She didn't recognize the young woman in the photograph, but somehow she still felt sorry for her.

It's either her or me, she thought as she slipped the vial of potassium carbonate out of her purse and into the drawer, along with a rusty nail and a piece of charcoal. *The makings of potassium cyanide.... Lovely stuff....*

She carefully wiped any potential fingerprints from the drawer handle with her shirt, then pushed the drawer shut with her hip. Finally, she crawled atop the desk, stood, and lifted the drop ceiling out of the way.

In a flash, she climbed up into the ceiling, slid the panel back into place behind her, removed a similar panel a few feet away, and slipped quietly into the women's restroom across the hall. A few precarious moments later, she slid the ceiling back into place and dropped a few feet to the floor from her perch atop the bathroom partition.

The knock at the door told her she should probably hurry.

"Honey?" Diego asked. "You doing okay?"

"I'll be out in a second," she replied, casting her dress quickly to the floor.

And as she stepped out once again into the darkened hall, she smiled. *He doesn't suspect a thing.*

***

ALTHOUGH their sweet, chocolatey smell permeated every corner of the halls, the air was also filled with an eerie stillness as David knocked on Sheila's door, brownies in hand.

The silence that followed left an ominous feeling in his gut. *Did I leave the oven on?* He brushed it off.

"Sheila?" he shouted, knocking again. *Silence.*

"Sheila!?!" he repeated, this time banging on the door with such vigor that he thought it would come off its hinges. *Still silence.*

Something isn't right. She said she would be here.

He wasn't quite sure how, but his hand ended up on the doorknob. It turned. *This is wrong,* he thought. *This is very wrong.*

Slowly, the door swung open, and he stepped inside.

"Sheila?" he shouted. "Sheila, are you here?"

The bowl of half-melted ice cream on the table confirmed his worst fears.

"Sheila!" he shouted. He ran frantically into her bedroom, found no one, and then ran into the spare room. It was also empty. That's when he noticed the light shining through the crack around the door at the end of the hallway. As he pulled the bathroom door open, he saw her, naked, unconscious, in a pool of her own blood and water.

"Oh, God," he said, feeling the sudden need to vomit.

Cautiously, he reached down to her neck and felt for a pulse. The slight flutter told him she was alive, but barely.

"Come on, Sheila. I'm getting you out of here," he said as he reached under her arms and lifted her out of the tub.

He quickly tied hand towels around her wrists. Then, in a fit of modesty, he wrapped her in a bath towel before dragging her out to his car.

***

CARLIE felt a tug at her shoulder as the passengers made their way towards the holding area to be debriefed. Instinctively, she turned and swung her fist, only to find it caught swiftly by none other than the man from the cabin.

She recognized him instantly by his chiseled features and long black hair that stood in stark contrast with the short haircuts of all the other Mikartan security personnel. She knew she had never seen him before in her life, yet somehow he seemed oddly familiar.

"Carlie?" he asked.

"Do I know you?" she replied.

Jonathan appeared to have to think about this for a moment, scratching his five-o'clock-shadowed face all the while.

"No.... No, I don't think so," he said, "but I know you. You're CIA. We've been expecting you."

She thought to herself, *have you ever had one of those days when you felt like the entire universe was just jerking your chain?* She quickly shook off the notion, however.

"I'm afraid you must have me confused with someone else," she said rather unconvincingly.

"The purple pill bar and grille has lovely food and always will," he said.

What the... wait a second, she thought. *I recognize that code... but where? Oh, my. He's...*

"And hast thou slain the jabberwock?" she replied, laughing so hard she feared she would cough up a lung.

At that, he replied, "The burnt umber crayon was lodged deep within his sinus cavity."

She smiled. "You're Martian Intelligence? What the hell are you doing here?"

"Shh. Keep it down," he replied. "I'm here for the same reason you are. Jack's an old friend of my father. Tell him I said hi."

It was at that moment when she realized that she had no idea where Jack was. She had been looking frantically around the room for several seconds before her data pad chirped to indicate an incoming message.

Carlie,

I have my mission. You have yours. Trust Jonathan.

Jack

Carlie smiled and relaxed. "Are we on the same side?" she asked.

"I don't know," Jonathan answered bluntly. "You tell me."

***

THE rubber wheels skittered on the tile floor as the EMT rolled the gurney through the emergency room lobby and into the back hall.

David jogged in behind them and walked over to the nurses' station. As he arrived, the head nurse turned and greeted him.

"Hello, sir. Are you the man who brought in the young woman?"

"Yes," he replied.

"The officer in the lobby would like to talk to you."

"What about?"

"He wants to ask some questions about where she lives and her motives. It's standard procedure in suicide cases."

"You mean she's..."

"No, no!" she shouted, waving her hands in an apologetic manner. "Sorry, I meant attempted suicide. I didn't mean to freak you out there."

He sighed visibly.

"Okay. Sure. I'll talk to him," he said as he backed away, turned, and left.

Chapter Twenty-four

OFFICER Warren knocked on Sheila's door—not that he expected anyone to answer, of course, but it just made him feel safer somehow.

A few seconds later, he knocked again, then pulled a lock pick set from his pocket and went to work.

When David reached the top of the stairs, he looked on with amusement as the officer fought with his picks.

"It's unlocked, you know," David said after a few moments.

Officer Warren sheepishly reached out and turned the knob with a sigh of embarrassment, then shivered as the door to Sheila's apartment swung slowly open. Upon taking his first step into the apartment, he knew this was going to be one nasty crime scene. His boots squished on the soaked carpet.

"So you found her where, exactly?" he asked.

"Over there," David replied, pointing at the bathroom door.

Officer Warren turned on the light switch in the foyer. With a shower of sparks from the frayed, water-soaked cord on the floor of the living room, the attached light flickered and died.

"Damn," he said, turning off the light switch and switching on his flashlight. He walked into the bathroom, turned on the light switch, swore when it didn't work any better than the one in the living room, and then turned it back off again. He carefully panned his flashlight over the bathtub, across the sink, and down to the floor between them.

That's when he saw the note....

***

DONNA Atkins muttered obscenities under her breath as she walked out of the briefing room and into the lobby.

"Martha?" she asked. "Could you call the hospital and see if there's any new word on Sheila?"

No sooner had she said this than the door swung open and Sheila entered.

"Rumors of my demise have been greatly exaggerated," she said with a wry grin.

"It's good to see you," Martha replied. "Things are crazy around here. We just got more bad news from the hospital. The President took a turn for the worse. His organs are shutting down. They don't expect him to last the night."

"Oh, I'm sorry," Sheila said. "I know you two were close."

Martha nodded grimly. "We were going to get married next summer."

Sheila sighed.

"Hey, you two! Get back to work!" Diego shouted jokingly.

Martha hadn't noticed his entrance, but somehow was relieved to see him.

"Martha, I'm going to be meeting with the province governor for lunch today. Could you be a doll and hold all my calls? K. Thanks. Bye."

Martha rolled her eyes. *Idiot.*

And with that, he was gone.

"Idiot," Martha muttered.

***

JONATHAN walked briskly through the halls of Mikarta Central Intelligence. On occasion, Carlie actually found herself struggling to keep up in Kinji's one and two tenths gravities, but somehow she managed.

Then without warning, he stopped... in the middle of a hallway. There were no doors nearby, and no emergency stairs outside the ornate, arched windows. Jonathan quickly slipped his hand into his pocket as though he were fishing for keys, then pulled his hand back out just as quickly.

How peculiar, she thought.

"Why are we stopping?" she asked.

"We're here," he replied, smiling.

Upon hearing this, she simply stood there, slack-jawed, wondering what Jonathan was smoking and where she could get some for herself, when the floor suddenly shook beneath her feet. Three seconds later, they began falling rapidly.

"Aaaaaaah!" she screamed.

"Relax," Jonathan said, laughing. "It only hurts at the bottom."

Thirty seconds later, with a shrill screeching sound, the falling platform began to slow, until it finally came to rest beside a door, the smoothness of its rather dull and uninspiring grey surface marred only by the number thirty-four painted in giant white numbers across the whole of its surface.

"I hate you," Carlie said, glaring at him indignantly.

"Too bad... honey," he replied.

"Excuse me?"

"Oh, did I forget to mention that?" he replied. "Mikarta Central Intelligence has your retina scan on file. You were as good as made. That's why your boss asked for our help. If anyone asks, you're my fiancée."

"What!?!"

***

SHEILA sat in her office chair, staring at the ceiling mindlessly while tapping her fingers rhythmically on the desk.

"Hey, could you hold the noise down?" Tim shouted from the next office.

Tim Luthier, Sheila thought—*pure genius or pompous ass? Hmm.... I guess those are orthogonal....*

"Whatever, Tim," she shouted back. "Hey, could you shower tomorrow? This whole place really reeks."

"Yeah, you know you like it," came his snarling reply. "Au naturale, with emphasis on the 'oh'... the 'oh, oh, oh'," he continued, laughing heartily.

She rolled her eyes, shook her head, and laughed.... *At him,* she corrected. *I'm laughing* ***at*** *him.*

And with that thought, she began tapping her fingers again. A moment later, she was shaken from her reverie by a knock at the door.

"Whatever, Tim."

And another knock.

"Give it a rest, Tim."

That's when the door opened with a cracking sound. Two men dressed in black suits stood at the door.

"Sheila Zarzycki?" the man asked.

"Yes?"

"You're under arrest for the murder of the president of Kinji."

And as they led her away past the gaping stares of her coworkers, she muttered, "You could have at least tried the knob."

***

CARLIE squinted as they stepped through the door into.... *Sunlight? How is that possible?*

"Welcome to Proxima Centauri III," Jonathan said, smirking.

Carlie stood dumbfounded for a moment, staring at... *his long, black hair blowing in the... Centauri, was it? Yes, Centauri breeze. Wait.... What the hell?*

"How...."

"It's a new prototype technology," he replied. "Radiation-free spatial folding—the next step in personal transportation technology. Only two problems.... First, it requires a reactor big enough to power an entire planet. Second, it interacts badly with temporal folding experiments.... Don't ask...."

But what are we doing here?

"You're probably wondering what we're doing here," Jonathan continued.

"Ya-huh," she meekly whimpered.

"This is our *real* base of operations—a carefully disguised base just outside Tirabia. The location on Kinji is just a facade to keep the locals happy. My office is about three blocks from here."

"So how do we get back?" Carlie asked.

Jonathan grinned. "Back?"

***

The clock tower in downtown Mikarta chimed noon in the distance as Donna strode from her office into the bustling streets of the French Quarter. Ahead, through the foggy mist, she could just make out the offices of Mikarta Central Intelligence.

Business lunch today, she thought to herself. *This had better not become a habit.*

As she approached Café Emilie, she paused. *What was the code? Oh, yeah.*

A moment later, a man approached in the most hideous suit she had ever seen.

"Hello, madam. How may I be of service?" he asked in a British accent that was even more fake than his hair.

"I'll have a table for two. Oh, and could I get a gin and tonic to start me off? I like a little buzz before my weekly haircut."

"Yes, madam. Right this way," he replied, directing her to a table where a young gentleman awaited her arrival.

"Paul, I presume?" she asked.

"Yes, and you must be Donna," he replied, smiling. "So you *are* as beautiful as you sounded on the phone."

She feigned embarrassment for a moment before sitting across from him. *What a charming fellow,* she thought, then suddenly realized, *"Oh, dear. I'm thinking in British English now,"* before shaking off the thought altogether.

"The information you requested about your colleague is in this envelope," Paul whispered, slipping the envelope to her under the table. "Be aware, though, that Mikarta Central Intelligence will disavow all knowledge of this conversation."

"And my second question?" she asked.

"You were correct. The province governor is on vacation on Tyson's Planet for the entire week," he replied. "Diego is definitely not dining with her in Mikarta."

She pondered this for a moment. *What else is he lying about, and why? Do I even want to know?*

"That's all I needed to know," she replied. "Thank you for your time. Here's a ten spot for the gin and tonic."

"As always, it was a pleasure doing business with you, madam."

And with that, she calmly walked away as though nothing were wrong... but something clearly was.

***

As she followed Jonathan across the Proxima Centauri III landscape, Carlie could see dozens of nondescript buildings on the horizon, nestled between rocky formations that protruded from the desert floor like teeth in the mouth of a sleeping giant.

The blue-green sky stood in stark contrast to the silvery grey sands that seemed to spread out endlessly before them, punctuated only by occasional chunks of rock and strange, cactus-like plants that bloomed in bright red, pink, white, and...

Green? The thought stuck in her mind as she pondered what sort of bizarre evolutionary path could have led to this oddity. *Green flowers. Never saw that one coming....*

"So where are we going?" she asked.

"My office," he replied curtly.

"Which is?"

"Secret."

"I see. And where is this office?"

"Also secret."

"Oh, dear me. I seem to have forgotten the time. I have to get home and water my plants," she said, her voice dripping with the sarcasm of a thousand software engineering interns. "Oh, that's right. You dragged me off to a desert halfway across the known worlds with no way home, and you're taking me to your office, but you can't even tell me anything about it?"

"It's an office."

"Yes, and?"

"And… it's secret."

"Oooh!" she growled.

***

MEMORANDUM

TO: ALL OFFICES

FROM: ALBERT FURLONG

RE: ID VALIDATION

It has come to our attention that a member of the Mikarta Liberation Army has been spotted consorting with key government officials in Mikarta. This represents a very serious security threat.

The MLA operative has been identified as a Miss Terésa Gonzales, though we believe she may be using the name Terésa Johnson. Her motive is unknown at this time.

Miss Gonzales was seen in a security camera tape of an incident at Dimpled Chad's Bar & Grille being escorted from the bar by one Mr. Diego Sanchez.

Mr. Sanchez has a cousin, Alfonse DiRoma, who is rumored to be a member of the Colonial Liberation Front. Several reports place him in the same cities as a number of bombings in the southern regions of Kinji's main continent, Surabé.

It is also unclear whether Mr. Sanchez is aware of Terésa's MLA connections, but until this can be determined, he is to be considered highly suspicious.

EOM

As Donna placed the memo back into the folder, the door behind her creaked open.

"Hi," Diego said.

She felt her skin grow suddenly pale.

***

THE doors opened with a whiz and a whirr as Carlie arrived at Jonathan's office... or at least she assumed it was his office.

"Is this your office?" Carlie asked.

"No. This is a portal to my office," he replied. "My office is..."

"Secret. I know. I know."

As they stepped into the small, empty room, Carlie was blinded by a white flash.

"Ow!" she screamed, covering her eyes with her arm.

"Sorry," Jonathan muttered. "I guess I should have warned you not to look directly at the retina scanner with your remaining eye...."

As her eyes recovered, she was standing in yet another room, this time with nice, cushy furniture that looked like it probably cost ten times what it was worth....

No matter, as long as someone else is paying for it, she thought.

Calmly, Jonathan sat down at his communications terminal.

"Hi, Jon. Who's your friend?" came the voice from the terminal. "She's cute."

"Whatever, Bill," he interrupted brusquely. "Listen, I need you to pull up the communications records on the President's staff. Look for any signs of new relationships, that sort of thing."

Bill smiled a smile that filled the screen as he replied, "We already did that. There's only one in the last few weeks... one Miss Terésa Gonzales. We sent out a memo while you were out."

He dug through the pile of paper on his desk for a few moments before he found the pertinent memo. After quickly skimming it, he nodded and grunted a bit.

"What about *her* phone records? Besides Diego, whom else did she call?"

"We're not sure," Bill replied. "She uses at least a dozen cell phones with different numbers—most of them stolen or abandoned by their previous owners. We know for sure that she has been working with Chuck Graham."

"Chuck 'The Slasher' Graham!?! Keep me posted," he replied, turning off the communications terminal and quickly crossing to Carlie.

"Come on. We have to go."

"Where?"

"Secret."

Carlie just rolled her eyes.

***

"What's up?" Diego asked innocently.

"Not a lot," Donna replied calmly. "I was just about to send a bunch of paperwork to the central office."

She quickly slid the remaining papers into the envelope and closed it.

"Whatever for?" Diego asked as Donna stamped the envelope for inter-office mail delivery to the central office.

“We need to hire a replacement for Sheila,” she replied, tossing it towards the outgoing chute a few feet away as she did so.

The envelope bounced off the wall and landed a few feet away. Slowly, Diego reached over and picked up the envelope. Part of its contents had fallen out.

Sheila watched in horror as Diego picked up the papers... then relaxed when he stuffed them back into the envelope without reading them.

“Did she quit?” he asked innocently while resealing the envelope.

A little too innocently, Donna thought.

“She was arrested for the murder of President Johnson.”

Diego dropped the package on the floor, blinked, paused a moment, blinked again, then turned and walked to his office without saying a word.

Cautiously, Donna walked over to the envelope, dropped it into the mail chute, then returned to her chair. As she reached her desk, she noticed an outside line go red.

I have to know, she thought. Cautiously, she pressed the speaker button.

"It is done," Diego said.

"Good," came the garbled reply.

...and then the line went dead.

Chapter Twenty-five

As waiters shuffled aimlessly through the Bourbon Grille, Terésa Gonzales let her eyes wander the room, taking in every nuance—every person, every object, all the way down to the last grain of salt on the table across the aisle—as any one of them could be a spy....

Well, maybe not the grains of salt, she thought.

As Chuck Graham stepped into the room, the crowd seemed to go about their business, but she could tell that there were *many* eyes glancing in his general direction. She couldn't believe that he would pick such an exposed location for a meeting... unless....

"Ah, Terésa, my dear," he shouted.

Okay, that's one way to make certain nobody cares... pretend that you don't care who cares... unless they don't care that you don't care that they care, in which case... oh! The pain! The pain!

"Hi, Chuck," she muttered, a look of sheer disgust crossing her face more reluctantly than a squirrel crosses a road in Texas.

"Good news," he began boisterously, then paused and continued in a more subdued fashion, saying, "It's over. We won."

"How's your mother?" she asked, returning his code.

"She's doing well, thanks. It's unfortunate that they found our 'evidence' a little early, but it looks like that proved to be to our advantage, eh?"

"Yes," she replied, "but I'm still not sure I understand how anything that's going on will lead to Diego's ouster."

"It's quite simple, really. Paul delivered the package earlier today."

"What about Sheila? Won't they let her out after the blame is shifted to Diego?"

Chuck shifted in his chair uncomfortably.

Terésa's eyes widened.

"She's going to have a little 'accident' in prison," Chuck said quietly.

Terésa smiled. *It is over. We have won.*

***

It's an odd feeling of delirium when your surroundings seem to swirl around you in bizarre patterns. Even stranger when you don't remember taking anything to deliberately cause such a sensation. Thus, Sheila felt completely disoriented for a moment, but regained her equilibrium a moment later.

My cell seems to be moving. How is that possible? It's ten thousand pounds of cement. Jeez! What was in that brownie? And why don't I feel hungry?

As she pondered this question, a bright flash filled the room, followed by a face... someone walking up to the cell holding... *a gun?*

And as the bars began to shimmer and fade out of existence, she realized that she was now standing somewhere else entirely. All she could see for miles was desert landscape with a blue-green sky, a few buildings in the distance, and a young man and woman standing a few feet away.

"Welcome to Proxima Centauri III," the man said, drawing a stun pistol.

And as her consciousness slipped away, she distinctly noticed how his long, black hair blew in the Centauri breeze.

***

As Chuck stepped out of the Bourbon Grille into the crowded streets of Mikarta, he smiled at the way the blue twilight glistened off Terésa's face like the glow of an angel's wings. However, his reverie was interrupted by an annoying sound. He couldn't quite place it.

"Terésa? What's that damn ringing?" he asked his companion.

"Oh, sorry. It's me" she replied, quickly whipping a cell phone from her pocket.

"Hello?" she continued, this time into the phone. "Yes, the white knight was eaten by the green beret.... Come again? Mr. Luthier? You're dropping out. Wait a sec."

She slapped her phone fairly hard. "Can you hear me now?" she asked. "Good. Okay, come again.... She's what? What do you mean she's not there? It's a prison, not a resort hotel!"

Her furrowed brow made her look even more evil than usual somehow as she screamed into the phone. "Well, *FIND* her, dammit!"

Chuck just stared at her, puzzled.

"Oooh!" she screamed, and threw the phone at the ground where it promptly shattered into about a dozen pieces.

"Bad news?" Chuck asked.

"The war is just beginning," she replied, then turned, shouted "Oooh!" again, and stormed off into the Mikartan night.

***

"Sir?" a young woman asked.

Jonathan broke his stride to stare at her for a moment before replying. She was truly a sight to behold, her long, dark hair flowing in even the modest breeze that blew through the hallway. As soon as he shook his head clear, he continued walking.

"Yes, Jeanine?"

"The prisoner is awake."

"Excellent. Inform control that I'll be right there. Carlie?"

She muttered an "Mmm hmm" in reply.

"I think you'll find Sheila fascinating."

"Didn't she kill the President?" Carlie asked.

"No," he replied, "but we want certain people to believe that we think she did."

"Who?" she asked.

"We're not sure. That's the problem."

Carlie chuckled.

"So what you're saying," she began, "is that it's a hopeless mission filled with insufficient information and even a bit of disinformation, with spies lurking around every corner, and with no real idea where to begin, and yet we're somehow supposed to make sense of it? Sounds like my kind of week."

With that, Jonathan smiled.

***

DIEGO stumbled as he stepped up the last step into the rotunda.

"Mr. Sanchez?" a gruff voice from behind him said.

"Yes?" he replied.

As he turned towards the sound, he found himself facing an armed guard.

"I'm afraid I have to place you under arrest," the guard said.

"For what?" Diego asked, totally baffled.

"For the assassination of President Johnson."

"Well... wh-wha-what about Tim?" he shouted, stuttering. "Are you going to arrest him, too? I mean, you've already arrested the rest of the staff, so why not go for the whole baker's dozen?"

As he continued his diatribe, the officer took Diego's arms, pulled them around behind his back and cuffed him.

"I will not be silenced. I will be heard!" he shouted. Then, his body went limp as the officer stunned him with a shock prod....

***

THE cool breeze from the air conditioning sent chills up Jonathan's spine as he walked down the hallway of Mikarta Central Intelligence.

As he stepped into his supervisor's office, he could immediately tell something was wrong.

"Jonathan, please have a seat," Phil said stoically.

Jonathan sat down in the "comfy chair", as it was known, and waited for the inevitable—a tongue lashing from Phil Ingood.

"Why did you bring her here?" Phil calmly asked.

"Because she didn't do it?"

"I know that, you know that... but we can't hold her here," Phil replied.

"We determined that she was in danger of assassination," Jonathan explained. "We had to get her out."

"I reiterate that we can't hold her here."

"Well, what if she asks for asylum?" Jonathan asked.

"The answer is still the same, Jon," he replied.

"Dammit, Phil! Somebody walked into the cell block with a phase pistol. We can't just ignore that!"

Jonathan shifted uncomfortably in his chair, trying to escape the haunted look in Phil's eyes.

"Look, Jon," he continued, "You know this is a restricted area. Technically, you aren't authorized to have *anyone* here."

"But...." he interrupted.

"No 'buts'. We let Carlie slide because her dad's an old friend of mine, but I can't sanction this place becoming known to a member of the Mikartan government."

"So what are you going to do?" Jonathan asked.

"We're bringing her out of sedation. She'll be blindfolded and released into the wild in an hour or so."

"You can't do that, Phil!" Jonathan shouted.

"I'm sorry. I have no choice."

Jonathan stormed out in disgust.

***

"But I don't want a small, secret inauguration," Tim protested.

"Mr. Luthier, in mere days, you've been promoted from secretary of state to the president of Kinji," Donna replied. "Don't let it go to your head. You weren't elected."

"That's why I must immediately give the appearance of being the rightful leader of Kinji," he countered. "There must be no question in anyone's mind that I am in charge."

"What did you have in mind?" she asked.

"Donna, my dear," Tim replied, "it's simple. Gather the military winds and the orchestra. They start with Hail to the Chief, then a bit of Hail Britannia, culminating in God Save the King."

Donna shivered.

***

CARLIE patiently waited for Jonathan's return. She couldn't help but notice how much more comfortable his office was than her cubicle. He had a nice chair and a computer that didn't still have vacuum tubes. *And peaceful,* she thought. *Ah, to have a real office with walls.... Silence, sweet silence.*

That silence was broken by the click of a door knob. Instinctively, she took up a defensive position beside the doorway. As the door swung open, she cautiously waited. No one entered.

That's when she heard it... a clicking sound.... *A gun being cocked?* she thought. Slowly, she reached down and pulled her sidearm from inside her knee socks.

In a flash, the intruder stepped into the room and drew his weapon. Carlie charged her sidearm, the screaming whine alerting the intruder to her presence. He spun. She spun.

Jonathan broke into laughter. "Nice reflexes," he quipped.

"Do you always draw your gun when you enter your office?" Carlie asked.

"Lately? You bet," he replied.

"They're letting her go, aren't they?" Carlie asked, a look of concern spreading across her face like a raindrop on a car window.

"Yeah," he replied. "Something about not being able to hold a civilian unless charges are pending."

Carlie paused. *If they let her go, she's as good as dead,* she thought. *We have to do something....*

"After they let her go, how quickly can you get me to her location?" Carlie asked.

Jonathan smiled. "How long did it take you to ask the question?"

***

The pomp is nauseating, Donna thought... *and the pomposity.*

As the band played the final bars of something almost but not quite entirely unlike Tea for Two, Tim stumbled—not entirely soberly—onto the platform. Chief Justice Charles d'Antoine stood in wait.

"Mr. Luthier," he began, "you have been charged with a solemn duty to serve the people of Kinji. The office of the President comes with many rights and even more responsibilities."

At least he's being charged with something, Donna thought sarcastically.

"Because you were not elected by the people," he continued, "your job is even harder than it normally would be. You must work doubly hard to ensure that you represent the will of the people."

"He never represented them before," Donna muttered. "Why should he start now?"

Around her, several members of the Parliament chuckled.

"It is an unenviable job, but I trust that you will be able to carry it out," Charles continued.

"I understand," Tim replied.

"Tim Luthier, do you promise to serve as the voice of the Republic, swear to be honest in all your dealings, and pledge to faithfully execute the duties of the president of Kinji?"

"I do."

"Then, as the duly authorized representative of the Kinji Judiciary Authority, I hereby inaugurate you president of Kinji."

The audience cheered wildly. *I bet he paid them,* Donna thought. *Dirty crook.*

And then it happened.

"My fellow Kinjans," Tim began, "as my first act as President, I hereby grant full pardon to any members of the Mikarta Liberation Army, provided that they put down their weapons today."

The crowd grew silent.

"And to show my sincerity in putting this war behind us, I have chosen a new Secretary of Defense from among its ranks...."

By this point, the crowd was so quiet you could hear the electrons in a sodium atom as they whizzed by.

"Miss Terésa Gonzales."

As she approached the podium, all Donna could think was... *this* ***can't*** *go well.*

Chapter Twenty-six

DAWN broke over the Mikartan skyline. As Sheila struggled to regain consciousness, she found herself lying in a field on the outskirts of the thriving metropolis.

As her blurry vision began to clear, she could just make out the shape of a person—a woman—standing over her.

"What took you so long?" Carlie asked.

Delirious and exhausted, Sheila just groaned.

"Come on," Carlie said, dragging her companion to her feet. "It wears off faster if you walk it off."

"Who... are you?" Sheila asked, still dazed.

"Carlie Floren... uh... Sinclair," Carlie replied.

"How long?"

Carlie turned her head in puzzlement. "Come again?"

"...since you got married?" Sheila asked.

"Six weeks. How did you..." Carlie replied, her voice trailing off.

"Carlie Floren... uh... Sinclair," she replied. "Sort of gave you away, there."

Carlie smiled sheepishly and began walking slowly. Sheila dutifully followed.

"So, Miss... Sinclair, was it?" Sheila asked.

"Yes?"

"Where exactly am I?"

"About five miles due north of Mikarta," Carlie replied.

"And I got here how?"

"That's classified."

"And you're here because?"

"Also classified."

"Where are we going?"

"To your office."

"Why?" Sheila asked. "Oh, wait... let me guess... classified."

"Wow, you catch on fast," Carlie replied, grinning ear to ear.

Suddenly, Carlie stopped.

"I'm probably not supposed to do this, but..." Carlie began.

"Do what?" Sheila asked.

With that, Carlie pulled her bag off her back and placed it on the ground. A moment later, she was holding an odd-looking vest.

"What is it?" Sheila asked.

"It's an optical/kinetic energy diffusion and optoelectric capture and extraction vest, or 'okey-dokey' for short."

"A wha...."

"It absorbs bullets and diffuses the energy impact across its surface area," Carlie explained. "It also absorbs most energy weapons fire... up to a point... and uses it to charge power cells for standard Earth-issue phase pistols."

"Come again?"

"You'll probably want to wear it for a while."

Sheila stood in stunned silence for a moment, then mumbled, "Uh... okay... err... okee... dokee?"

"Yyyyeeeeaaaahhhh...." Carlie replied, followed by a long sigh.

***

INSANITY is a funny thing. Most people think everyone else is. Oddly enough, that suspicion is largely what keeps them from being so, and at the same time, causes them to occasionally question that fact. Indeed, it is when everyone else starts to make sense that we most question our own mental state, and in so doing, remain sane.

Thankfully, this state is usually only temporary. When other people *continue* to make sense for an extended period of time, however... that is when sanity ends.

And, in fact, that is precisely how Donna felt right now. The boardroom was dim, its inhabitants doubly so. As the presenter pushed the button to show the next slide, a c-shaped character appeared from one side, chomped its way across the title, then came back from the other side while pulling a rope which, in turn, pulled the new title onto the screen.

The mindlessness of the situation did not escape her, but suddenly it didn't matter anymore.

"We will reinvigorate the paradigm," the man said, "and thus reinvigorate this campaign. But first, we have to complete all of the action items on our agenda."

Ugh. Manager-speak, she thought.

"Can someone tell me what our target demo for this campaign is?" another said.

Why are we campaigning now? There's not another election for five years!

"I believe it's the Gen-triple-Y-ers."

"Great," said the presenter as he flipped to another slide, this time with the old slide appearing to incinerate itself, revealing the new one behind it. "We'll just incorporate the latest profiles into the mission statement and drive adoption with techniques that work on a targeted focus group."

Donna snapped. *I can't take it anymore!*

"What in Hell is WRONG with you people!?!" she screamed. "Don't you people have MINDS!?! I mean, there ISN'T A CAMPAIGN. WE WON!"

"Miss," the speaker replied calmly, "we feel that it is imperative that we continue to hammer our message home to ensure appropriate election results in the next election."

"It's not for FIVE YEARS!"

"Miss, please calm down. You're getting hysterical."

"I'm... getting... hysterical. I'm surrounded by MORONS! You know what, forget it. I can't take it anymore. I'm out of here."

With that, she stood and left the room, shutting the door behind her with a slam. The room was momentarily silent.

"So," the speaker continued, "what's next on our agenda?"

***

"It goes down tonight," Terésa whispered.

Her companion simply sat there in silence, his ski-masked visage betraying little emotion. That's when Terésa saw it. She looked deep within his eyes and saw... nothing.

"Excellent," he replied.

Terésa shivered.

***

A grey, smoggy haze bathed the Mikartan skyline in a dingy, dreary soup as Sheila and Carlie made their way through the crowd in Millbrae Square, its dirty, wind-worn stone arches contributing further to the overall sense of disrepair. Indeed, the deep shadows cast by the buildings in the late evening sun left the place feeling downright gloomy.

As they approached the famous Fontana del Bartolomeo, Carlie thought she saw a familiar face in the distance.

Was that someone I know? No, she doesn't seem familiar now. Maybe I just read her profile at some point....

But her thoughts were interrupted by her traveling companion.

"Donna?" Sheila shouted. "Donna!?! Hey! Wait up!"

Carlie quickly increased her pace to catch up. Suddenly, she felt an odd thud as a boy on a skateboard tripped her and sent her flying momentarily through the air. She hit the ground with a grunt.

Where is she? Where did she go? Dammit! You were supposed to stay with ***me****.*

Then she saw it out of the corner of her eye. The light reflecting off a metallic case through a distant window made her blink reflexively, and in a flash, the contents of the now-open case—a sniper rifle on the third floor of the King Center—were exposed moments later.

She watched in horror as Sheila stood there talking to... to someone who looked oddly familiar. As the sniper raised his rifle, Carlie began running.

"NNNNNNOOOOOOOOOOOOOOO!" she shouted, flailing her arms and trying to be as obvious as possible....

But it was too late. Sheila's limp body collapsed to the ground in a heap.

Carlie's eyes narrowed as she stood over Sheila's still form. She slowly reached for her sidearm as she scanned the window for signs of motion. Seeing none, she made her way into the alley adjacent to the building, but the black limousine that filled the narrow drive stopped her dead in her tracks.

If I don't get out of here, I'm dead, she thought as she quickly ducked back around the corner onto the main street. Cautiously, she peeked back around the corner, only to be greeted with a shower of bullets. She quickly pulled her head back around the corner, reached around with her sidearm, and fired in the general direction of the car.

The shooting suddenly stopped.

Carlie stood for a moment and scratched her head. *I can't be that lucky....* As she stuck her head back around, though, the bullets promptly resumed. *This is getting ridiculous,* she thought. *I'll call for someone.*

She quickly reached down for her cell phone. As her fingers brushed against it in her pocket, she heard something behind her click.

Oh. Shit.

***

DONNA watched as her friend fell limp before her. *Who is this woman chasing her? Is she a police officer? Mikarta CI?*

She suddenly had a feeling that she should be anywhere but here and began to run across the plaza. That's when she felt a hand on her shoulder.

"Paul!" she exclaimed.

"Shh," he warned. "It's not safe to talk here. Meet me at our usual location for lunch tomorrow."

"I'll see you there," she replied.

She turned back to see if the woman was still there beside Sheila, but she was gone. When she turned back around, so was Paul.

***

JONATHAN Park's phone rang. It wasn't all that unusual.... *Okay, so it* **is** *that unusual,* he thought. *What's up?*

He looked down at the caller ID and was even more perplexed. *An Earth cell phone? That's a little odd,* he thought, so he placed the call on speaker.

"Hello?" he asked.

The only response was an odd, rhythmic beeping... like someone pressing a button on the keypad. He vaguely recalled having studied Morse code once. *I can do this,* he thought.

"S?" he said. "M. S. Wait... that can't be right. S... O... S... Okay. Good so far."

"Need a hand?"

Jonathan spun around faster than a conservative senator caught by TV cameras at a gay bar, only to find himself face-to-face with his boss, Phil.

Phil began almost immediately. "That's s... h... e... i... l... a... s... h... o... t... k... i... n... g... c... e... n... t... e... r... k... i... d... n... a... p... m... e...."

"Somebody locate that phone," Jonathan said to no one in particular. Then, upon scanning the room and finding it otherwise unstaffed, he slid his chair over to the computer to do it himself.

As Jonathan finished keying in the tracking request, his screen changed to show a detailed street map of Mikarta.

"So, what are you sitting on your ass for?" Phil asked.

"Jacob," Jonathan shouted into his radio as he walked towards the door, "call the paramedics to King Center. Man down. Mike, I want a special forces team at Fourth street and California Avenue. Tell them to wait for me. I'll be there momentarily."

As Jonathan stepped out the door, he paused for a moment, stuck his head back inside, and added, "Oh, and Phil?"

"Yes?"

"Bite me."

Phil laughed.

***

CABINET Secretary Brock Peterson stood as the president entered. The other members of the cabinet followed suit moments later.

"Take your seats," Luthier said.

The cabinet members quickly did so.

"Our first order of business," Luthier continued, "is to approve my nomination for secretary of defense. As a former MLA leader, Miss Gonzales is the perfect choice to lead our war against these terrorist factions that threaten to destroy our budding democracy."

"Hear, hear," Brock shouted.

"Hear, hear," they all replied.

"All in favor?" Brock asked.

All seven hands were quickly raised.

"Opposed?" he asked, largely for formality.

"It's settled, then," Luthier replied.

"Now, on to our next order of business," the Cabinet Secretary said. "We need to address the recent terrorist attacks in Mendala. Attacks in our northern province are becoming more frequent."

"Nuke them all," Tim replied.

The remaining cabinet members just sat there, jaws agape.

Chapter Twenty-seven

THE hallway in the abandoned cannery reeked of rotting fish, its shadowy corners cold and uninviting. Carlie groggily opened her eyes.

Sodium thiopental, Carlie thought. *Potent barbiturate. Very nasty.*

Her wrists chafed against the ropes as she struggled against the cheaply made plywood chair. She couldn't see much—*partly a result of the medication,* she suspected—but she could distinctly make out another chair about three feet away. Beyond that, the room faded into obscurity.

In the distance, she saw signs of movement. As her eyes struggled to focus on their distant form, a spotlight illuminated the chair, blinding her further.

"Carlie Sinclair," a man's disembodied voice boomed from the eerie blackness.

"Who's asking?" she shouted in reply.

Suddenly, the chair she had seen earlier was illuminated by a spotlight shining down from the ceiling. As she turned her head around, she realized that it was not the only one. She was surrounded by about a dozen similar chairs, all illuminated in a menacing fashion. Occupying these chairs were various men and women, none of whom looked too pleased to be there.

"Carlie Sinclair," the now-visible man continued, "you have been found guilty of treason against the Republic."

"Without a trial," Carlie noted.

"We have no need for such niceties," the man replied. "When you helped Sheila Zarzycki escape from prison, you became an enemy combatant under article 317 of the Articles of the Kinji Republic."

"Article 317?" Carlie replied. "There is no article 317. There are only 312."

"President Luthier has added eight more," the man replied. "We are operating in a state of martial law."

"Luthier?" she asked. "Did you say... President... Luthier? Hey, wait a minute. You look famil...."

And then everything went black.

***

President Luthier stood as Terésa entered.

"Terésa, my dear," he said with a smirk. "You were right. One little nuke and the terrorists are scurrying around like cockroaches when you turn the kitchen light on."

"See, what did I tell you?" she replied.

"What do you think we should do about the situation in Pilatia?"

She thought for a moment before replying, "Pilatia?"

"There was a bombing on a train in the garment district this morning," he explained. "Nobody claims responsibility."

"First, we should send in troops to keep the peace," she suggested. "Plant someone with an assault rifle on every corner."

"Will that help?" he asked.

"No, but people will *feel* safer...."

"Wonderful," he replied.

***

THE police barricade blocked access to the warehouse from five blocks in every direction. As he stood there, he noticed a familiar face.

"What's the word, Carl?" Jonathan asked.

Carl turned and smiled. "Hey, Jon," he replied. "We're ready to move in on your signal."

"Sir?" asked a voice from behind him.

Jonathan turned. Before him stood a young girl in her late teens or early twenties.

"Yes?" he asked.

"We are receiving a message from the KAF."

Kinji Armed Forces? Jonathan scratched his head. *What could they want?*

"What do they want?" he asked.

"They have ordered you to stand down."

***

SHEILA groggily opened her eyes and reached up to rub them. The sharp pain in her wrists told her immediately that she was restrained. She winced.

As her eyes came into focus, she could make out.... *Oh, crap. Hospital room. Why couldn't it have been a Turkish prison?*

"Where am I?" she asked to no one in particular.

The empty room remained silent in reply.

***

CARLIE awoke to the feeling of being dragged by her arms down a hall. Her legs were bound with rope, and her arms were being held by two soldiers. Three other soldiers followed behind with rifles pointed in her direction.

As they pulled her through a set of double doors, she had a sinking feeling.

"Excellent! Excellent!" Luthier exclaimed.

Luthier....

"You bastard!" Carlie shouted.

"Ah, Carlie, my dear," Luthier replied. "I *really* hate to do this. Nothing personal, you understand."

With that, the two soldiers stood her against a wall and took up positions along the perimeter of the room. There, they picked up rifles and stood at attention. The three remaining soldiers stood beside them.

Only five of them, she thought. *One of me.... Could happen.... There's a chance....*

As if on cue, the doors swung open once again and eight more soldiers entered, rifles at the ready.

Or not....

***

"Sir," the girl added, "they say that if you enter that building, you will be interfering with national security directive three-break-alpha and will be subject to court martial."

Jonathan paused for a brief moment....

"Tear gas and cover fire *only*," he said. "If we can't go *in* yet, we'll just have to drive them *out*."

"Sir?" the girl asked.

"Yes?"

"They also said in the message that Carlie is an enemy of the state and is being executed. They said that any attempt to rescue her would constitute an act of treason punishable by death."

Jonathan stood there.

Carl turned towards him and grimaced. "Jonathan?"

"Open fire."

***

The soldiers stood at order arms, their rifles resting on the ground, touching their boots.

"Ready!" Luthier shouted.

The soldiers snapped to right shoulder arms and disabled the safeties on their rifles.

Carlie shivered. *So this is it?*

"Aim!" Luthier shouted.

The soldiers drew their rifles and aimed at Carlie.

Suddenly, the window overhead shattered as a foreign object flew through and bounced across the ground.

The gunfire outside drew their attention momentarily as the tear gas began to fill the room.

Carlie took advantage of that moment of distraction and flung herself to the floor.

"Fire!" Luthier shouted as he realized what was happening... but it was too late.

"At what?" one soldier shouted, already engulfed by the smoky haze.

"We have to get out of here, sir," Terésa said urgently.

Luthier stood, obviously still in shock. Through the ashen veil, Carlie could barely make out their figures as they ran up the stairs along the wall, opened a trapdoor, and disappeared onto what she could only assume was the roof.

As the air slowly cleared, she made out something else in the distance.

"Carlie?" Jonathan shouted.

Carlie sighed.

***

The shuttle slowly descended towards the capitol building.

"We need a plan," Luthier said angrily.

Terésa squirmed uncomfortably. "We *have* a plan. This changes nothing."

"Carlie knows we were there," Luthier replied.

"She can't prove it, and she knows it," Terésa answered.

"No, we need to deal with Mikarta Central Intelligence," Luthier insisted. "We must send in troops to secure the facility."

"We *need* to provide a show of force against our neighbors," she countered. "We have limited forces at our disposal, and going up against Mikarta CI this early would be too risky. We must show our strength *first*. Pick a planet with minimal defenses."

The shuttle's landing struts touched the ground with a thump.

"Okay," Luthier replied as the hatch swung slowly open. "How about Proxima Centauri III? We could conscript the locals to build up our military, too."

"I like the way you think, Tim."

***

Jonathan stepped cautiously into his office. Everything seemed to be in order. As he flipped open the laptop on his desk, though, he noticed something odd—a bright yellow electronic sticky note on his screen.

> *Jonathan,*
>
> *Call Donovan.*

Jonathan reached into his pocket, pulled out a rather odd looking data pad, and began pressing buttons.

***

THE sharp pain in her shoulder made Sheila wince in pain as she struggled to sit up. Slowly, she eyed the room, its nondescript features rendering it almost completely unrecognizable... but one small flaw betrayed its location: the window.

As she stared out the large picture window before her, she immediately recognized the blue-green sky.

"Have a nice nap?" a man's voice asked, seemingly out of nowhere.

Sheila spun her head around with a snap, then quickly regretted it.

Oh well, she thought. *There's no better place to get whiplash than a hospital....*

The man hovering in the doorway—a doctor, she presumed—was an older man in his fifties, bespectacled, wearing a white lab coat with a name tag that read simply, "Dr. Bob".

As she opened her mouth to speak, he quickly interrupted.

"Welcome to the Proxima Centauri Ops medical ward," the doctor said. "A lot of people are going to get canned for bringing you here, but while you're here, we'll give you the best care in the sector."

She tried to laugh, but the pain in her side was too much, so she winced instead.

"Get some rest," he continued. "I'll be in to check on you in a bit."

As the door shut, the room shook slightly.

Wow. Must be some cheap construction.

Then, the room shook again.

Chapter Twenty-eight

THE Mikarta Central Intelligence orbital outpost above Proxima Centauri III sprang suddenly to life, the normally black windows around its outer hull now glowing with purposeful intensity.

Nearby, giant hangar doors crept slowly open like mouths preparing to devour their next meals. As one wave of bombers flew out to begin their next run, the previous wave flew back in for supplies.

The universe sighed.

Chapter Twenty-nine

Donovan answered the call. Despite the suit, Donovan's chiseled features and short, dark hair reminded Jonathan that this was a military mission, and Donovan was the general.

"Jonathan," he began, "what brings you to call?"

"There was a note," Jonathan replied.

"Ah, yes," Donovan said, chuckling. "I set that up to appear today, didn't I? Well, no matter. Diego said that you were finished with the antidote. Have you solved the distribution problem?"

"I think so," he replied. "We seeded it into the drinking water, but we still need some time to do a small-scale test."

Donovan looked pensive. *I wonder why he doesn't know this already,* Jonathan wondered.

"It didn't work."

"What do you mean, 'it didn't work'?"

"If it had worked," Donovan replied, "history would record that the disaster never occurred."

As Donovan held up an old newspaper clipping to the camera, Jonathan turned white as a sheet.

"November 13? That's tomorrow! You have to send me back again," he begged. "We can try distributing it in some other way."

"Jon, you know I can't send you back again. You'd die. Besides, that's not your primary mission. You have to stop Luthier from finding the portals at the Mikarta CI headquarters on Kinji."

Jonathan scratched his head. "You really think that Luthier caused your time displacement?"

"I don't know how it could be anything else," Donovan replied. "He certainly didn't find the portals on Proxima Centauri III."

Jonathan grimaced.

***

"TABLE for two," Donna told the man in the hideous suit. "And a coffee. I like a little buzz before my weekly haircut."

"Right this way," the man replied.

As she sat down at the table at Café Emilie, the look on Paul's face immediately told her that something was terribly wrong. He said not a word as he reached into his pocket and produced an envelope.

Donna opened the envelope and read it to herself.

> *Donna,*
>
> *I'm afraid I have bad news. It appears the information I gave you earlier was from a less than reputable source. I have reason to believe Diego was, in fact, working in concert with Mikarta Central Intelligence to prevent a far more serious threat.*
>
> *My sources have recently made me aware of a biological weapons research*

facility working on a substance to neutralize cutatox, a bacterial byproduct of Staphylococcus Cutis-Exitiabilis. I do not know its location, but I will give you another message if and when I find out.

I have reason to believe that Diego was visiting this facility at the time of the assassination attempt, and that meetings related to this project are the most likely explanation for the secret meetings and poor cover stories.

That's not the worst part. President Luthier is married to one Terésa Gonzales—a known terrorist originally from Lenora Prime—and has been for many years. I believe that her involvement with Diego was merely a means of gaining access to the government of Kinji—for what purposes, I do not know.

More when I know more,

Paul

***

Carlie stepped into the Mikarta Central Intelligence building. The normally empty halls were lined with computers, desks, chairs, and other random junk.

As she walked towards the lift, a set of rails slowly began to rise from the floor. She stepped back and watched as two giant doors dropped a couple of inches, then slid slowly into pockets under the floor.

The platform quickly slid into place a few moments later, filled with people and equipment. No sooner had the rails dropped than the people began sliding equipment off to the side.

"What's going on?" she asked.

"Don't ask us," the man replied. "They just told us to move this stuff, so we're moving it."

With that, Carlie stepped onto the platform with them, pulled a control pad out of her pocket, and punched 34.

***

SHEILA stood and hobbled to the window. One look at the sky told her all she needed to know. The dozens of small flashes of light in the distance were painful even from a distance. She knew that they could mean only one thing.

The room shook again, this time harder.

They're getting closer, she thought, *and they're nukes.*

As the door swung back open, the doctor didn't mince words.

"Good, you're up," he said. "Let's go. We're leaving."

***

As the door opened onto the desert surface, the bright flashes in the distance gave her pause.

Should I turn around now? No. They might need help evacuating, she thought, so she quickly jogged to the nearest building and ran inside.

The flurry of medical personnel told her that this was the medical center, its normally full rooms mostly empty. A few personnel were helping move the immotile patients out while others were grabbing holographic storage cells of patient information.

I'd just get in the way here, she thought, but then she saw someone familiar out of the corner of her eye. *No, not someone. Two someones,* she thought.

"Jonathan!" she shouted. "What's going on? Can I give you a hand?"

"We're being bombed," he said.

Carlie rolled her eyes.

"And sure," Jonathan added. "Grab an arm."

Carlie slipped an arm behind Sheila's back to help steady her.

"Oh," Jonathan said, smirking in amusement. "You meant to ask *who* was bombing us."

Carlie smiled a sarcastic half smile, half grimace.

"Kinji."

The exterior door opened automatically as they approached it, and they walked through. Outside, bombs continued to fall while Proxima Centauri fighters scrambled into the air to fire back at the bombers.

"Wait a sec," Carlie replied. "Aren't they on our side?"

"They don't know we're here, remember?" he replied, "and they're not going to know. The base is indistinguishable from civilian buildings, but once they're on the ground.... Let's just say that our orders are to scorch the earth."

"Self destruct?" she asked.

"Catastrophic spatial cascade," he replied. "We'll shift every atom in the entire base by several feet in random directions."

Carlie instinctively ducked as one of the bombers sped past, flying just a few hundred feet over her head.

"Wow," Carlie replied in awe.

"You want to know the worst part about it?" Jonathan asked.

"What's that?"

"Our orbital outposts are supplying them," he replied. "We have the power to stop the bombing...."

"But if you did, this base would be discovered," Carlie replied.

Jonathan nodded.

Carlie shivered.

Chapter Thirty

"Are you planning to go topside today while you can still breathe the air?" Skylarov quipped.

Donovan Jenkins shivered.

"This plan still makes me nervous, Mikhail," he said.

"Relax," Skylarov replied. "Nothing can go wrong. You've tested the antidote, and you know you can make this work."

"I know it will work," Donovan countered, "but it just doesn't seem right to play games with people's lives...."

"We won't have to. The Mikartans have assured me that the antidote will work," he replied. "Every trace of the toxin should be destroyed by the time it reaches the drinking water supply. If all else fails, though, we can roll back time to stop the test."

Donovan grimaced.

"And if we can't do it? What if I'm wrong? What if time doesn't flow both ways?" he asked.

Skylarov frowned. *Then we should be glad we are only going to release the toxin in* ***one*** *town.*

"I don't know," Skylarov replied. "I don't know."

***

THE cabinet stood as President Luthier entered the room.

"As you were," he said.

Schmuck, Terésa thought.

"Gentlemen," he continued, "mission accomplished."

Terésa's ears perked up.

"Proxima Centauri III is fully under the control of the Kinji Armed Forces," he continued. "We are experiencing a few minor hiccups, however."

Hiccups? Terésa thought.

"Hiccups?" Terésa asked.

"While the military forces on the main continent have been largely destroyed," he replied, "certain rogue elements of the Centauri military continue to operate on other continents."

Terésa frowned. *This could damage our popularity in the next election,* she thought.

"This could damage our pop..."

Luthier cut her off.

"We believe," he continued, "that they are being supplied by weapon construction facilities underground in the mountains above Tirabia. We intend to eliminate the insurgent threat by constructing barriers to travel between cities."

"What do you have in mind?" Cabinet Secretary Peterson asked.

"We will have armed military checkpoints," Luthier replied, "and we will require identification to move from one place to another. If an insurgent attack occurs in a city, everyone who entered that city in the previous week will be rounded up and summarily executed."

The room grew eerily quiet.

Terésa smiled as Luthier continued.

"Today, Proxima Centauri III, tomorrow, the universe."

***

DONNA quickly stepped away from the conference room door and back to her desk.

Tomorrow, the universe?

***

CARLIE felt a slight tingle as they stepped through the portal onto a lift platform on Kinji.

"What's going to happen with all this stuff?" Carlie asked. "There's no room here."

"Come on," Jonathan replied. "I'll show you."

He pressed the number 0110 on his keypad. The lift plummeted again, this time slowing as it neared the bottom.

"Secret labs start with a zero," he continued. "That way no one pushes them accidentally."

As the door opened, they found themselves stepping into... an inky void. Carlie couldn't see anything, including her companions. Then, a small light appeared, partially illuminating her surroundings.

"It helps to carry a flashlight," Jonathan remarked.

With that, he reached out and pressed a few buttons on a control pad. As he pressed the final button, the giant metal door next to it crept slowly open.

Beyond that door lay a large storage vault with rock walls. A series of crude steel shelves lined those walls, filled with containers covered in large radiological warning stickers. The shelves had only a small gap on both ends—one for the doorway through which they had just passed, and one for a similar doorway at the other end.

As they approached the second door, it opened for them, revealing a brightly lit, metal-lined hallway, with what appeared to be a rock floor and ceiling. The whole place looked like someone had quickly thrown metal panels along the walls to hold up the lights, then put in a few beams between the walls—*just enough,* Carlie mused, *to keep the walls from falling over.*

Her musings were briefly interrupted by a medical technician. He took Sheila and helped her into a waiting wheelchair, then quickly disappeared into a lift with Sheila in tow. After the lift doors closed, Jonathan and Carlie began walking in the opposite direction.

As she walked through the doorway, Carlie turned and looked back where she had been. The room at the other end of the storage room was gone; a row of shelves stood where it had been. Carlie shivered.

The corridors seemed to stretch on for an eternity in an endless spiral, with door after door lining the walls, each with a number on it—section 11, section 12, section 13.... Finally, they reached a door and stopped in front of it. As the door slid open, she saw a shuttle bay—larger than any she had seen previously—its shiny metal standing in stark contrast to its otherwise austere surroundings.

Dozens of scientists scurried around like hamsters in a wheel, each working on their own pet projects at various workstations around the perimeter, while technicians serviced a small shuttle parked nearby.

As the duo approached, the hangar bay doors slowly opened, and beyond them, they saw.... *Snow*. The snow fell in clumps and was vaporized by the heat of the energy field covering the entrance.

The view down the side of the mountain was breathtaking, its snowcapped neighbors jutting up from the verdant fields below like giant whitecaps rising up from the ocean just before a storm.

"Lenora," Jonathan explained. "Welcome to Lenora Prime."

Chapter Thirty-one

"OUR next target is Tularis Prime," Luthier continued.

"What's on Tularis Prime?" Secretary Peterson prodded.

Terésa grimaced. *Time to trot out the old dog and pony show,* she thought as she reached out and pressed a button on the wall. A projection screen descended from the ceiling, and the lights began to dim.

"Tularis Prime," she began as the first slide came into view, "is one of the seediest systems in the known worlds. In addition to being the home of one of the more ruthless mob bosses, it is also the location of a research facility currently engaged in the mass manufacture of weapons of mass destruction."

Secretary Peterson's jaw was agape. "We have no such intelligence!" he shouted.

"We have it on good authority that our information is accurate," she interrupted. "We believe that there are large stockpiles of plutonium on the planet's surface. This will become clear once we have seized control of the planet."

Secretary Peterson scowled.

"Finally," Terésa continued, "we have reason to believe that the Tularian government is providing material support for the terrorist factions on Proxima Centauri III. This alone would be sufficient grounds for an invasion."

"The plan," Luthier interrupted, "is to start with a bombing run against key strategic assets, then send in ground troops to clean up whatever forces remain. We leave in 18 hours."

As the lights faded back to full brightness, Terésa smiled.

"Any questions?"

***

"Did you say Lenora Prime?" Carlie asked incredulously. "That's millions of light years away!"

"Just outside Adalia, specifically," he replied, grinning. "Or, if you look out your left window, at a distance of twenty light years, you can just make out the faint glow of Tularis."

Carlie raised her eyebrows, then asked, "Okay, what's really going on here?"

"What do you mean?" he replied.

"I know my theoretical physics," Carlie replied. "This isn't possible. Folding that distance in a single jump would take a power source the size of a small planet."

No sooner had she said this than a scientist interrupted her.

"Sir, I just wanted to make you aware of a slight change in facility utilization," she said.

"A wha-"

"The Earth scientists arrived early, sir," she replied.

"No, no. This will not do," he countered. "Have they found the portal chamber yet?"

"No," she replied.

"See that they don't," Jonathan warned. "The consequences could be dire...."

***

In the cold recesses of the supply station above Proxima Centauri III, Chuck Graham smiled. He watched in silence as Luthier's men loaded the bombs onto the ships.

Things are going swimmingly, he thought. *Soon, Lenora Prime will be nothing but a smoldering ruin, and that idiot, Luthier, will be blamed for it. Best of all, Terésa will be dead. The plan is perfect.*

"Cutatox is one of the deadliest known poisons," the scientist explained. "In small quantities, it will kill or disfigure a large number of people. In the quantity we will be distributing, we estimate the entire population of Tularis Prime will be obliterated."

Terésa did not mince words. "When do we begin?"

"Tomorrow," Luthier replied.

Any day now....

***

Carlie changed the viewscreen to the next channel just as the KNS News logo appeared. She was stunned. *They get KNS here?*

> "You're tuned to KNS, the Kinji News Syndicate," the reporter said. "Voters were in a state of shock today when they were denied entrance to polling places by KAF troops. President Luthier held a press conference a few minutes ago."
>
> "Fellow Kinjans," he began, "today marks a sad day for our democracy. Threats

of terrorist attacks at the polling places have forced our hand. We cannot allow them to put our citizens in jeopardy, so we have postponed the parliamentary elections indefinitely."

Luthier waited for the noise to die down as the crowd of reporters murmured their disapproval.

"It is most regrettable that these actions are necessary," he continued, "but Kinjans should be assured that the government will continue to function as it normally does through this difficult period in our planet's history. I have selected an interim parliament to continue our wartime operations. I have no doubt that they will perform admirably."

With that, the reporter reappeared.

"KNS will continue to bring you coverage of this story as it develops."

"In other breaking news," she continued, "the death toll from Mikarta is still rising after a strike presumed to be in retaliation for recent surgical strikes against Proxima Centauri III. The lone attack ship was quickly destroyed by Kinji missiles, but not before launching a number of explosive devices, most of which made landfall. Kinji security forces have ordered a full evacuation of nearby areas until the damage can be assessed and any risks to public safety contained."

The reporter paused for a few moments, waiting for the B-roll to end. When she reappeared on the screen, she concluded her report.

"For the Kinji News Syndicate, I'm Trisha McKeever."

Jonathan entered just as Carlie turned off the viewscreen in disgust.

"Something wrong?" he asked.

"Everything is wrong," she replied.

Jonathan nodded knowingly.

"So what are you researching here?" Carlie asked.

"Well, we're doing immunological research," he replied. "The Earth team... I'm not sure. We don't talk to them much. There are parts of the base that are off-limits to them, including the portal chamber. Beyond that, they pretty much keep to themselves in sections nine through thirteen."

"Can I see?"

Jonathan stiffened, paused for a moment, then relaxed.

"Sure. Why not?" he replied. "I'll take you there."

***

The supply station shimmered in the light reflected from Proxima Centauri as its orbit took it slowly into the planet's twilight. The station's lights dropped to daytime levels, and the giant sun shield was slowly deployed to reduce the radiation levels inside.

The shuttle bay doors slid slowly open once again as the third wave of fighters and bombers made their way into the staging area—a polar orbit near the folding gate at Proxima Centauri IV. In a few hours, they would fold into orbit around their destination in waves and reduce it to ashes.

Lenora, Chuck thought. *At last, you will be my burden no more.*

***

CARLIE watched as Jonathan slid his card through the reader in section II. The light above turned green momentarily. Then a warning horn sounded as the giant door swung slowly open.

The room beyond was stark, its dark, shadowy innards seeming to absorb the light like a sponge soaking up ink. The crude metal grillwork of its raised floor, coupled with the dim lighting and hooks around the walls, made her wonder if she had just walked into a research lab or a slaughterhouse.

The room was basically empty, with no real furniture, no personnel, and no visible entrances or exits other than a set of metal bars in front of a long hallway that seemed to extend far into the distance. Indeed, the only hint of the lab's purpose was a row of large freezers down one wall, along with a refrigerator nearby.

On the refrigerator was a sign that read, "People food."

The room was also quiet—eerily so—except for one faint sound that seemed to echo from the distant recesses of the caged hallway.

Click, clack.... Click, clack, click, clack.... Chirp.... Click, clack, click, clack....

That's when they noticed the sign on the row of freezers.

Lizard food.

Chapter Thirty-two

PRESIDENT Luthier addressed the troops by viewscreen. Dressed in a military uniform, he strode to the podium.

"Many members of the press have expressed concern," he began, "about our mission to Tularis Prime. We have not been attacked by the military of Tularis Prime, true, but they pose a far greater threat to us and our allies than you can possibly imagine.

"We have reason to believe that the Tularian government is engaged in the design and construction of weapons of mass extinction—deadly biological weapons that could literally wipe out the population of an entire planet.

"Although our scientists are busy working on countermeasures, we currently do not have the means to protect ourselves from these weapons, and thus they represent a substantial escalation in the threat posed by the Tularian government.

"In addition, we believe that the government of Tularis Prime is actively diverting funds to support the Colonial Liberation Front, a known terrorist organization. We believe that our reasons for going to war are sound.

"Make no mistake, the next few hours will be the most important hours in our war on terror. All of Kinji stands with you. Godspeed, gentlemen."

The viewscreen went black.

***

CHUCK watched the bombs rain down on Tularis as wave after wave of Kinji ships carpeted the planet from space.

One more wave before the fun begins, he thought—*one more wave before the Lenoran people breathe no more.*

His exuberance was interrupted by the viewscreen, however. He had told the computer to monitor any communication between the attack fleet and Kinji.

This conversation, he thought, *promised to be... entertaining....*

"President Luthier," the soldier began, "We have a small problem."

Chuck smiled.

***

LUTHIER grimaced as the viewscreen sprung to life. *A "small" problem,* he thought. *Why is it that small problems never are?*

"How small?" Luthier replied. "By small problem, do you mean that one of the ships is disabled, or by small problem, do you mean that Earth has joined the fight alongside Tularis Prime?"

"Neither, sir," the soldier answered. "Wave 15 has been compromised. We detected an unexpected balance problem in one of the warheads during their final self test."

"One missile?" Luthier chided. "That's pretty small."

"That's not the problem," the soldier continued. "The missile passed its tests a few days ago, so that had us worried. We opened it up and found a container that has us even more worried."

"A... container?" Luthier asked.

"Biohazard, sir," he replied. "Cutatox, we think."

"Stand by," Luthier ordered. "Hold wave fifteen until you receive further instructions."

"Aye, sir," the soldier replied. "Standing by. Dirk out."

As the viewscreen went black, Luthier began dialing immediately.

"Terésa!" Luthier shouted. "What the ***hell*** did you do to my ships?"

Terésa sat in stunned silence.

"You put cutatox in one of the missiles," Luthier continued. "What the hell were you thinking? Did you think we wouldn't notice?"

"Did you think I didn't have a backup plan?" she replied, smiling.

"Oh, no.... No!" he cried.

***

As they stood at the doorway to Section 11, Jonathan froze. Above the metal bars, he could just make out two lights—one red, one green. The red light was lit.

"What's wrong?" Carlie asked.

"Red light," he replied.

"What?"

"Red light. Red light. Red light!" he whispered furiously, nodding in the direction of the cage-like structure.

"Is that bad?" she asked.

Jonathan looked at her, eyes widened in fear. "Red," he said.

And in the distance... *click, clack, click, clack....*

***

LUTHIER strutted and fretted his hour upon the staging area on Kinji.

I don't even know where she is, he thought. *Can I stop her? Maybe we found the only rigged bomb. Maybe she's bluffing.*

Or maybe the cutatox is on the surface already. She's setting me up! That bitch is setting me up!

Deep greenish sky.... She must be on Lenora. It's the only place that makes sense. We'll bomb Lenora instead. It's the only way....

Luthier gave the order.

"Men," he shouted at the viewscreen, "cease bombing. You have a new mission. You are to divert to Lenora Prime, effective immediately. Your mission is to hunt down Terésa Gonzales and terminate her."

"Sir?" one pilot asked. "What about the bombing run?"

"I'm sending you target coordinates on Lenora Prime. The bombing run will proceed as planned; only the list of targets is different. Dismissed!"

***

HE knows!

Terésa's jaw hung agape as she realized what this meant. *Chuck set me up to take the fall instead of Luthier. He was never going to destroy Tularis Prime at all!*

I'm a fugitive now, she thought. She looked out her window at the dark blue-green Lenoran sky and shivered.

Luthier may be an idiot, but he knows he isn't safe as long as I'm alive. If I stay here, he'll find me even if he has to destroy the planet to do it. There's no place to hide here.

With that realization, she walked quickly out of the office and got into her private shuttle. Moments later, she was gone.

Chapter Thirty-three

November 12, 2359

THE skies over Lenora Prime turned almost imperceptibly lighter as nearly a hundred bombers folded one by one into an orbit near its L2 Lagrange point.

One by one, the bombers appeared like tiny twinkling lights in the distance—tiny specs of white against the deep, blue-green sky—and then began their inevitable descent planetward.

***

LUTHIER smiled. *Just a few more minutes,* he thought, *and it will all be over.... **She** will be... all over....*

"Commence the first bombing run," he ordered... "now."

***

JONATHAN jumped as the ground beneath his feet shook violently. Alarm klaxons started honking and the giant door to section 11 began to close.

"Run!" he yelled.

With that, he grabbed Carlie and pulled her through the door and into the hall outside, then pulled out a phase pistol and stood and watched as the door slowly closed to a crack.

Suddenly, giant metal claws reached through the narrow opening.

Carlie screamed. "What is that!?!"

The creature emitted a guttural snarling sound as the door strained to close.

"I'm not sure," he replied, firing three shots at the beast, "but I think he's hungry."

The lizard screamed in pain and retracted its claws. With the lizard no longer holding it, the door slowly finished its slide, then latched shut with metal pistons as big as your arm.

Carlie's eyes widened as she stared at Jonathan.

Jonathan merely shook his head...

...and then the next shock wave hit.

***

From his private shuttle above Proxima Centauri III, Chuck Graham smiled.

It is over. ***I*** *have won.*

***

Jonathan and Carlie made their way through the winding corridors. As they neared the main room, the comm pad in his pocket began beeping incessantly.

"Excuse me," he said. "I have to take this."

With that, Jonathan quickly slipped into a broom closet and closed the door behind him.

"Jonathan, what's happening?" asked a somewhat older Donovan Jenkins.

"We're under attack," he replied. "There's nothing in your logs about this."

"I had just returned from shore leave to find our entire research team eaten," Donovan answered. "I kind of had other things on my mind."

"Yeah. I think that just happened."

Donovan cringed.

"We have to evacuate to Alpha Centauri Base," Jonathan continued. "We're going to destroy the portal after everyone is out."

"You can't," Donovan replied.

"What?"

"You still have to go back and prevent me from starting the experiment," Donovan continued. "Besides, if you destroy the portal, it will leave a radioactive residue behind. It will be detected, and you'll mess up the timeline even further."

"But sir," Jonathan interrupted, "this thing is dangerous to use during temporal folding, and they're experimenting with an Ackerman crystal. I don't think we should just leave this behind...."

"Don't worry," Donovan replied. "Nobody ever finds the portal gear. I was there, remember? All you have to do is stop Luthier, and the rest should take care of itself."

***

PAUL jumped as the shock wave shook the facility under the Puccini Mountains of Lenora.

"What's going on?" he shouted.

"Sir," another man shouted from a console near the wall. "We're receiving an emergency message from the Kend'hara."

"Put it on."

The shaky voice at the other end of the comm channel chilled him to the core.

"This is the The Kend'hara shuttle Phoenix 13 to anyone who can hear me, over," the young man said.

"This is the research station Lenora Alpha," Paul replied. "We read you, over."

"We have lost our hull integrity. Engines are critical, and we're coming in hot. We are in need of an emergency landing, and it's gonna be ugly."

"Copy that," Paul replied. "Jill, open hangar doors. Deploy emergency braking barricade."

"Estimate arrival in ten... nine... eight... seven... six..."

"Everybody brace!" Paul shouted.

"four... three... two... one...."

***

CARLIE smirked as Jonathan stepped out of the closet.

"What's so funny?" he asked.

You're the last guy I expected to come out of the closet, she thought, biting her lip to avoid grinning ear to ear.

"Nothing," she replied quickly, then began giggling uncontrollably.

Jonathan rolled his eyes.

"Well, come on, then," he said as he began pulling her through the winding corridors once again.

"To where?" she asked.

"Alpha Centauri Base," he replied. "We're being bombed. We have to go *now*."

"Sheila?"

"She'll be fine."

"Are you blowing this portal up, too?"

"We can't. I don't have time to explain."

He's worried, she thought. *Something is very wrong.... Very wrong, indeed.*

***

SPARKS flew like a million angry wasps after a hapless child poked their nest with a stick. The sound of metal shearing permeated the hangar deck with such ferocity that even the bulky hearing protectors were of little use, leaving the deck crew grasping those hearing protectors and writhing in pain from the intense squeal.

By the time the Phoenix 13 came to rest in a smoldering heap against the crash barriers, it had cut deep gouges in the deck floor like a wildebeest that got too close to a lion.

Paul sighed. *So,* he thought, *what else is gnu?*

He watched as the emergency hatch swung open listlessly and a young man stepped down, followed by a young woman.

"Ensign James Kurtz reporting for duty, sir, and this is my wife, Allison. We're the science team Donovan requested."

Military, Paul thought. *Great. Just what we need. And Earth military, even.*

"What's going on out there," Paul asked.

"It's a war zone, sir," he replied. "They came out of nowhere with no warning... Kinji ships... eight hundred... maybe a thousand... bombers, fighters... the works. The captain didn't want to send us down in the middle of it, but he said it was urgent, so...."

"I have to make a call," Paul said curtly as he spun on his heels and walked towards the comm station.

"Greetings from hell," Paul said as Jonathan's face appeared on the viewscreen. "Any clue why Kinji is bombing Lenora?"

"Kinji? Bombing Lenora?" he sputtered. "I figured Earth was bombing us after their people disappeared. Oh, yeah... they're missing. I just noticed. Probably the mechs. Last I heard, Kinji was too busy bombing Proxima Centauri III and Tularis Prime to care about Lenora...."

"If so, they missed their target by half a galaxy," Paul replied.

Jonathan grew pale. "You think they found a way to trace the portal traffic?"

"The timing is pretty coincidental," he replied.

"Terésa," they both said simultaneously.

"He's going after Terésa," Paul said.

"But why?" Jonathan asked.

"I'm not sure," he replied, "but with the internal power struggle that this could cause, now is the perfect cover to take out Luthier... while his forces are here."

"Everyone, get to work rounding up the wayward lizards, and tell Kinji to expect visitors from the east," Jonathan quipped.

"I'll meet you there soon," Paul muttered as he closed the channel.

***

DONNA staggered home from the bar. As she slipped into her apartment, she kicked something—an envelope, crudely shoved under the door. She bent and picked it up, then threw it in the general direction of a pile of papers as she collapsed onto the bed.

No, she thought. *I need to read this.*

Dearest Donna,

The Kinji military is attacking Proxima Centauri III. We're going to visit grandma Lenora.

Paul

She knew what this meant... and it wasn't good news.

Donna quickly regained her faculties as best she could—a cold shower and lots of coffee. Her bloodstream was a cocktail that would make even a drug company proud.

Lenora Prime, she thought. *They're evacuating to Lenora Prime? Terésa is from Lenora Prime.... This is not good. Not good at all....*

Then, she noticed that the message light on her data pad was blinking. The text of that message was even less pleasant.

Kinji attacking. Must keep grandma safe. Tomorrow, watch for three wise men from the east.

Chapter Thirty-four

As they stepped out of the portal onto the metal arrival ramp on Alpha Centauri Base, Carlie slipped on the corrugated deck plating and landed with a thud.

"Have a nice trip?" Jonathan joked.

Carlie groaned.

"Come on," he said, helping her to her feet. "We have to fold to Kinji."

Jonathan practically dragged her down the corridor as she limped along, struggling to keep up.

When they reached the hangar deck, a shuttle was waiting. Minutes later, the shuttle Prometheus folded from Alpha Centauri to Caldera, through the Mars gate, passing just beyond Jupiter in a slingshot at near light speed to a gate temporarily placed in orbit near Pluto for a space race, then folded one last time to Kinji.

"Why the long fold?" Carlie asked.

"Harder to trace," Jonathan replied.

She nodded.

As they descended into the atmosphere above Kinji, the city of Mikarta slowly emerged through the clouds. A blackened shell of its former beauty, the skyline was dark now, the city lit only by the headlights of military vehicles circling the streets.

The landing struts hit with a thud as Jonathan planted the shuttle on a patch of barren ground a few miles outside the city. Before the dust settled, Jonathan was armed and reaching for the evac ladder.

Carlie slid down first, dropping to the ground, then limping in pain. Jonathan quickly followed, then retracted the ladder by remote control.

As they began jogging towards the city center, Carlie heard the sound of tires crackling along the barren desert floor. Moments later, a jeep slid to a screeching halt in front of them.

Nowhere to run, Carlie thought. *It's over.*

As the dust began to settle, they heard a woman's voice call out to them through the dingy haze.

"Carlie? Jonathan? I heard you needed a lift."

As soon as the woman turned off the jeep's headlights, they saw....

"Donna?" Jonathan asked.

"Who were you expecting?" she replied, smirking. "Oh, and Paul says hi. Wait... I thought he said *three* wise *men*."

"Paul's a wise *guy*, if that means anything," Jonathan replied with a grin.

***

Luthier sighed as the channel opened. This time, the message was audio only, but he could make out Terésa's voice as plain as the nose on his face.

"Still here, asshole," she said.

Luthier howled with rage as he obliterated the innocent pieces of furniture around him, his chair splintering as it hit the wall.

"I may be damned to hell," he shouted, "but I'm taking you with me!"

He closed the channel, then opened a channel to the ships in orbit around Lenora.

"Men, there comes a time in every nation's history when it must do things that it finds distasteful in the name of freedom and liberty... to preserve the ideals that it holds dear.... History may judge us harshly for what I am about to do. If so, let history remember that everything I do, I do for our planet and its people."

"Terésa Gonzales," he continued, "is a genocidal monster. She attempted to unleash a devastating biological weapon attack on the people of Tularis Prime. We prevented that disaster, which would have killed tens of millions. We believe that she is holed up somewhere on Lenora Prime. The population of Lenora Prime, sadly, must be sacrificed to ensure that this woman can never harm anyone again."

"To that end," he concluded, "I am ordering the release of the very biological agent that she wished to inflict upon Tularis Prime. It is regrettable that some twelve thousand people must perish to ensure her demise, but compared with the deaths she would cause, that will seem but a trifle. And so it is with great sadness, but great resolve, that I hereby order the installation of cutatox warheads on all of the remaining missiles. Once all of the missiles are so armed, we will launch them simultaneously to obliterate all human life on Lenora Prime. That is all."

Chapter Thirty-five

November 13, 2359

DONNA's jeep pulled up to the back gate of Mikarta Central Intelligence headquarters. Paul was waiting for them when they arrived.

"Are you sure he's in there?" Jonathan asked.

"He isn't in the capital building," she replied. "The Proxima Centauri freedom fighters bombed it from orbit."

Jonathan shivered.

"With the gates locked, there's only one way in," he told them. "The designers built a secret entrance in case the facility was ever compromised. There's a telephone booth under the adjacent square. Dial the right number, and we're in."

"Do you know the number?" Carlie asked.

"No, but how hard can it be?" he asked. "It's only a twenty-digit number. 1-1-1-1-1, 1-1-1-1-1, 1-1-1-1-1, 1-1-1-1-1. Nope. 1-1-1-1-1, 1-1-1-1-1, 1-1-1-1-1, 1-1-1-1-2. Nope."

Carlie stared at him, wide-eyed in terror.

"I'm kidding," he said, smiling an impish grin. "Of course I know the number."

Carlie relaxed visibly.

"Donna," Jonathan continued, "I want you to do something for me. If I don't make it back from this mission, I need you to deliver this letter to a courier. I don't have time to explain."

Donna nodded her acceptance as she took the small envelope from Jonathan and stuffed it into her shirt pocket.

The quartet walked quickly across the plaza and down the rightmost staircase on the other side. When they reached the bottom, they turned around and saw, between the two staircases, a smaller plaza nestled into the hill at ground level, with a stone wall along its back edge and a matched pair of restrooms built into the hill under the plaza itself.

Between the restrooms stood a stone archway, the endpoint of a pedestrian tunnel that led from the adjacent park to the street level on the other side of the plaza. When they walked into the tunnel, they found an old-style Earth telephone booth with a communications terminal inside.

As they entered the phone booth, Jonathan apologized to Donna. "I'm afraid there's barely room for two," he said.

"That's cool," she replied. "I'm not really cut out for this spy stuff."

"On the contrary," he countered. "You're a regular Nancy Holmes."

She looked at him with a puzzled expression. "Drew."

"Ah, yes. Drew. My bad."

Donna shook her head in bewilderment.

"Stand back," Jonathan said.

Paul and Donna stepped back a few steps as Jonathan pressed a few buttons on the keypad.

"Hold on," he said to Carlie.

"To what?" Carlie asked.

"The phone," he replied.

"What?"

And with that, the floor of the booth began falling rapidly under their feet, bringing the phone and part of the walls along with it. Fifty feet down, it came to a screeching halt.

"Off," he shouted.

By the time Carlie's foot hit the concrete floor, the booth had already started its rapid ascent towards the ceiling.

"Yikes...."

***

DONNA cringed as she watched them disappear into the bowels of Mikarta. She quickly slipped the letter into her blazer pocket and began walking towards her jeep.

"Did you catch the number?" Paul asked.

Donna just smiled knowingly. *34152-41798-62405-00110.*

***

LUTHIER stood as the door slid open.

Jonathan smiled.

Carlie just stared. *This is going to get ugly;* she thought.

"You're too late," Luthier shouted, a spark of recognition slowly crossing his visage. "As soon as I press this button, our cutatox bombs will leave Lenora lifeless."

Luthier smiled as his hand reached down towards a red button on the console.

"You..." Jonathan said, dumbfounded.

Slowly, Luthier's hand approached the button as Jonathan drew a phase pistol.

"Nooooooooo!" Jonathan shouted as he jumped towards Luthier, firing three rounds and hitting him with two.

Simultaneously, the doors to the room slid open again and two armed security guards entered, weapons drawn.

As Luthier fell to the floor, they fired, striking Jonathan repeatedly in the chest.

"Noooooo!" Carlie shouted as she jumped towards Jonathan. "You bastards!"

The moment she hit the ground, she drew her sidearm and fired. The first guard collapsed, knocking the second off balance. The second guard, in turn, fell over the railing and hit the deck eight feet below with a sickening crunch.

"Nice shot," Jonathan whispered. Then, with a timid smile, he closed his eyes.

Suddenly, the viewscreen activated again. The face of Terésa Gonzales smiled at Carlie.

"Thanks for cleaning up my mess, kiddo. I always knew I could count on the ECIA to do what they do best."

With that, Terésa played a recording... imperfectly edited, and audio only, but very direct and to the point. Carlie listened in horror as in death, Luthier gave the order that he could not give in life.

"Commence the... bombing run," he ordered... "now."

"I did it!" she cried. "I killed them all!"

And then, with his dying breath, Luthier uttered six words that would haunt Carlie for the rest of her life.

"My god," he whispered. "What have I done?"

...and then was heard no more.

Chapter Thirty-six

DIEGO smiled as the cell doors opened. *We apologize for the inconvenience,* they said. *Like that's really supposed to make things better.... Schmucks.*

A young woman stood just beyond the prison gate. *It's good to see a friendly face,* Diego thought.

"Hello, Mr. Sanchez," the woman said. "My name is Carlie. Carlie Sinclair. I'm here to take you to see President Johnson."

"He's alive?" he asked.

"No thanks to that rat, Luthier," she replied.

"I'm afraid he was little more than a pawn," Diego countered. "Terésa is the real mastermind."

"Either way, I owe my life to a certain Jack Sinclair," President Johnson said as he walked into the room.

Diego immediately sprang to attention at the President's entrance.

"As you were," Johnson replied.

"Sheila?" Diego asked.

"I've granted her a full pardon," Johnson answered, "which certainly makes sense given that she didn't really do anything.... She'll be back from Alpha Centauri Base in a few weeks. For once, I didn't have to force her to take a vacation...."

Diego laughed.

***

JACK Sinclair relaxed in a hotel room on Caldera IV. His rest was short-lived, however; the viewscreen came on not ten seconds after his head hit the pillow.

"Go away," he said groggily.

"Jack?" Carlie asked.

"Oh, it's you," he muttered.

Carlie brushed off the insult.

"What's this I hear about you and President Johnson?"

"How do you think he got off the planet before the bombing?" Jack asked. "Oh, and visitors from the east? Did you *want* to get caught?"

Carlie smirked. "You got the message to Donna."

"They would have spotted me in a second if I roamed the streets during the day," Jack replied, "but yes, I have my ways."

Carlie rolled her eyes. *That's why I married you,* she thought.

***

"MY fellow Kinjans," President Johnson began, "rumors of my demise are... how should I put it... fabricated to entrap the guilty."

The crowd cheered with a volume that belied their meager numbers.

"However," he continued, "I'm getting too old for this."

The crowd chuckled in acknowledgment.

"And so, I pass the torch of leadership on to a new generation. Today, I restore the vice-presidency of Mr. Diego

Sanchez, whose position was wrongly stripped from him in what was, I might add, a rather foolhardy and desperate attempt to rout out my assailant."

The crowd again cheered with enthusiasm.

"And finally, it is with a heavy heart—or more to the point, a somewhat *damaged* heart—that I resign my position as the president of Kinji."

The crowd murmured in confusion.

"As my first act as president," Diego announced, "I am calling for a new election to replace that which was delayed indefinitely by my predecessor... or... his predecessor... or... well, to put it bluntly, Luthier. For too long, our planet has been torn by strife as a result of the reckless actions of a fool and a madman... uh... woman.... By calling for this election, I wish to assure the people that the democratic process is alive and well on Kinji."

"In addition," he continued, "you will have the opportunity to vote in a new election for the president of Kinji. Things have gotten kind of confused, and we're really not sure what the Constitution would tell us since the entire Supreme Court was obliterated by a nuclear attack two weeks ago."

Diego paused to take a sip of water.

"Rather than try to handle things by the seat of our pants," he continued, "we're just going to start over. It's easier that way."

The crowd chuckled.

***

SHEILA paused as she approached the makeshift presidential office suite on the outskirts of Mikarta.

There's no place like home, she thought. She kicked her heels together really hard, but only succeeded in bruising her feet. Realizing her mistake, she muttered, "Damn. I knew I should have picked the red shoes this morning."

Carlie stood waiting for her as she entered.

"Hey, Carlie," Sheila shouted. "Long time, no see."

Carlie just smiled.

"What's the news on Jonathan?" Sheila asked.

Sheila was a bit nervous when Carlie grabbed her by the arm and pulled her into a small closet, with a nameplate that read, "The Gatwood Room".

"This doesn't leave this room," Carlie replied.

"I hope it will fit," Sheila joked.

Carlie's glare told her that she wasn't kidding, so Sheila's grin quickly faded.

"He... doesn't exist," Carlie said.

"Come again?"

Carlie seemed to choose her next words very carefully, Sheila noticed.

"As far as our records show," Carlie continued, "Jonathan Park was never born. He never died. He never existed."

"The body?"

"Gone," she replied.

Sheila shivered.

***

Chuck Graham frowned as he stood and walked towards the door to his room. *As long as Terésa breathes, I won't be safe.*

As he reached for the door handle, it began to turn slowly from the other side. He quickly retreated behind his desk and hid under it.

Through the cracks, he could just make out the shape of Terésa Gonzales herself. Slowly, cautiously, he reached into his pocket and drew out a phase pistol. As she opened the door to leave, he stood, aimed, and fired, but the door blocked his shot. Terésa ran.

"Security!" he shouted, though he knew full well that she would be long gone before they could stop her.

Chuck sighed.

***

CARLIE, Sheila, and Donna sat at a table in a conference room at Mikarta Central Intelligence.

"Sheila," Carlie began, "it gets weirder. I think I recognized the person who shot you, but I need your help to find him. I think he was part of the staff."

"Have you seen him recently?" Sheila asked.

"No," she replied.

"He must be one of Luthier's staff, then," Sheila suggested. "If the network will stay up long enough, maybe Donna could bring up a list of everyone he hired."

Donna turned towards the computer terminal at the end of the table and logged into their personnel system.

"Does anyone look familiar?" Donna asked as she flipped through the records one by one.

"No, no, no, no..." Carlie said.

Donna kept clicking the "Next" button.

"Wait!" Carlie shouted suddenly. "That's him!"

"Felix Finch," Sheila said. "Luthier hired him before the assassination. He was on Luthier's personal staff...."

"I have a home address for you," Donna interrupted.

Carlie smiled. "Let's see if we can make this canary sing," she replied.

***

FELIX laughed at the standup comedian's act. More to the point, he laughed at the standup comedian....

The knock at the door broke his concentration momentarily.

"Come back tomorrow," he shouted, then turned back to the viewscreen.

The door opened with a crunch as the screws holding the hinges sheared off suddenly. Felix was standing before the door hit the floor.

"Felix Finch?" the police officer asked.

"Y-yes?"

"You are under arrest for conspiracy to assassinate the president of Kinji."

Felix turned, ran towards the window, and dove headlong through it, landing on the rooftop below. As he ran down the ridge, he could see a fire escape ladder just ahead.

The helicopter appeared out of nowhere. As the officers inside took careful aim and fired a warning shot just past his ear, Felix stopped, raised his hands, and waited for the inevitable. Moments later, he was lying face down on the rooftop, handcuffed.

***

CARLIE stepped into the apartment. It smelled musty—a cross between stale TV dinners and beer, with a tinge of sweaty gym socks. *If this guy is the ringleader, I'm Abraham Lincoln,* she thought sarcastically.

The room was a mess. Pizza boxes littered the entryway, with cans of beer and soda covering the floor... and there, under the table, was a cardboard box looking oddly conspicuous.

If she had learned one thing about criminals, it was this: they weren't too bright. Before you go hunting for evidence in hidden places, you should eliminate evidence hiding in plain sight. So as she opened the box, what she saw surprised her somewhat.... Magazines.... *Pornographic* magazines....

I'd be lying if I said I was shocked, but I was sort of hoping for something more significant—a gun, a knife, a bomb....

That's when she noticed that the closet door was slightly ajar. As she opened the door, piles of paper fell out, nearly knocking her to the floor. Carlie poured through it and found... love notes from some girl named Lisa....

More like hate notes, she thought. *Wow, what a loser....*

I'd rather gouge my eyes out with a wooden spoon, one note said. *If you were the last man on Earth and I were the last woman, the human race would die with us,* read another.

Carlie stopped reading after the fourth suggestion that he take a vacation to a highly exothermic region reserved for condemned souls....

Nothing, she thought. Exhausted, she collapsed on the couch. As she slumped down into its spongy recesses, she stared across the room with a glazed look. The far wall was nondescript—a white plasterboard surface with nothing hanging on it. It was trimmed with cheap wooden baseboard that looked oddly more recent than the rest of the wall.

Carlie begrudgingly slunk across the room to the wall and began tugging at the baseboard, a large chunk of which easily pulled loose in her hands.

Behind it, she found rat poison, vials of charcoal and iron oxide, a damp white powdery substance—*potassium carbonate, perhaps—was this guy making cyanide?*

She also found a large quantity of a shiny, silver-white powder sealed in a highly fractured glass vial. She thought that it looked somewhat like aluminum or aluminum oxide, but the thin layer of oil on top reminded her of something from high school chemistry.

Sodium metal in its pure state reacts violently with water, including water vapor in the air. First, it releases hydrogen gas by binding to the oxygen atom in the water. This hydrogen then combines with free oxygen in the air to form water vapor. With a high enough concentration of water, or if the sodium is in a powdered form, this reaction can be so hot that the hydrogen actually burns, the professor had said as he threw a tiny chip into a pot full of water. Carlie remembered getting wet despite sitting on the opposite side of the room.

It's the perfect fuse for something nasty, she thought, *but what?*

Then, she found it. The block of material taped to the vial felt oddly like modeling clay. *Some sort of plastic explosive. Powdered sodium in a glass vial, plastic explosives.... This is basically a live land mine....*

Carlie stammered. "Uh... we need someone from the bomb squad in here. NOW!"

Chapter Thirty-seven

SHEILA entered the holding cell. "Hi," she said. "Remember me?"

"You're Sheila, right?" he asked.

"Yeah."

"Sorry about trying to shoot you earlier," he said matter-of-factly. "I was just doing what they paid me to do."

"No hard feelings," she replied, biting her bottom lip as she said it. "Look, I don't want to be here any more than you do, so let's just get this over with. Tell me what I need to know, and I'll stop bothering you."

"What would you like to hear?"

Yeah, that's about right.... Tell me what I want to hear, she thought. *Looks like I'll have to do this the hard way.*

"The truth," Sheila replied.

"The truth?" he asked sarcastically. "You can't *handle* the truth."

Sheila's fist broke his jaw on the first punch.

"Let's try this again," she replied.

***

CARLIE sat nervously waiting for the bomb squad. The fractured glass was basically a hair trigger, its contents just waiting to explode and ignite the plastic explosives attached to it.

Jack Sinclair arrived with the bomb squad, took one look at it, and said, "Yep. We're screwed."

Carlie grimaced. "The police team has already evacuated the building," she began in a very proper, very fake British accent, "so thankfully it is only we who are screwed."

Jack laughed. "Normally, our best bet would be to neutralize the plastic explosives by digestion, but that might cause the vial to fall, potentially triggering whatever explosive material is left."

"Maybe we could neutralize the trigger instead," Carlie offered.

"Any reaction would be dangerously exothermic," he replied.

"What do you propose, then?" she asked.

"We leave the building, then launch a missile at it from outside," he replied. "Lots of collateral damage, but no human casualties."

"I think we can do better," Carlie said.

"What did you have in mind?"

***

SHEILA sat patiently in the holding cell, a shock prod in hand.

"Who sent you?" she asked.

"I don't know," Felix answered.

"Wrong answer, asshole," she replied.

With that, Sheila stuck him with the shock prod and sent several hundred volts surging through his body. He twitched for several seconds before Carlie pulled it away.

"Let's try again," Sheila continued, a little more agitated this time. "WHO SENT YOU?"

"I'll never talk," he replied.

She turned the voltage up. This time, his body shook violently.

"That was the second lowest setting out of ten," she told him. "I won't go above five because you would likely lose consciousness at six... but I could keep going at four all day."

Felix set his jaw in preparation for another jolt.

"No," she continued. "That's too easy. Did you know that the human body can survive for up on three minutes without oxygen?"

With that, she lifted him up by the shirt, slammed him into a wall, and began to crush his windpipe with her arm.

"I'm going to ask you one last time. Who sent you."

"Chuck!" he whispered hoarsely. "Chuck Graham!"

Sheila set the shock prod to 10. As the unconscious body of her former attacker hit the floor, she smiled.

"No hard feelings."

***

CHUCK Graham stumbled out into the street in front of Dimpled Chad's Bar & Grille in Mikarta. As his foot hit the sidewalk, he heard a click.

"Chuck Graham?" the voice said.

"Ye-Y-Yes," he replied.

"You're under arrest for conspiracy to assassinate the president of Kinji," the voice informed him.

Chuck knelt down slowly and placed his hands behind his head.

***

CARLIE carefully filled the syringe with anhydrous oil. She slowly pushed out most of the oil as she slipped the needle into the container of sodium. In a single draw, she pulled most of the sodium powder into the syringe.

"It's not big enough," Carlie exclaimed.

"I think she's challenging your manhood," one bomb squad officer joked.

Jack shrugged. "Don't move or it will squirt everywhere and probably go off. I have an idea."

Carlie whimpered.

Jack pulled a can of compressed freon out of his bag.

"What do you think that will accomplish?"

"Plastic explosive is fundamentally a combination of a plastic and an explosive, which is usually nitroglycerine—or the homemade kind is, anyway. At sufficiently cold temperatures, the nitroglycerine becomes much more stable."

"The fire will heat it right back up," Carlie replied.

"Not if it is just a brief flash," Jack explained. "Most of the trigger's energy will be spent blowing itself away from the plastic explosives. Cut that strap there."

Jack pointed to the strap that held the material in place. Carlie slowly cut the strap.

Please don't break the glass. Please don't break the glass, she thought.

The strap broke with a snap. The syringe sticking through the rubberized skin of the safety glass held the tube in place.

"Okay," Jack began. "I'm going to cool the plastic explosives."

He began spraying the freon in the general direction of the clay-like substance, watching it intently as ice crystals began to form on its surface.

"On the count of three, yank the syringe, throw it out the window, and smash the vial with..."

Jack looked around the room. Carlie looked around the room. The only thing visible was the three-foot section of baseboard that Carlie had ripped from the wall....

"Baseboard," they both said in unison.

"On three," Jack said. "One... two... THREE!"

Carlie threw the syringe as hard as she could. The pressure produced by the sudden oxidation of the powdered sodium blew the plunger out of the syringe. The syringe then became a self-propelled rocket as the sodium began to rapidly oxidize through the hole where the plunger had been. By the time it hit the window, it was emitting a plume of bright orange flame three inches long.

As the baseboard smashed the vial, it, too, turned into a giant plume of fire, which quickly reduced itself to a smoldering heap of burning clay-like material.

"It's on fire," Carlie said. "Should we run?"

"No," Jack replied. "That's just the plastic burning away. It's not hot enough to explode by itself. We'll just let it burn itself out."

"Fire extinguisher?" she asked?

"Sure. Why not."

That's when the syringe rocket shot back through the other window. The curtains quickly burst into flames, followed by the carpet.

Jack quickly sized up their surroundings in two words....

"*Now* run."

Chapter Thirty-eight

SHEILA and Donna smiled as they walked up the steps into the unused warehouse that had been pressed into service as a temporary hall of justice. The doors opened lethargically, their motorized hinges no longer functioning, pushed instead by a young man who looked more like a hockey player than a staffer.

As they reached their seats, the judge stepped in.

"Order in the court!" the bailiff shouted. "The honorable Justice Carlos Gonzales presiding."

Donna's ears perked up. *That name sounds familiar,* she thought....

The judge sat down gracefully like an eagle swooping to catch its prey. Donna watched in amazement.

"Prosecution," the judge began, "you may call your first witness."

The prosecutor twitched nervously in his seat.

"Your honor?"

"Yes?"

"The only witness was found dead in his cell this morning."

The judge motioned to him. "Approach the bench, please."

The prosecutor stepped slowly forward.

"Do you mean to tell me that you have no witnesses to call?" the judge asked.

"Yes, sir."

"Do you have any evidence?"

"It was destroyed in a freak fire," the prosecutor replied timidly.

"You do realize that I will have to drop all charges, do you not?" the judge asked.

"Yes, sir."

"Well, then, I'm sorry. There's nothing more that I can do unless you want an extension."

"I don't believe it would be a prudent use of the court's time, your honor," the prosecutor replied.

"Very well, then," the judge continued, this time directed to the entire court. "If there are no witnesses and no concrete evidence to tie the defendant to the alleged crime, I'm afraid there is nothing more that I can do."

Sheila's eyes widened. *He's getting off? No. This can't be happening.*

"I find the defendant not guilty by reason of lack of evidence," the judge continued. "Bailiff, please escort the defendant to the rear exit."

***

CHUCK Graham stepped out of the courtroom into the alley behind it. As he walked towards the waiting taxi, he heard something rustle behind him. He looked around, but saw nothing.

Must have been the wind, he thought.

As he reached down to pull the door handle, he glanced at the driver. An older gentleman looked up at him.

"Where can I take you today?" he asked.

"Anywhere but here," Chuck replied.

As he pulled the door open, a reflection in the glass caught his eye. Slowly, he turned around, and his eyes widened in terror.

"You...."

***

"Hey, Sheila," Carlie shouted from across the food court.

Sheila turned to see Carlie and her husband walking towards her from the Hubert's Grille.

"Hi, Carlie. Still in town, I see."

"Until Friday," Carlie replied. "Hey, what's this I hear about you crushing some guy's windpipe?"

Sheila blushed. "I guess I got a little carried away."

"You'd better be careful," Jack said. "I think my Carlie might be rubbing off on you."

Sheila laughed as Carlie playfully slapped him on the shoulder.

Chapter Thirty-nine

A month later (December 25, 2359)

Sheila relaxed on her couch and flipped the viewscreen to KNS.

"Let's see how the election is working out," she said to herself.

"We'll bring you more on this story as it develops," the reporter said. "And in other news, suspected mob boss Chuck Graham was found dead today."

Sheila's face turned pale, then slowly changed to a smile as she realized what this meant.

"According to police, Graham, a suspect in a number of suspicious deaths over the past five years, was *himself* found dead by a group of children when his body floated ashore on the East Fern River."

Couldn't have happened to a nicer guy, Sheila thought.

"Police say he died of a gunshot wound to the back of the head. Graham was forty-three."

Only one thing saddened Sheila. *I wish I could have pulled the trigger.*

"In other news," the reporter continued, "Vice President Diego Sanchez was elected as president of Kinji in a landslide, receiving a record 95% of all votes cast. His opponent, Roger Hammerstein conceded before the final polls even closed. We now take you live to the state house where President Sanchez is about to make his acceptance speech."

"Wrote it last week," Sheila said as she turned off the viewscreen. "I'm sure he'll do fine."

***

Terésa Gonzales smiled as Alfonse Di Roma stepped onto the train car in New San Francisco. She kissed him passionately as they made their way into a row of seats.

"Happy to see me?" she asked.

"Always," he replied.

"Then you'll be happy to know that Graham had an... accident."

Alfonse smiled.

It is over. We have won.

***

Diego smiled at the cameras as the press conference continued. He glanced over at Donna standing offstage with her new boyfriend, Paul, and smiled. *Ah, young love,* he thought. *I remember what that was like... before she tried to have me killed....*

He shook off the thought. *There's no time to worry about Terésa,* he mused. *She'll get hers in the end.*

With that thought in mind, he smiled ear to ear and turned back towards the podium.

"My fellow citizens of Kinji," he began, "today is a great day for our democracy. You are all aware of the election results, I'm sure."

The audience chuckled.

"But that's not why this is a great day for democracy," he continued. "That's why this is a great day for me."

The audience chuckled a bit more.

"Today is a great day for Kinji because of what I am about to announce. At noon today, representatives from a dozen colony worlds signed a historic treaty. This peace accord promises to unite us in a common goal: the peace, prosperity, and protection of our colonies against common threats.

"This treaty has not been easy. Indeed, some of the finest minds of our generation have been beating their heads against a wall for three weeks trying to hammer out something that we could all agree to. In the end, we really only agreed on one thing: we won't shoot you if you don't shoot us."

The crowd laughed audibly this time.

"And so, with its humble beginnings, this Colonial Earth Alliance was created, forged in the fires of war, tested by the fiery wit of bureaucrats sitting around a conference table, and dedicated to the mutual defense of the outer colonies... and we unite this day in the hopes that this alliance will remain strong throughout the decades ahead. Have a Merry Christmas, and good night, everyone."

...and somewhere beyond the lights, beyond the cameras, beyond the crowd, former President Johnson smiled.

Chapter Forty

Three years later (February 15, 2363)

VLADIMIR Rejndorv stepped into the nuclear storage vault. *This should be safe,* he thought. As the door slammed closed, something behind him disturbed his comfort. The snarl, low and guttural, sent shivers up his spine.

Slowly, he turned back towards the exit and saw it. There, in the corner of the room, sat a full-grown mechlizard.

Cautiously, he slid sideways towards the doors. Sensing his attempt at escape, the lizard raced to block his path.

Rejndorv backed away in terror now, desperately searching the room for anything that might be used as a weapon. *The storage shelves,* he thought, but as he reached out to grab a shelf along the back wall, his hand slipped right through it.

Am I dead? Am I a ghost?

Vladimir Rejndorv tried to steady himself against the back wall, but again, his hand passed right through it into... *into what?*

As he slid slowly through the holographic shelves, the mechlizard watched in confusion.

The base computer sounded an alarm. "Warning! Quantum lens temperature exceeds safety limits. Catastrophic failure in fifteen seconds."

That's when he saw the button. On a control panel across the room, dozens of blinking lights and buttons stared back at him, but one in particular caught his attention.

> *Emergency escape portal system. Press this button only in the event of an emergency.*

"Quantum lens temperature is now at 600 Kelvin and rising," the computer uttered. "Catastrophic failure in ten seconds...."

Rejndorv could feel the effects of the temporal distortion field tearing at him as he moved towards the control panel.

"Failure in five seconds.... Four.... Three.... Two.... One...."

Then, in one last desperate act, he pressed the button and was gone....

The research core computer turned off its voice notification system automatically once it realized that the room was empty. It progressively disabled life support in sections 14 through 1, since no one was there, either.

It detected a small blip indicating possible life in the nuclear storage vault, so it decided to keep life support online in section 15, just in case... and as the lights dimmed, the mechlizard turned, pressed the door release with its tail, and walked out into the darkened corridor.

Chapter Forty-one

Three years earlier

DONNA stepped cautiously into the courier's office. A young man greeted her, smiled, and asked if he could help her.

"I'm not sure what to do with this," Donna replied. "I was told to give this to a courier."

"Certainly," the man replied, taking the envelope.

The man stared at the envelope for several seconds, scratched his head, and stared again.

"This is a joke, right?" he asked.

"No," she replied.

"Okay," the man answered, "but I won't guarantee that this *planet* will still be around in five hundred years...."

Donna looked down at the package, read the delivery date and location, and buried her head in her hands.

I have to know, Donna thought as she reached into her pocket and drew out a small knife. She opened the package with it, then skimmed the note inside.

"Do you have a pen?" she asked.

"Sure," the man replied, handing her a ballpoint.

She quickly scribbled something at the bottom of the note, resealed the package with a bit of packaging tape, and handed it to the man behind the counter.

As she walked out of the courier's office, Donna sighed. *That kind of week,* she thought.

Chapter Forty-two

Five hundred years later

DONOVAN Jenkins frowned as he read the note.

> *Donovan, if you are reading this, I am dead, and I have failed.*
>
> *Jonathan*
>
> *P.S. Luthier is a patsy. —Donna.*

This is bad, he thought. *Very bad.... Oh well. No point worrying about it now.*

As Jonathan Park entered his office, Donovan furrowed his brow.

"Jonathan," he began, "I have a mission for you."

Part III:

The Rise of Terror

March 7, 2360

Chapter Forty-three

March 7, 2360

KURT Lawrence coughed in the acrid air.

As the delegates to the first Colonial Congress gathered on Kinji, the sun beat down on them like water on the rocks below Niagara Falls. Today, the delegate from Tularis Prime, Kacey Watson, would be inaugurated as the first president of the Colonial Earth Alliance.

As for Kurt, he was just here to support his big sis. He didn't care if she was president of the colonies or starring in a community theater play. He was always there for her. Of course, his parents had to take him. He couldn't wait until he turned 16 so he could learn to fly himself. *Nine more years,* he thought. *What a drag.*

But today was different somehow. He could sense the anticipation in the air. Today marked a new dawn for these recently united colonies. A few minor skirmishes aside (mostly arising out of a terrorist coup d'état), the transition of power had been a peaceful one, much to the continued amazement of all involved.

As the moment drew near, the projection screen behind the platform changed from a blank screen to random shots of the crowd. Suddenly, his face appeared in a close-up shot.

Kurt resisted the urge to shout "Hi, Mom," because his adoptive mother was right beside him. Instead, he relegated himself to waving furiously at the camera.

As the cameras began a slow pan across the stage, he saw "Kacey-bear" walk across stage. She smiled as she saw his face in the crowd and waved a cute little finger wave in his direction.

When she reached the podium, she pulled a note from her pocket. *She never did trust the prompter,* Kurt mused.

"Citizens of the free colonies," she began, "welcome. First of all, I would like to say thank you. Thank you to all of you who voted for me, thank you to all of you who didn't vote for me—a little less thank you, maybe, but thanks anyway...."

She paused for the laughter to die down.

"Thank you to the government of Tularis for nominating me as their delegate, thank you to all of the people who worked hard to make today possible, including the staff, the members of the press, and you, the members of our audience... but most of all, thank you to all of the members of the colonial military forces, both for providing security for this meeting and for protecting the people of the free colonies during the last few months."

The crowd began to applaud, so she paused for a few moments before continuing.

"I know things have been kind of crazy lately, but today marks the dawn of a new era—a new age of enlightenment—a new hope in a universe of despair. Today marks the induction of twelve... eleven... excuse me... eleven new delegates to the Colonial Congress. Mr. Dumas of Lenora will be inducted later, at his own request."

Kurt could sense her displeasure as she said those last few words. She wanted the Colonial Congress to all be inducted together... but she wouldn't let his refusal dampen her spirit today. *She would never let anyone rain on her parade. That's just the kind of girl she is,* Kurt thought.

"As a part of this ceremony today," she continued, "we have a representative from the government of Earth, Secretary of State Sandra Baker. To you, we extend this olive branch as a symbol of peace between our worlds. The free colonies pledge to support trade relations with Earth and to work together for the common good."

Kacey reached out and extended her left arm, olive branch in hand, in the direction of an older woman who stepped quickly onto the stage. With her right hand, she shook the woman's hand and froze for a moment, cross-armed, to pose for the cameras.

Suddenly, the crowd began to murmur in confusion.

"What's going on, Daddy?" Kurt asked.

"That's Robert Dumas," his father replied. "He was supposed to be sworn in at his home on Lenora Prime. I don't think anyone was expecting him to be here."

Kurt watched wide-eyed as Dumas pushed his way through the crowd. As he neared the stage, he slowed down. A man in a black suit pulled him aside for a moment and whispered something into he ear. Dumas nodded approvingly.

"What's going on?"

"I'm not sure, son," his father replied. "We'll know in a moment."

The next few seconds were a blur. The ground shook as a giant fireball erupted from beneath the platform, incinerating the front row and collapsing the raised stage into the pit below it.

The temporary stage lights that stood precariously perched just beyond the raised platform promptly fell into the platform, setting off a shower of sparks. Then, the surface of the stage caught fire. Not three seconds after the lights fell, the stage was engulfed in flames.

As the stage burned, emergency crews rushed to try to get the delegates off the now sunken stage. As the first fire extinguisher was discharged to clear a path through the flames, the second explosion hit. This one was contained in the pit. Pieces of wood and other materials flew everywhere.

Suddenly, a hand fell from the sky and landed in Kurt's lap. The ring on the young woman's finger looked eerily familiar.

"Kacey!" he screamed.

He felt his parents struggling to pull him away as he desperately reached towards the fiery stage hoping to somehow save her... but it was too late for that now....

And so, Kurt Lawrence did the only thing a seven-year-old could do.

He cried.

Chapter Forty-four

Three Weeks Later

The reporter frowned as he read the opening line.

"This is Michael Jobs reporting for the Kinji News Syndicate, KNS," he said. "In colonial news, Robert Dumas was sworn in as the president of the Colonial Earth Alliance in a secret ceremony on Lenora Prime earlier today."

The viewscreen cut away to an image of Robert Dumas smiling a quirked smile as he stood at a makeshift podium that oddly resembled an oil drum.

"My fellow citizens of the colonies, it is with great sadness that I announce the death of the last of the injured delegates to the Colonial Congress," he said. "Kacey Watson was a good woman, and deserved better. She will be truly missed."

Liar, Kurt thought. *You probably killed her yourself.*

"And so it is with a heavy heart that I, as the next in the line of succession, accept the position of the president of the Colonial Earth Alliance in accordance with colonial law. I promise that, as president, I will honor their memories by doing my duty to protect the colonies against tragic acts such as this one, to defend the colonies against undue influence by foreign governments, and to ensure that this attack on colonial soil does not go unpunished."

You'll honor her memory by defiling it, Kurt thought. *I hope you burn in hell.*

"We have reason to believe that Earth paramilitary officers were instrumental in planting the explosives that killed the remaining members of the Colonial Congress. We will actively pursue those responsible, but the government of Earth is being uncooperative. As a result, I am invoking immediate trade sanctions against Earth. All ships flying between Earth-controlled and free colonies will be subject to search and seizure of any cargo."

"Passengers will be allowed to carry personal items, but may not import anything from Earth-controlled colonies. Effective immediately, anyone leaving the free colonies bound for any destination on Earth will have their personal belongings catalogued and recorded for determination of prior ownership upon readmittance."

"Citizens of Earth-controlled colonies will be confined to their planet of current residence until further notice. Any attempt to travel among the free colonies will result in immediate deportation."

"We will be announcing additional sanctions and restrictions in the days and weeks ahead. We apologize for any inconvenience this may cause, but we are doing this for your protection. Your safety is our priority."

Chapter Forty-five

Thirty-one years later (January 1, 2391)

One would not normally associate a dimly-lit cockpit with romance; indeed, Kurt Lawrence rarely found anything of the sort here, but that never stopped him from trying.

I smile at Cassie. Cassie scowls. I roll my eyes. It seems to go that way every day; Kurt thought. *Personality of a turnip, that one.*

Kurt sighed—*Cassie Harmon, my sweet*—then smiled at Cassie, received his daily scowl, rolled his eyes, and turned back towards the viewscreen. As the small cruiser approached the Ouroboros Nebula, the image began to tear violently.

"Why are we doing this again?" Cassie asked pointedly.

"Antibiotics," Kurt replied. "There's an Earth shipment coming through this sector in about thirty seconds."

"Why aren't we trading for the antibiotics we need again?" Cassie asked, reiterating her original question a bit more precisely this time.

"Because our president is a tool," Walter replied.

Kurt hadn't noticed when he entered. He probably watched the whole embarrassing exchange a moment ago. *Little weasel should stick to computer programming,* he thought.

As if on cue, an Earth transport vessel folded into the open space just beyond the nebula's edge. With sensors temporarily blinded by the fold, they were a perfect target.

"Docking spikes," Kurt ordered.

Two long metal spikes shot from their ship like harpoons in search of a whale. Within moments, they had pulled themselves alongside the transport.

In a blinding flash, cutting torches sliced into the Earth ship's hull.

"Sixty seconds, people," Walter said.

Kurt shrugged it off.

Before the manipulator arm had finished removing the section of hull plating, the crew stood ready to run. Kurt stood among them.

As they passed into the storage bunker on the other side, Kurt shivered. *Refrigerated storage is the worst,* he thought. Then, he spied his prize: a stack of boxes along the far wall.

"There!" Kurt shouted.

Cassie grabbed the antigrav platform and slid it across the floor to the far wall. One by one, they threw the boxes onto the platform. Once it was loaded, they slid the platform back across to their homemade entrance and shoved the boxes through before stepping back themselves.

Fifty-seven seconds after their arrival, the manipulator arm slammed the makeshift door back in place and welded it to the hull.

"Folding in two!" Walter shouted. "One! FOLDING!"

When the sensors on the Pegasus came back online three seconds later, they saw only empty space.

***

Colonial Earth Alliance Portable Base 3 glistened in the sunlight reflecting off of the third Tularis moon. Tularis itself was technically a gas giant, but two of its moons had just enough atmosphere to viably support colonies. Tularis I, A.K.A. Tularis Prime, was a mining colony—population 350 million. Tularis III was a military test site—population 300, give or take—all underground in an old fallout shelter. The portable base resting precariously on its surface was a *secret* military test site—population thirty.

The crew barely even blinked as the shuttlecraft Isis folded into the upper atmosphere overhead. The ship landed gracefully in the waiting landing bay except for a few concrete posts that happened to get in its way.

"Kurt's driving," one of the deck hands shouted to an amused audience.

As it slammed to a halt, the docking ladder slid down to the deck, hit the deck, and promptly fell off, followed quickly by one of the landing struts. The ship teetered at an odd angle for several seconds before finally rolling backwards until its engines were touching the ground.

"Uh... little help here?" Kurt shouted.

As they stepped down via a rickety stepladder, Marc turned to the viewscreen across the shuttle bay.

> "You're tuned to TANN, the Terran Alliance News Network," the young blonde reporter began.

Marc couldn't help but notice Walter drooling out of the corner of his mouth. *Eww. Gross.* He chose to ignore it... *for now*.

> "In colonial news, twelve people were killed and thirty wounded after a car bomb exploded just outside New Paradise on Kinji. Due to the news embargo, details were sketchy from the

> scene, but the Kinji News Syndicate expects to have a reporter on location within the hour."
>
> "In more local news, raiders disrupted cargo lines near Kensington 7 today, stealing medical supplies. No casualties were reported in the incident."
>
> "With your TANN update, I'm Emily Bernsen. You're watching TANN, the Terran Alliance News Network, with news updates every hour on the hour."

Marc just shook his head.

***

WILSON Phelps frowned. *It's gonna be that kind of day again,* he thought as he turned off TANN. *Every time some terrorist gets a hair up his ass, I have to go track him down. Bloody waste of time if you ask me.*

But no one asked him. They just paid him to show up, dig through rubble, and figure out who built the bomb. This one promised to be no different than all the rest. Plastic explosives or dynamite with a crudely improvised trigger—probably a trip wire or a cell phone—and a blast radius of about thirty feet, hidden somewhere obvious like under a table or behind a plant.

So once again, his day was interrupted by an urgent message. Once again, he would have to leave the comfort of his apartment here on Tularis Prime and travel to some godforsaken place only to find nothing useful... *again*.

When the head of Colonial Investigation appeared on his viewscreen, though, he quickly reevaluated his opinion.

"Wilson," Frank shouted, "we have a problem."

Frank Oslow was a bald man, diminutive and portly. If Wilson didn't know better, he'd swear he saw the guy in a really old movie involving a flying house.

"What's up, Frank?" he asked.

"It's Europa again."

"Isn't that a little out of our jurisdiction? I mean, I know they're technically CEA, but they have no military, and they're in the Sol system. Doesn't the Terran Alliance have someone qualified?"

"This one's a real gem—more up our alley," Frank replied, still somewhat shouting to be heard over the din of jackhammers, sirens, people shouting, and the occasional sound of a cutting torch slicing through steel beams or a circular saw dicing up timbers.

Wilson frowned.

"Well, what do we have?" Wilson asked.

"It involves two latex balloons," he replied, "filled with what we think was potassium and water, a block of plastic explosives, and a housing made of porcelain."

"Porcelain?"

"Fragmentation bomb," Frank answered. "Yeah, whoever built this was a real sick bastard."

Wilson grimaced. *These kinds of days are the worst,* he thought as he grabbed his coat and hat.

"I'll take a look," he muttered.

***

ERIK Hanssen stared out the window at the fields on Tularis Prime.

"Daddy?" Anna asked. "Why are you so sad?"

Erik sighed. *If only you could have lived here fifty years ago, little one,* he thought. *You could have known the waters running free, with clear blue skies that were empty apart from a supply ship now and again. You could have enjoyed years of peace and comfort... instead of this.*

"The world is not as it used to be, hon," he said, "and I suppose that is as it should be, but... sometimes I grow weary of change."

"What do you mean?"

"Do you remember when we used to have plenty of food to eat?"

"No," the young girl replied.

"I do," Erik said longingly. "I remember when we could live off the land... when we had enough land to live off it."

"But the soldiers need the wheat and the corn so they don't go hungry," she said innocently.

"As do we all, my child. As do we all."

***

MARC chuckled as his friend, Kurt, celebrated his thirty-eighth birthday. His real birthday wasn't for another couple of weeks, but he preferred to celebrate it on January 1st for the fireworks. Kurt had, of course, insisted on flying the crew to Tularis Prime for the party.

Unbelievable, Marc thought. *"It's my party and I'll fly if I want to," he had said. What a smartass....*

As Kurt blew out the candles on his cake, Marc saw a troubled look on his friend's face. The crowd cheered, but Kurt barely smiled at all.

"Speech! Speech! Speech!" they shouted.

"My friends," Kurt said, trying to silence them a bit, "today is... an interesting day. We're about to be invaded by a bunch of geeks."

Marc chuckled. *Kurt never was much of a speaker,* he mused.

"The CEA is transferring their latest pet project to our base. Right now, all I can tell you is its name: Omega Dawn.

They want it finished within the year, and even though the portable base isn't really finished, they're moving in a team of a hundred civvies anyway. Apparently, the words 'spartan accommodations' didn't put them off sufficiently. Maybe I should have said 'open latrines' instead."

The crowd chuckled.

"Anyway, I'm assigning Marc and Kimberly as military liaisons to the project. Keep me informed and crack the whip as needed."

Marc looked at him cautiously.

"I need someone I can trust on this one, Marc."

Marc nodded. *Trouble.*

***

WILSON cringed at the devastation. *It never gets easier,* he thought as his eyes scanned the sea of broken glass, wood, and bricks.

"Casualties?" he asked.

Frank stepped up beside him and nodded.

"Twelve dead, " Frank replied. "Probably thirty people hurt, some minor, some critical."

"Any leads?"

"Just one. They saw a redheaded girl wander through just before the explosion."

"That's not much to go on," Wilson said, "but it's better than nothing, I guess...."

***

MARC Hanssen stepped into the research lab. (They called it a research lab, though it was really more like a cargo bay, complete with piles of crates lining the back wall.) In the middle of the vast expanse, three civilians stood around a large, flat display table.

He could barely make out some sort of schematics on the screen, but what he saw looked incredible—miles of circuit traces dotted with tens of thousands of components. It reminded him of some of the primitive computer schematics they learned back in school—real, rad-hardened components as big as your thumb, not these wimpy little prefab circuit blocks that had become so popular lately.

The circuit had only a couple of inputs—power, ground, trigger—and a series of outputs that were marked with antenna markings.

How very strange, he thought.

"Hi, guys," he said, barging in.

The scientists stood there in their lab coats and looked at him like he'd said something amusing. The sole girl scowled at him.

"Uh... and girls," he stammered.

The girl smiled briefly, then turned back to her work, slinging her cherry-red hair to one side with an "I'm better than you" sort of air.

"Don't worry about Kristen," one scientist said. "She was ordered back to work right in the middle of her shore leave. I think she's looking for an excuse to punch someone before she leaves again tomorrow."

The rest of the scientists laughed.

"I'm your senior military liaison, Lieutenant Colonel Hanssen" Marc said, paused, then pointed in the girl's general direction before adding, "but you can call me Marc."

"You?" another scientist asked. "You're the liaison?"

"Yes," Marc replied (somewhat self-consciously).

"You just don't look like the type," the man replied.

Not a nerd, Marc mused before speaking his mind.

"Not brainy enough for you?" Marc asked.

"You don't look like military," he replied.

"And you are?"

"Trent Carlson."

"And you think so because?"

"My grandfather was military," the boy replied, "before the... incident."

"Was? What happened to him?" Marc asked.

"He was ordered to seal off a hatch," he replied. "It... condemned the mother of two young kids to her death... left them orphans...."

The man paused, a pained expression on his face. Marc had just opened his mouth to say something when Trent suddenly resumed his side of the conversation.

"He snapped under the pressure, ended up in an asylum, and eventually committed suicide, sir."

Marc looked into his eyes to see if he was kidding. He wasn't. Marc shivered.

"So what is this thing?" Marc asked.

"Doomsday device." Trent replied.

Again, Marc looked into his eyes. Again, he shivered.

"In the event of an all-out war," Trent explained, "this device is capable of blotting out a sun... permanently. We call it the StarKiller. It's a weapon of last resort. Nobody wants to see it used, but we were told to build it, so... we're building it."

Yeah, and Eichmann was just following orders, Marc thought. *This assignment is really going to suck.*

***

"You know," Wilson said, "we might have one lead."

Frank looked at him like he was speaking in Hit'ui.

"It's probably unrelated," Wilson continued, "but I saw an alert in my email this morning."

"Well, get on with it," Frank replied grumpily.

"A member of the CEA military—a young woman—was listed on the passenger manifest of a transport that arrived here two days before the bombing."

Frank smiled. "Did she have red hair?"

Chapter Forty-six

The next day

KRISTEN stepped out of the tube car into the deep blue artificial evening light of Europa's underwater city, Trinity, and walked hurriedly to the door of her hotel room. As she pulled her keys out of her pocket, a blue flash nearly blinded her, its repetition unsettling in a mildly amusing sort of way.

When the police siren followed a moment later, she knew something was wrong.

"Kristen Farmer?" the voice bellowed through the loudspeaker.

"Yes?"

"Please stay put with your hands in the air."

She wondered for a moment if someone was trying to mess with her head—after all, three of her best friends were police officers—but something in the tone of the man's voice told her that this was quite real and quite serious.

She watched as a uniformed officer stepped slowly from his car, weapon drawn.

What the....

As he approached her, she thought she heard the words "turn around," so she did, then placed her hands behind her head. A moment later, she felt the man clumsily pull her arms down and behind her back.

As the cold steel of the handcuffs snapped around her wrists, she suddenly wished she had taken her shore leave on Kinji instead.

Europa sucks, she thought. *What was I* ***thinking****?*

***

"SIR," Marc said, tugging on the shoulder of Kurt's uniform, "we seem to have a situation. Kristen didn't report in this morning."

"A deserter?"

"I doubt it, sir," Marc replied. "She's one of our best. She was home on Europa for shore leave to visit her brother and...."

Kurt flipped a switch.

> "You're tuned to TANN, the Terran Alliance News Network," the woman said. "Terror suspect Kristen Farmer was arrested today on Europan soil. She is believed to be a close associate of Kurt Lawrence, who is a member of the Colonial Liberation Front, a known terrorist organization based on Kinji."

Kurt flipped the switch again.

"Next question," he said.

"What do we do?" Marc asked.

"We move," he replied. "That's why this thing's portable...."

Marc nodded.

***

WILSON smiled. *Interrogation,* he thought ironically. *Now **this** is useful.... If I had a dollar for every useless lead we've gotten... well, I sure as hell wouldn't be working here....*

"Hi," he began. "Do you know why you're here?"

"Did I win something?" she asked, a fake ear-to-ear grin only thinly masking the venom that boiled beneath the surface of her otherwise delicate features.

"Who do you work for?"

"Colonial Earth Alliance Officer, serial number 0112795464l8," she replied.

"We know what you did on Tuesday," he continued. "Were you under orders?"

"On Tuesday, I was on shore leave," she replied.

"Why did you do it?"

"Do what?"

She isn't an idiot. She's not going to just tell me what I want to know. Time to step up the questioning.

With that thought in mind, Wilson slammed his hands down on the table and moved his face close to hers, scowling at her across the few short inches between them.

"We show your point of origin as Tularis III," Wilson snapped. "Is that where your terrorist base is located?"

Kristen raised an eyebrow and stared at him.

"Tell me why you planted a car bomb in New Paradise!" he howled.

"You're a fucking nutjob," she replied, scowling.

"Where are you from!?!" he demanded angrily. "Are you from Tularis III!?!"

"Colonial Earth Alliance Officer, serial number 0112795464l8."

Wilson stormed out of the room and slammed the door. Frank stood awaiting his arrival in the hallway.

"Learn anything?" Frank asked.

"Nope," Wilson replied.

"It's there," Frank muttered. "I'm sure of it."

***

The sun's ruddy glow glistened brightly off the new-fallen snow as Tularis slowly crested the horizon. The pine trees rustling in the light morning breeze shed their wintry load a little more with each passing moment as a flock of very confused birds circled overhead.

Marc stood and watched the scurrying structural engineers shore up some missing hull plates before departure. *T-minus five minutes.*

As the seconds ticked by, time seemed to slow to a crawl. He bemusedly watched Kurt barking orders, Cassie and Walter taking them, and Kimberly flipping him off as she stepped back inside the hatch. Then, Kurt gave the signal. That was his cue.

Cautiously, Marc yanked the giant locking clamp that kept the ship in place... and it promptly began sliding slowly, unswervingly down the hill.

"Shit!" Kurt shouted over the comm system from his seat in the navigation pod.

Marc quickly yanked back on the handle, but it was too late. The base was now skidding like the world's largest sled down Apricot Hill, its smaller central hub section skidding at ground level, the much wider outer ring mercifully remaining a few feet up.

The engineering team ran quickly to get out of the way of the main body (from which they were downhill) while Marc just laughed. Then, as he turned around, he saw it... the aft pylon sliding straight towards him.

Oh, crap.

***

Frank smiled as he stepped into the troop transport.

"We've got them now!" he said enthusiastically. "Tularis III is just five hours away."

"What do you hope to accomplish with this little trip?" Wilson asked.

"We're going to catch the terrorists!"

"You know they'll probably just shoot you," Wilson replied.

Frank stared blankly.

Wilson just shook his head.

***

MARC dove into the snow bank as the pylon passed inches above his head. He felt a slight discomfort as the pylon unmercifully shoved his legs deeper into the snow. Moments later, he realized that it had passed, and he lifted his head.

The sight behind him looked like something a ten-year-old would do with a bottle rocket. The craft careened towards a cluster of houses—*probably unoccupied, but you can never be too safe,* Marc thought. *Around here, they could quite easily be booby trapped—maybe even filled with nuclear devices with hair triggers....*

Then, just as it was about to smash the houses to ribbons, the navigation thrusters fired for a brief instant, lifting the ship just high enough to avoid them. It crashed to the ground with a thud on the other side, whereupon a grove of trees stopped its continued descent.

Marc started running in its general direction.

"Don't bother," Kurt shouted through the radio, laughing. "Damn, that was fun!"

***

THE transport ship Chaucer's Revenge passed outside the limit of influence for the Mars folding gate as it passed the orbit of Saturn. Only past this point would it be safe to use the ship's folding drive without any risk of disrupting the Mars gate.

Of course, the gate on Earth, or GlobeGate as it was affectionately known, was well within this range, but the two gates were synchronized with data passed through a permanent microfold so that they could never become active at the same time. This ship had no such advantages, and being a large troop transport, was physically too wide to safely navigate the commercial folding gates directly.

Frank frowned. *Wilson is right. This is stupid. I'm about to walk into a war zone.*

"Fifteen minutes to fold," the navigator shouted.

If I walk out of this, I'm going back to finish law school, he thought. *Life's too short for this crap.*

***

KIMBERLY smiled as Kurt entered the engineering control room.

"What's the status, Kimmie?" he asked.

"SNAFU," she replied. "What did you expect?"

Kurt smiled a wry grin. *We're alive,* he thought, *so we're doing better than I expected....*

Marc chuckled. "Everybody okay?"

"Yeah," Kimberly replied, "but the nav thrusters overheated from firing in the atmosphere. They weren't rated for that. We'll have to do some serious repairs or we'll be doing pretty much a beeline once we get past the atmosphere."

"Folding drive?" he asked.

She shook her head slowly.

"Worry about that outside the atmosphere," Kurt ordered.

Marc looked at Kimberly. Kimberly looked back. Marc shivered.

Looks like I picked the wrong week to quit huffing kittens.

With that final thought, Marc sat and watched in horror as the ground grew ever more distant through the viewport. He watched as the blue atmosphere outside transitioned rapidly to black. He watched as the planet became a small disc. He watched as the Tularis sun itself shrank to a point of light while the nearby Ouroboros Nebula grew to a bright wash. Then, he fell asleep and watched a herd of sheep jump a fence to bite Kurt on the backside. Marc smiled.

***

THE transport ship Chaucer's Revenge settled on the surface of Tularis III near a CEA base. As the rear hatch opened, the eerie stillness was broken only by the scratchy sound of a tumbleweed blowing past.

Frank stepped out cautiously, the snow under his boot crunching like a fresh corn chip in a good Mexican restaurant. The entrance to the base was wide open, its buildings in a state of disrepair that would make even a Lenoran refugee balk.

"Pack it up," he shouted. "Nobody has been here for years."

"What do we do with the girl?" Wilson asked.

"I guess we let her go," Frank replied, "and see where she goes."

With that, they left as quickly as they had arrived.

Chapter Forty-seven

Marc rubbed his eyes as the yellow glow of emergency lighting roused him from his slumber. His cabin actually got more light through the viewport from the Ouroboros Nebula glowing in the distance, so he made a mental note to get brighter emergency lighting.

As he rolled over towards the bedside table, he reached for his headset and winced at the sound of people screaming into his ear.

That kind of day, he thought.

Stepping out of his cabin, Marc immediately had to jump out of the path of an engineering team that brushed past him, narrowly avoiding a head-on collision. When he had regained his balance, he spotted Kimberly running to catch up with the other engineers. He, in turn, started running to catch up with her.

"Kim!" he shouted.

Kim slowed her pace slightly and turned her head to see who was calling her. This proved to be a bad idea, as she promptly ran headlong into the bulkhead at the end of the corridor.

"Ow..." she said as she turned and resumed her frantic pace, this time with Marc alongside her.

"What's going on?" Marc asked.

"Engineering is trying to straighten out some engine control problems," she replied, "and I'm trying to make sure those wastes of perfectly good oxygen don't screw it up... again...."

"So basically," Marc began.

"We're screwed."

Marc nodded and replied, "So... same as yesterday, then?"

"Pretty much," she replied.

As they rounded the bend, they saw twelve engineers huddled around a panel. Piles of optical cabling lay strewn about like a bowl of brightly colored plastic spaghetti. Several of the cables were discolored, blackened from an explosion in the panel below it.

"What's the damage?" Kim asked.

"Repeater with no power," an engineer replied. "The ion drive wasn't designed for atmospheric use, and shut itself down while drawing a full load. The back current blew out the primaries in the step-down transformers that power parts of the control network."

"Spare?" she asked.

"Nope," the engineer replied. "We think the regulators in the device can handle the full voltage for a few minutes."

"See," Kimberly replied, "this is why I have to be here...."

She ripped open a panel nearby, pulled out a step-down, then tossed it to the engineer.

"Goodbye, life support controls for this deck, hello ion drive. Hope nobody wants to adjust the thermostat for a few hours."

***

THE radio announcer keyed the microphone as a young intern frantically shook a piece of wire copy outside the window. He smiled at the girl, put the prepared copy aside, and injected a station break.

"You're listening to TANR, Terran Alliance News Radio. We're going to take about a thirty second break and be right back. Stay tuned to TANR."

As he turned off the mic and started a commercial playing, the intern ran into the room.

"We have another bombing," she exclaimed excitedly.

"And that was an emergency?"

"It's a bombing," she replied, puzzled.

"We get twelve bombing stories a day around here."

"It's on Earth."

He keyed the mic.

"In a breaking news story, a bomb exploded today in New San Francisco, killing more than eighty people and injuring several hundred.

"The bomb apparently was planted in the subway system underneath the George W. Bush Memorial Waste Management Facility. The resulting 'shit storm', as one observer called it, caused two trains to derail while passing each other, killing a number of passengers and nauseating the rest.

"In a related story, residents of several suburbs of New San Francisco are raising quite a stink over the full evacuation resulting from the mandatory waste disposal shutdown. We have no word yet on when people will be able to return to their homes and businesses, but this disaster is expected to leave about three million people homeless for several months. The Terran Red Cross is setting up emergency shelters across the bay in the Marin Headlands and in nearby Sacramento. Amtrak is also providing free transportation for evacuees on its bullet trains.

"We'll have more news on this breaking story as it develops. You're listening to TANR, with weather and traffic reports four times an hour."

***

WILSON cringed when his viewscreen beeped again. *Another pointless trip?*

Frank's face appeared on the screen.

Yup. This stinks.

"Wilson, old boy," he began in a fake British accent that would embarrass even a five-year-old.

"Yes, Frank?" Wilson replied dryly.

"Guess who I'm sending to help investigate the New San Francisco subway bombing?"

"Whoa there! Aren't we at war with Earth?"

"Our military is at war," Frank corrected. "This is a civilian matter. We don't allow politics to get in the way of humanitarian aid. Besides, they don't get many bombings on Earth. Their teams really aren't trained for that sort of thing... and we were available."

"Crap," Wilson replied.

"And plenty of it."

Wilson wept audibly.

"It could be worse," Frank said in a mock consolatory fashion.

"It could?"

Frank thought for a moment, then answered, "Never mind."

***

KURT frowned as he stared at the blinking red lights on the main control console.

"What's the status, Kimberly?" he asked.

Her voice came through the comm system so clearly that he almost thought she was in the room.

"We're almost done," she replied. She paused, then added, "There. We're done."

The indicator lights changed from red to green a moment later.

"Confirmed, Kim. You're done. Get back up here. We need you here on the bridge."

"On my way," she replied as the door opened to his left.

Kurt noted that this bridge was designed correctly, with all of its entrances to the front left and front right. *Why would anything bigger than a shuttlecraft have a bridge entrance at the rear? That's just begging for a surprise attack,* he mused.

"Where are we going?" Marc asked as he walked onto the bridge, followed shortly thereafter by Kimberly, hand scanner at the ready.

"Back into the Ouroboros Nebula," Kurt replied. "We overshot it pretty badly."

Before them, the star field on the viewscreen slowly changed as they swung around in a long, slow arc back towards the nebula's outer ring.

***

WILSON cringed as he surveyed the subway station. The smell of freshly dumped human waste conspired with the usual smell of stale human waste to overwhelm his senses even through the hazmat suit's charcoal filter.

Who would have thought when I started working for Colonial Investigation that I'd be on Earth, in a subway station, wading knee-deep in sewage?

About a dozen intelligence agents from the Earth Central Intelligence Agency were already poring through the rubble.

James Moore hovered over them all like a vulture circling its prey. The head of the ECIA anti-terrorism unit, James lived for moments like this and was pretty transparent about his excitement.

Wilson walked over to him.

"Wilson?" James asked. "Wow. I haven't seen you in ages. What brings you here?"

"Apparently, Colonial Intelligence thinks there may be a connection between your bombings and ours," he replied. "Personally, I think they're full of... well... this...."

James laughed. "You're welcome to look around. We've pretty much scoured the place already, though."

"Find anything?" Wilson asked.

"Zilch."

Wilson rolled his eyes, then frowned as something embedded in a remaining section of a shattered wall caught his eye.

"What's that?" he asked, pointing.

James frowned. "I don't know...."

He continued to study the metal fragment for a few minutes, then pulled it from the wall with pliers and walked across the room to a gathering of scientists.

Wilson watched and waited. After what seemed like an eternity, James walked back over, accompanied by three armed police officers.

"I'm afraid you're going to have to come with us," James said sadly.

Wilson froze.

***

The portable base glistened as it passed into the outer ring of the Ouroboros Nebula, clouds of microscopic dust flashing as the particles ionized against the charged hull plating, then jumped violently away from it.

Deep within the bowels of the base, thirty civilian scientists continued their power core testing, shield design, materials engineering, and theoretical studies of spacial folding.

A few decks up, Kurt sat on the bridge, wondering what his superiors were thinking when they stuck a bunch of civvies on his station.

A few seats over, Marc stood, peering over Kimberly's shoulder, watching the ship's power readings take huge dips, and wondering what his superiors were thinking when they asked the scientists to test such a horrible weapon in the first place.

And there, in the darkness, they waited.

***

DAWN arose on Proxima Centauri III. As the first rays of sunshine crested the horizon, a faint ticking sound echoed through the dark alley.

Tick, tick, tick....

Nearby, the monks at St. Anthony's Orphanage arose for morning prayer as they did every morning.

"Ave verum corpus, natum de Maria virgine," they chanted.

Tick, tick, tick.

In a few short hours, they would make their way from the catacombs of the centuries-old monastery to the upper chambers to prepare breakfast for the children.

"Vere passum, immolátum in Cruce pro hómine."

Tick, tick, tick.

In a few short hours, the children would wake to the smell of a freshly cooked meal.

"Cuius latus perforátum, fluxit aqua et sánguine."

Tick, tick, tick.

In a few short hours, these refugees from war-torn planets would once again be welcomed into the loving arms of caring teachers at the nearby school.

"Esto nobis, praegustátum"

Tick, tick, tick.

In a few short hours... their world would change forever.

"mortis in exámine."[2]

Tick.

[2]Hail, true body, born of the virgin Mary, who truly was spread out as a sacrifice on the cross for mankind, whose pierced side flowed with water and blood. Be for us a foretaste in the test of death.

Chapter Forty-eight

"WHAT's going on?" Wilson asked as the guards pulled him away from the bombing site.

"We have our orders," the guard replied gruffly, yanking him alongside.

As they rounded the bend, a guard pulled a cloth bag over his head, handcuffed him, and shoved him rudely into some sort of vehicle.

Wilson waited for what seemed like hours before he was yanked back to his feet on what sounded like a concrete floor.

He tried to keep his feet under him as they pulled him blindly through twisting passages that smelled of leafy green vegetables. His mind raced as he wondered what could possibly be going on. Finally, the reflected sound of his footsteps told him that they had entered a much larger room. A few steps later, they pushed him down into a chair and walked away.

As the bag was removed from his head, Wilson struggled to focus his eyes. After a few moments, he could make out the features of his old friend, James.

James looked at him with sadness. “I suppose you know why you are here,” he said.

Not the slightest idea.

“Uh... no? What’s going on?”

James frowned. “The fragment,” he replied, “was from a colonial military detonator. It appears that this was an act of war.”

“That’s crazy!” Wilson exclaimed. “Why would they send me to help you investigate the bombing if our side planted it?”

“To keep us from finding any evidence, perhaps?” he replied as he walked behind the chair where Wilson sat.

“Well,” Wilson said, “I sure did a bang-up job of it, then, what with me leading you right to the most damning piece and all?”

James smirked.

“That’s why I’m letting you escape.”

***

“MONSEIGNEUR Canard!” the seminarian shouted as he ran across the piazza.

The headmaster immediately recognized the young man as Earl Watts, one of his best and brightest at the seminary. He slowed his pace to allow Earl to catch up.

“Ah, Mister Watts,” he said as Earl approached. “What brings you here at this hour? Shouldn’t you be at morning prayer?”

The young man paused for a moment to catch his breath before speaking. The monseigneur noticed that the young man had not yet changed into his ceremonial robe. Clearly, he had something on his mind that was more pressing than his normal daily routine.

“There’s a problem at the orphanage,” Earl replied, still wheezing slightly.

"What sort of problem?"

That's when the young man said the most horrifying thing someone can say to a caregiver.

"One of the children is... missing...."

In thirty years, I've never lost a kid, he thought. *I'll be damned if I lose one the day before I retire.*

"I'll be right up."

***

"Excuse me... escape?" Wilson asked.

As the sound of sliding doors announced James's exit, Wilson suddenly realized that the room was otherwise empty.

He saw a shuttlecraft docked at a port on the opposite side of the room. As he tugged on his handcuffs, he realized that they were loose; his hands slipped easily free.

He quickly made a beeline for the shuttlecraft and climbed aboard. Sitting at the console, he keyed in the Mars folding gate as his destination, then activated the transport. The moment he pressed the final button, the door at the other side of the room opened, and three armed guards ran in, pulse rifles at the ready.

The shuttlecraft door slammed shut as the first rounds impacted the outer hull. Three seconds later, the shuttle began its ascent.

He could hear the soldiers' chatter over the shuttle's comm system as he left the ground.

"Fire pulse cannons!" a voice shouted.

"We can't, sir," another voice replied. "The power grid just went down. Backup power, too. They found a toasted squirrel carcass nearby. Probably chewed the lines. We should have it back in about five minutes."

"That's not good enough! Scramble fighters to intercept!"

"Long range communication is down as well."

"Then use short range to someone who has long range."

"We can't. The transponder in that shuttle stopped transmitting, and the ship never registered a flight plan. We have no way to locate it once it leaves tracking range in three... two... one... tracking lost...."

The next words were unintelligible, but he concluded it was probably for the best. As the shuttle left the atmosphere, it took a circuitous path to the Mars gate that took it in a slingshot around Jupiter, past the dark side of Earth's moon, past Venus, the sun, then in the general vicinity of Mercury, before finally ending in a stable orbit around Mars.

From there, the shuttlecraft passed through eighteen folding gates, including gates in the Kinji, Proxima Centauri, and Lenoran systems before arriving back at Tularis Prime and landing.

They don't pay me enough for this crap....

***

MARC wandered into the engineering lab.

"Hi, guys," he said to no one in particular.

Trent stood and nodded at him as he walked over to the console of a test chamber.

"How are the tests going?"

"Watch," he replied as he pressed a button.

Suddenly, the entire deck shook violently, and the lights dimmed.

"Yield?" Marc asked.

"If we weren't protected by a shield," Carl replied, "this entire deck would have collapsed in the artificial singularity we just created, along with three decks above and below."

"How much bigger will this thing be?" Marc asked.

"We're at the limits of our testing facilities," he replied. "That was a one percent yield. The next test is ten percent. We'll do it outside."

"Thanks," Marc replied.

Trent chuckled.

***

THE comm screen lit up like a Christmas tree as Kurt sat down in the captain's chair. On the screen, it read, *Incoming message, Priority Orange.*

Kurt pressed a code into the keypad on the arm of his chair. A moment later, he saw Kristen on the viewscreen.

"Is this a secure channel?" Kurt immediately asked.

"Yes," she replied.

"Are you okay?" he asked.

"I was detained by Europan security forces," she replied. "I swear I can't tell if they're allied with us or Earth. Almost seems to depend on the day of the week."

"They're walking a tightrope," he replied. "They're a CEA world, but they're in the Sol system. It's like being the lone gorilla in the reptile hut."

Kristen smiled.

"Where are you?" she asked. "I need to get back to work."

Kurt shook his head. "We're coming to you. Where are you?"

"I took a shuttle to Proxima Centauri III."

"We'll be there in an hour," he replied. "Kurt out."

***

MONSEIGNEUR Canard huffed as he raced up the steps to the orphanage main office on the third floor above the piazza (which itself was on the third floor of the building on one side, but at ground level on the other). He arrived at his office thoroughly out of breath.

As he turned the knob, he realized that he had left the key in his living quarters four floors below.

Damn, he thought. *Maybe there's someone else around with a key.*

He looked around at the empty hallway and sighed, then trudged slowly towards the steps.

No sooner had he reached the bottom of the first flight of steps than Earl appeared, running the other direction.

"Earl, my boy!" Monseigneur Canard exclaimed.

Earl smiled and held up his keys.

"Ah yes," Canard chuckled. "Oops. I did it again...."

Earl shook his head.

Canard shuffled up the flight of steps and breathlessly stumbled across to the door, unlocked it with Earl's keys, and tossed the keys to Earl, who promptly dropped them on the floor.

"Where..." Canard began, then paused to catch his breath, "where was the child seen last?"

Earl thought for a moment before replying, "I *think* he was last seen at lights out last night."

"Oh, dear," Canard replied. "Who, and in what room?"

"Chip Hardy. Room 212D."

Canard brought up the building diagram on his computer terminal. On the screen, he saw room 212D and a green dot. *Good. No one opened any windows,* he thought. *He has to be somewhere on the floor.*

"I have a hunch," Canard said, "that he hasn't gone anywhere at all."

Earl looked at him quizzically.

"Come again?" he asked.

"Closets, Earl. Closets. Go get him."

Earl walked out towards the living quarters.

***

The shuttlecraft Isis passed slowly out of the Ouroboros Nebula and entered the folding gate in orbit around Tularis Prime. He entered the coordinates for Proxima Centauri IV into his computer, and the folding gate took care of the details.

It is a strange experience being in a ship as it folds. First, everything shimmers in a very disorienting way, almost like a special effect in a cheesy science fiction movie. Then, you feel this sudden sense of awareness that the universe is infinite and you are finite. This gives way to a sense of unease as you realize that you are in two places at once, and thus far less finite than you were ever meant to be.

Now, this feeling of simultaneous existence in two places—the perception of bilocation—bears further explanation. With ordinary bilocation, if such a thing were even possible, one would expect to simultaneously perceive two locations at once. Indeed, it is remotely plausible that this is what you might perceive if you folded without a ship around you, assuming that the radiation levels were not sufficient to kill you before you had time to describe the feeling. However, when folding inside a ship, this is not at all what happens.

Instead, simultaneously, both you and your ship are in two places, but at any given instant, any given piece of you and/or the ship is in one place or the other, so in effect, you are both inside the ship in the first place and floating in space in the second place while simultaneously being safely inside the ship at the second place and floating lifelessly in the cold vacuum of empty space in the first.

Worse, you are also in every possible combination of fragmentary arrangements thereof—your head might exist in one place while your body exists in the other, you might be missing appendages, missing internal organs, missing the chair underneath you, and so on. Of course, this feeling is momentary, but it is still very disorienting and disconcerting.

And then, just as you begin to realize the horror of these infinite possible timelines converging simultaneously—timelines in which each of those infinite combinations actually plays out—as you realize that an infinite expanse of extradimensional space is now folding down into a single finite point in four-dimensional meatspace, things start to shimmer again. It is at this point that more and more of the infinite pieces of your being "stick" in a completely different and (at least biologically) utterly unexpected spatial frame of reference, until finally, after a few seconds of what borders on madness, you are "all there" in the new location (or at least as much as you were before).

So it was for Kurt as his shuttlecraft emerged from the folding gate around Proxima Centauri IV. A few moments later, he set a course for Proxima Centauri III, where Kristen anxiously awaited his arrival, then went to sleep for the remainder of the trip.

***

Tick, tick, tick.

Boom.

The floor shook as the explosion shattered several support posts beneath the monastery. A nearby gas main ruptured in the blast, sending flames fifty feet into the air before the leak detection system shut off the flow.

Monseigneur Canard immediately turned on the viewscreen in his office to check for any news updates, only to watch the power fail a moment later.

Stupid Proxima Gas and Electric, he thought.

That's when he smelled the smoke. He quickly pulled the fire alarm and started running towards the stairs.

As he jogged down the stairs, something felt wrong, but he couldn't put his finger on it. When he reached the bottom, he put his finger on it. The teachers of the school were gathered on the piazza. Among them stood Earl.

"Earl," Monseigneur Canard shouted, "did you find him?"

"Who?"

"Chip!"

Carl turned white as a sheet. "I assumed he would come out when the alarm went off," he stammered.

"Damn," the monseigneur shouted, then made a sign of the cross and muttered "Forgive me, Father, for I have sinned" before running back to the steps. He felt as though his feet were going to collapse under him by the time he reached the second floor, but he pressed on.

As he reached the door to the interior hall at the top of the steps, he touched the handle and recoiled in pain.

The knob is hot, he thought. *It's an inferno in there. If I go in, I may not be coming out.*

Then, thoughts of a scared child hiding in a closet washed over him and he girded himself. Taking his jacket off, he wrapped it around his hand, grasped the door handle, and turned it, keeping the door between himself and the flames.

The heat from the fire inside dried his skin uncomfortably as he stared at the wall of flames between himself and his destination. Placing the jacket over his face, he ran through the flame into the hallway beyond, turned left, ran down another corridor, and opened the door to suite 212.

By the time he reached the suite, the vinyl floor covering was beginning to bubble from the fire on the floor below. He had perhaps seconds to find the boy and get out before this room, too, would be consumed by the flames. Then, he heard something—a sound so subtle that he might easily have missed it—someone pounding a fist against... a trunk?

On the floor at the foot of Chip's bed was a trunk painted to look like a treasure chest. The pounding sound appeared to be coming from *inside*.

As he walked over to the chest, a gas main in the wall burst and exploded, sending plaster everywhere and exposing the burning wall joists for all to see. A moment later, a section of ceiling buckled near the window, the ceiling joists already badly scorched and failing under the weight of the floor above.

Quickly, Monseigneur Canard flipped up the latch and opened the trunk where a very scared Chip Hardy sat quivering.

"Come on, boy," he said, pulling the child to his feet. "We're going to get you out of here."

***

KURT awoke with a jolt as the shuttlecraft Isis made landfall on Proxima Centauri III. The autopilot had registered some sort of navigational glitch when he keyed in the destination coordinates, but he had ignored it. *I should have known better than to trust my instincts,* he thought as he surveyed the barren rocky precipice on which the shuttle was perched perilously.

As he reached for the comm screen controls, the entire shuttle shifted uncomfortably. He reached for the flight controls instead, keyed in a slight correction, and waited for the computer to make the necessary calculations. A few moments later, the engines fired up for all of a half second. The shuttle then jumped into the air a few feet, landed again on the adjacent slope with a thud, and skidded to the bottom, bouncing painfully the entire way.

I should have known better than to trust this crappy machine over my instincts, he thought as he reached for the communications controls.

A moment later, Kristen's face appeared on the screen, giving him a glare that could freeze molten lead.

"Kristen," he asked, "Did you say 28 degrees 5 minutes 16.7982 seconds west by..."

"No," she promptly interrupted, "I said *east*."

"...east by 85 degrees, 8 minutes, 53.5108 seconds north?"

"South."

Kurt shook his head and sighed.

"See you in a few hours," Kristen muttered as she closed the channel.

***

CHIP stumbled as Monseigneur Canard helped him out of the trunk. Suddenly, a burning beam fell and blocked the only door that led out of the suite.

The window, Canard thought. *We have to jump.*

Canard quickly ran to the window and tried to open it. It was stuck.

"Am I going to die?" Chip asked.

"No," he replied. "You're not going to die for a long time."

Looking around the room, the only thing massive enough to break the thick glass was the treasure chest. Canard reached over and, with all the strength he could muster, lifted it over his head and brought it crashing down on the window.

The window pane cracked, but did not completely break. Canard threw the trunk again, breaking out a small section of the window just large enough to crawl through. With that, Monseigneur Canard leaned out the window.

"Get ready to catch someone!" he shouted.

***

As Kurt's shuttle sat down on the landing pad in Carrulus, near Proxima Centauri III's southern pole, he marveled at how green the grass was at such a latitude, then remembered that the entire planet was somewhat closer to a much smaller, cooler star than most habitable worlds, resulting in no real polar ice to speak of and large, uninhabitable deserts covering the vast majority of the planet.

Without artificial irrigation, even Tirabia (at the "sunny side" northern pole) would be uninhabitable, he reminded himself. *In fifteen years, when this pole is on the sunny side, Carrulus will be 55C (131° F) in the shade. And I don't even like to think about the flare storms....*

Kurt cringed. *I **hate** Proxima Centauri III.*

The rear hatch opened with a grinding noise that sounded like a food processor commercial before stopping with a clomp that could make even the largest pachyderm jealous.

As he stepped out, he noticed something else for the first time.... *No birds,* he mused. He wasn't sure whether it was a climate thing or simply that nobody had thought to bring them. *Just as well, though,* he thought. *At least they don't get caught in the engines.*

He closed the hatch on the shuttle with the press of a button. The motor bearings groaned under the strain.

I should really get that fixed, he thought.

He looked around and saw an empty field with hundreds of shuttle pads, all empty. Today was April 17th—Proxima Centauri Day—the day when the Proxima Centauri government was formally incorporated. Like similar holidays in most of the less desirable colonies, everyone took the day off work and used it as an opportunity to get as far away as possible....

As he began the interminable walk across the empty field towards the city streets beyond it, he found himself overcome with an impending sense of boredom, so he passed the time first by imagining his friends as cartoon characters, then by solving sets of third-degree polynomial equations in his head, then by thinking up inappropriate things to write in his log, and finally by coming up with crude pickup lines before resigning himself to the pointlessness of it all and starting to whistle show tunes he'd learned on Stavromula Beta.

Eight arduous minutes later, he reached the main city gate. They called it a gate even though there wasn't actually anything resembling a gate—more like a cheap archway made of three rusty antenna tower pieces.

In his mind, Kurt imagined tumbleweeds blowing through the town, but in truth, it wasn't really *that* empty. An electric car buzzed along the roads every once in a while, and the corner diner was obviously open. Its "Open 24 Hours" sign flickered and buzzed in a sickly attempt at attracting customers, but in actuality, it did a far better job at scaring away any passersby who might otherwise have expected a modicum of routine cleaning and maintenance.

The lot was filled with cars, a throwback to a time when such transit made more sense. The city itself was a no-fly zone, much to the chagrin of anyone coming to visit, and largely to prevent precisely such occasions. And there, sitting in a window booth, was Kristen, her head leaning on her clenched fist, rolling her eyes in his general direction.

Yup, he thought. *It's gonna be that kind of week.*

***

A crowd of people on the piazza looked on in horror as Monseigneur Canard called to them for help. A few quickly scrambled over to catch them if they jumped from the second story window.

Earl watched Monseigneur Canard lift Chip up and out of the window. He watched in horror as the ceiling overhead sagged ever lower, seemingly ready to burst. Then, the crowd shouted "GO!"

Earl watched as Monseigneur Canard released Chip. The child fell with a grace that can only be described as amazing, then landed in the upstretched arms of the crowd below. Then, it was Monseigneur Canard's turn.

Earl watched as he crawled out onto the ledge. Earl watched as the entire facade of the building suddenly collapsed. Earl watched the crowd run away from the building in terror, and Earl watched as a burning section of the wall and roof above it collapsed on Monseigneur Canard.

Chip started to run towards the steps, but a firm hand grasped his shoulder.

"No," Earl said. "It's too late. He's with God now."

And so, as his home was consumed by the flames, Earl watched, standing in silence, staring vacantly as it collapsed, piece by piece. He watched as the fire department arrived and sprayed foam at the charred wreckage. He watched as the hours passed. He watched the dying embers glow dimly against the night sky, its vermillion incandescence spreading like blood over this stone sepulchre, and thought only one thought.

I should have gone. It should have been my life....

Chapter Forty-nine

WILSON stepped out of his shuttle on Tularis Prime. *And now, back to my apartment for a long nap,* he thought, but as he stepped through the door, he immediately knew it couldn't be that easy.

The red message light on his viewscreen throbbed monotonously. *Not again,* he thought.

He reached up and pressed the message button, and his boss's face appeared. *Please, not again....*

"Wilson," he began. "Welcome home. I trust you had a nice trip. While you were out, we lost the Kinji Ministry of Defense. Come as soon as you get this message."

Wilson walked over to his bed and collapsed. *It can wait.*

***

KURT swore as the back door to the shuttle hinged downwards by about eight inches and jammed. They turned and walked back towards town. Then Kurt suddenly turned and ran at the door, slamming it with his shoulder before staggering away, holding his arm in pain.

Kristen giggled.

Kurt then pushed the button to close the door. It closed. Finally, he pushed the button to open the door. It opened, groaned, and stopped a little farther open this time.

"Ladies first," he said.

Kristen stared at him like he was nuts, then squealed as he lifted her up over his head and dropped her through the opening at the top. Then, she screamed as she fell six feet to he floor below.

"You okay?" he asked.

"Yeah, no thanks to you," she replied.

He then grabbed a bundle of cables, used it as a handhold to pull himself up higher, tucked his foot against a latch plate along the side of the doorframe, and pushed himself up high enough that he could swing through the opening and drop down to the floor. As his feet hit the ground inside the shuttle, the door groaned and continued to open.

Kristen held up the wrench that she had just yanked out of the mechanism, then looked at him and smiled.

***

WILSON was still groggy from an acute lack of sleep as he walked into the front door at Colonial Investigation on Alpha Centauri V. He had barely stepped one foot through the door before his boss was on him like a bulldog on its owner's leg.

"Wilson, my dear boy," his boss said, wrapping his arm casually around him, again using such a fake British accent that Wilson had the urge to sign him up for sensitivity training.

"Where is it *this* time?" Wilson asked.

"Kinji," Frank replied. "Dirty bomb."

"Uranium?"

"Cow dung."

Wilson laughed, then stiffened as he noticed Frank's icy stare.

"It spread fecal matter across twelve city blocks," Frank continued. "Cleanup could take months."

Wilson tried hard to stifle a giggle, but failed miserably.

"Considering I just came back from a subway that got flooded by a sewage treatment plant," Wilson replied, "I don't see how this could be worse."

"You haven't smelled cow dung on a hot Kinji summer day, have you?" Frank asked.

Wilson cringed. *So pretty much the way Mikarta normally smells, then?*

Almost before he knew what was happening, he was on a transport shuttle en route to Kinji.

***

THE shuttlecraft Isis shot a shower of sparks as Kurt grazed the hangar doors, then plunged it wing-first into the hangar deck, cutting a swath of destruction that ended only when the nose of the shuttle impacted a support pylon at the far end of the hangar.

Kristen stared at Kurt, his hands gripping the control stick like a life vest, knuckles white with terror.

Kurt merely whimpered, "Is it over?"

Kristen shook her head. "Maybe next time you should try *closing* your eyes...."

As they stepped out of the shuttle onto the hangar deck, Marc stood waiting.

"We have a problem," Marc began.

"*You* have a problem?" Kristen replied sarcastically.

"We're nearly out of fresh water," Marc continued non-plussed. "We also need to put in for food within the next couple of days."

"Eat the military team first," Kristen replied.

Marc turned to Kurt.

"What's gotten into her?" Marc asked.

Kristen stared daggers back at him.

"But really, we need to do a supply run," Marc said.

"Go," Kurt replied, then immediately regretted it.

"Cool!" Kristen shouted, faking a valley girl accent. "Can I go? We could turn it into a pajama party!"

Kurt scowled.

***

Wilson could smell the odor before his foot hit the pavement on the landing pad outside of town, the scent burning his nose and making him suddenly queasy.

He stepped quickly into the transport pod and buckled his restraint, pulled the door shut, and placed a respirator over his face as the pod drove him towards the city center. By the time he got there, neither the pod's filtration system nor the respirator could adequately filter out the putrescent stench.

When the pod door finally opened, Wilson's eyes began to tear so badly that he could barely make out the face of his friend, Carson Peterborough, a member of the Colonial Investigation forensics team.

"What's the story?" Wilson asked.

"It stinks," Carson replied jokingly. Seeing Wilson's icy stare, he became suddenly serious. "Witnesses say the explosion came from a white van, no plates. We've looked at the wreckage, but there's not much left. The VINs were filed off, no vehicles reported stolen nearby—basically, we have no leads."

With that, Wilson began tossing piles of debris to one side, looking for anything that might provide some hint as to the identity of the bombers.

***

THE hangar doors crept slowly open as the crew of the small cruiser began their preflight checks. The doors stopped about halfway open—*plenty wide enough for this mid-sized ship,* Marc thought. I'm just glad Kurt's not driving.

"You going to open those the rest of the way?" Marc asked.

The crackle on the radio was quickly replaced by a young man's voice.

"We can't," the engineer replied. "The drive motor's counter is miscalibrated. It thinks the door is open. It's on the schedule to be fixed tomorrow."

And as he finished saying that, Marc distinctly thought he heard someone say "I'm glad Kurt isn't flying."

Marc smiled. *I hope he didn't hear that....*

As the shuttle cleared the doors, Kurt's voice blared from the radio.

"Things are getting rough out there," Kurt's disembodied voice said. "Don't screw up."

Marc cringed. "We copy that," he replied. "We're clear of the doors and are on our way."

Walter muttered, "I'm glad Kurt's not driving."

Marc just glared.

***

WILSON collapsed on the bench as the evening sun set slowly over the horizon, its crimson glow reflecting painfully off of every vertical surface, including the windows on the building across the street in front of him. He closed his eyes and swore that he would get revenge for this assignment.

"You didn't find anything either, I take it?" Carson asked.

Wilson shrugged. "I found a shell casing, twelve screws, a contact lens, two washers, a cardboard box with a handwritten message in magic marker claiming the world would end last year, and at least eight copies of bibles stolen from hotel drawers."

"Anything useful...."

"Oh, why didn't you say so?" Wilson asked. "Then, no."

Carson sighed, then stretched, brushing a tree limb with his arm. For one brief moment, Wilson thought he saw something.

Was that... a flash of light? On that building?

"Carson," Wilson began, "do that again."

Carson stretched again.

"No, no, not that. You hit a tree branch and it moved the shadows on that building. I thought I saw something shiny."

Carson shook the branch.

There it is again.

"I definitely saw a flash of light coming from the side of that building," Wilson exclaimed, pointing. "I'm not sure what it is, but I don't think it belongs there. Here. I'll show you."

Wilson shook the branch.

"I see it," Carson replied. "We'll get somebody up there with a ladder."

***

THE light cruiser Nemesis folded into the center of the Ouroboros nebula and waited.

"We're early," Walter said. "Any second now."

And waited.

"Okay," Walter said. "They should be here.... Our mole onboard said they would be here by now."

"I don't like this," Marc said finally. "We should go...."

As he said this, the transport ship folded in.

"They're here!" Marc shouted. "Let's move, people!"

Cassie and two other soldiers ran into the airlock, sealing it behind them. By the time they arrived, automatic cutting torches had already cut out a large section of the hull.

Cassie swung a metal assist arm over to the panel and pressed a button to turn on the giant magnets, then used the arm to swing the massive panel out of the way.

One by one, they pulled their hand trucks through into the freezer hold and began piling boxes of supplies on them.

"Thirty seconds," Wilson shouted over the radio as they lifted the last box off the last hand truck and pulled it inside.

"Ooh, wait," Cassie said, looking at one box off in the corner. "Peanut butter."

She lifted it onto the hand truck and started back towards the opening.

"Wow, this is heavy," she muttered.

Then, the first shot hit the wall next to her.

"Get down!" she shouted as she threw the box into the airlock and dove for cover behind the pile.

Three Terran Alliance soldiers broke into a run towards the makeshift doorway as Cassie struggled to push the hull plating back into place. As it neared the gaping hole in the hull, one of the soldiers managed to get his arm through the gap.

"Get out!" she shouted to them, holding the plate in place until everyone else had cleared the airlock. Then, she hit the button to close the airlock door.

"Go!" she shouted through the radio to Marc.

Marc pulled the ship away and watched in horror as Cassie and the three Earth soldiers were sucked into the lifeless vacuum of space.

"Folding," Walter said.

The small cruiser flickered, then vanished with a flash of light as they appeared alongside the portable base near the edge of the nebula... and there in the darkness, a tiny transmitter floated out of the airlock, dropped by the arm of the now-dead soldier, sending out its signal for all the universe to see.

Ping.... Ping....

"You are cleared to dock," Kurt's voice said through the radio.

"Kurt," Marc replied, "It's Cassie.... She... didn't make it."

At that, all hands went suddenly silent.

Ping....

***

"Remarkable," Carson said as he stared at the fractured metal cylinder. "It appears to be a fragment of a drive shaft... embedded in the side of a building."

Wilson took it and rotated it slowly in his hands. As it reached the halfway point, he saw an aberration in its otherwise smooth surface. Slowly, he leaned closer, closer, closer, until he could recognize what he was seeing.

Letters... and numbers....

Wilson smiled and pointed at the code, which simply read AXS23498XR7493274.

"I believe ve have a VINner," Carson replied in a mock German accent.

At that, Wilson stared at him for several seconds before shaking his head in disbelief, then burying his face in his hands.

***

Marc somberly stepped out of the small cruiser onto the hangar deck as Kurt stepped in from the hallway beyond.

The look in Kurt's eyes said everything and nothing all at once.

"If it means anything," Marc said, "she died saving every one of our lives."

Kurt just stood there, staring through him as though he weren't even there.

"Kurt?" Marc asked. "You okay?"

"I'll never be okay," Kurt said, then turned and slowly walked away.

***

When Frank heard a knock at his office door, he immediately opened it... and quickly regretted that decision as Wilson entered rapidly, reeking of manure.

"Find something?" Frank asked.

"Yeah. We have a VIN," Wilson replied.

"Couldn't you have just called me?"

Wilson shrugged. "I wanted to tell you the good news in person. We traced it back to a car rental place outside of town. Now we just have to follow up on it and try to find out who rented it."

"Well, what are you waiting for?" Frank asked.

"Personally?" Wilson replied, "I'm waiting for your office to smell as bad as I do."

Frank looked unamused.

"That and it's night there right now. We'll start again in twelve hours."

Frank just glared.

***

Erik Hanssen arose with the sun as it began its slow arc across the skies over Tularis Prime. Like every morning, his wife, Sarah, was already out milking the cows and gathering eggs for breakfast. His granddaughter, Anna, still slept up in the loft, and his grandson, Marc... well, he was off gallivanting around the galaxy as usual.

Erik smiled as his granddaughter came down the steps.

"Anna, dearest," he told her, "go fetch some eggs from mommy."

Anna quickly scurried out the door. Once she was out of the house, he turned on the news. *No point scaring her,* he thought.

"You're tuned to the Colonial News Channel, with news updates three times a second."

Showoffs, he thought. *I remember a time before we had virtual news anchors.*

"Tularis Prime," the reporter began, "is once again under the microscope as colonial and Terran forces clashed in the Ouroboros Nebula."

Nothing new, Erik thought.

"As with most border skirmishes, no real territory changed hands, but the continued escalation of attacks in this region has resulted in politically charged debate about the war and its effects on the local population."

"We'll have further coverage as more information becomes available. You're tuned to the Colonial News Channel, with updates three times a second."

He shut off the TV as Anna entered.

"Everything okay, Papa?"

As good as it ever is, he thought.

"Everything is fine," he said. "Everything is fine."

***

THE girl behind the counter at UWreckIt Rental Cars looked way too young to be renting cars. *She can't be a day over thirteen,* Wilson thought.

"Are you old enough to work here?" he asked.

"I'm twenty-two," the girl replied.

"Forget I asked," Wilson said. "My name is Wilson Phelps of Colonial Investigation."

The girl turned suddenly pale.

Wilson chuckled. "Don't worry," Wilson said comfortingly. "We're not investigating you."

She relaxed noticeably.

"So wh-what do you need?" the girl asked.

"We're trying to track down a vehicle. Well, no...." He paused for a moment and collected his thoughts. "We've found the vehicle... or pieces of it, anyway. We're trying to find out who rented it."

"Pieces of it?" she asked.

"Bombing."

Again, that look.

"What was the vehicle?"

"White van. Here's the VIN," he replied, handing her a slip of paper.

The girl's fingers suddenly started clicking keys rapidly as her eyes darted in alternation between the screen and her visitor.

"That van is scheduled to be returned today," she replied. "It is rented to a Mister..."

She stared at the screen blankly.

"Yes?" Wilson asked.

"John Doe."

"Address is probably fake, too," Wilson replied.

"26192 Peach Street," she replied.

Wilson keyed it into his data pad, then grimaced.

"Unless they added another 250 blocks..." Wilson muttered. "Okay, do you have any surveillance cameras here?"

"Of course," she replied, smiling.

"Could I see the footage?"

The girl paused, keyed something into her computer, and frowned.

"It looks like someone erased the data files on the local drive," she muttered to herself. Then, she looked at her wristwatch.

"Oh, I see," she continued. "That was over two weeks ago, so our copy was purged already. I'll have to ask my manager to request the archive from our security firm."

"Could you call him?" he asked.

***

Kurt sat quietly in his favorite chair in front of the viewport in the crew mess. He saw Marc's reflection as he approached, but did not immediately acknowledge his presence. After a few seconds had passed, he turned and addressed him.

"Marc."

"Kurt."

The two men said nothing, yet said everything. Marc smiled a smile that said, "I know you loved her." Kurt nodded, crooking a smile that said, "Yeah." Marc lowered an eyebrow in a way that said, "I'm sorry." Kurt grimaced in a way that said, "I know. It's not your fault."

And so they went on this way for about five minutes before Marc finally spoke.

"Come on. I'll buy you a drink."

Kurt nodded and stood in a way that said, "Okay, but don't expect me to like it."

With that, Marc put his arm around his childhood friend and walked with him to the bar.

***

Wilson could feel his eyelids sticking to his eyeballs as he stared at the screen for the fifth straight hour. His boss, Frank, had long since gone home.

"There has to be something here," he said to no one in particular.

The images, however, revealed little. The three men were nondescript in every way—blurry faces, plain-looking clothing, short haircuts—that was the only thing remotely unusual—and the pictures just didn't reveal anything of interest.

Indeed, the only pictures that were particularly clear were images of the counter itself—pictures taken from directly overhead....

This is hopeless, he thought.

Then, something in the corner of the frame caught his eye. As the man pulled a billfold from his pocket, Wilson saw an emblem on the man's ring. He couldn't quite make it out, but it seemed oddly familiar.

It looks like my uncle's special forces ring, he thought. *He fought in the Earth military before he resigned his commission in disgust a few years ago. If these guys are former special forces, he might be able to identify them.*

So he resolved to get some sleep and call his uncle in the morning.

***

ERIK skimmed the local headlines on his data pad.

Kinji parliamentary elections... pass. Lenora conspiracy theory... pass. Town meeting on relocation? What's this?

As he selected the entry, his data pad showed a text bulletin from the Colonial News Channel.

> *NEW UMBRIA, CAMALDOLI PROVINCE, TULARIS PRIME (CNC): In light of recent skirmishes in the immediate area, the New Umbria city council is holding an open planning meeting at 1900 hours on Sunday night to discuss emergency relo-*

> *cation plans in the event of an attack on Tularis Prime. All residents of New Umbria are invited to attend and participate in the discussion.*

Erik thought for a moment. *Sunday night, seven. Sure. I can make that.*

Then Erik set the pad down and continued making breakfast.

***

WILSON woke with a jolt as the viewscreen turned itself on at full volume.

Darn RF remotes, he thought as he pulled the remote control out from under his pillow. *As least those old IR remotes didn't work unless you pointed them at the screen.*

As he started to turn it off, though, the images on his screen changed. The text on screen read, "Terran special forces invade Polaris Colony."

That's when he saw them—three men who looked suspiciously like the men from the security camera footage. Like the men on the security video, one was wearing a special forces ring on his right hand.

Suddenly, the incoming message light blinked and a chime sounded. Wilson switched over to the incoming video conference call.

"Did you just see that?" Frank asked.

Wilson simply laid his head back on the pillow.

"Those looked like the guys from the tape!" Frank shouted.

"They were. Look, it's three A.M. Wake me up at noon," Wilson muttered, then shut off the screen.

***

ERIK spun around as Anna Hanssen ran in after school. The nine-year-old had a keen intellect that belied her young age.

"Grandfather," she asked, "are you going to the meeting today?"

"Which meeting would that be?" he asked innocently.

"Oh, Papa," she replied mockingly. "I mean the meeting about evacuation plans."

I guess she heard about it at school, he thought. *Kids today....*

"Well?" Sarah prodded.

*Of course my wife takes **her** side....*

"Of course I am, honey."

"That's better," Sarah replied.

With that, Erik turned on the viewscreen and flipped to colonial news.

"In colonial news," the young woman said, "Kinji officials are one step closer to capturing the terrorist bombers responsible for the recent manure bomb in Mikarta. After comparing security camera footage from a nearby vehicle rental firm with footage from recent Terran Alliance troop activities, the bombers have been conclusively identified as members of the Terran Alliance Special Forces."

"The Terran Alliance," she continued, "has officially denied the charges. However, despite their claims to the contrary, the Colonial Alliance has called it an act of war. The previous cease-fire has all but dissolved, with massive fighting along the borders between Terran and Colonial space, and the Colonial Earth Alliance has handed down an official declaration of war."

She paused briefly, then said "We'll have more news in just a moment, but first, here's a look at your local weather."

Erik changed the channel. On the screen, he saw the TANN logo as a baritone voice pronounced, "You're tuned to TANN, the Terran Alliance News Network, with news updates every hour on the hour."

An older gentleman appeared on screen a moment later.

"Riots erupted in the streets of New Paradise on Mars as evidence of attacks on Earth ships by Colonial Earth Alliance troops was leaked to the underground media," the news anchor said. "Protests have also broken out in Darfour, Regina, Nashville, St. Petersburg, Texarkana, and Parker's Crossroads. The CEA military has disclaimed all responsibility for the attacks, claiming that...."

Erik shut off the viewscreen. Anna's terrified expression chilled him to the core. *This can't end well.*

"We are evacuating, right Papa?" she asked.

"I hope so, mijn kleindochter[3]," her grandfather replied. "I hope so."

***

KURT stared at the viewscreen as he made his report about the incident and sent it to Colonial Central Command. A moment later, the screen sprang suddenly to life, and a balding man in his fifties appeared.

"Commander Lawrence," the man said, "I'm afraid I am the bearer of bad news."

Admiral Murrow was one of the few leaders Kurt actually respected, so he was momentarily caught off guard by the bluntness of his greeting.

"What is the news?" Kurt asked.

"As of today, you are officially disavowed. You're on your own."

You mean we weren't already? Kurt thought, but held his tongue.

"Moreover, the CCC has been under siege off and on all week," the admiral continued. "If we lose contact, your standing orders are to assess the situation, and if it becomes clear that we are losing the war, you are to collapse Sol. If

---

[3] My granddaughter (in Dutch).

for any reason that becomes impossible, you are to collapse another star of strategic significance."

"Are those orders official?" Kurt asked.

"Of course not," he replied. "Officially, this conversation never took place, your project does not exist, and your mobile base was destroyed with all hands presumed lost the day before Sol exploded."

Kurt nodded his assent.

***

THE polished granite columns of the New Umbria town hall stood in stark contrast with the modern architecture of the nearby buildings. The city council chamber inside, in turn, stood as an exercise in contradictions. Its modern sound system and lighting were neatly integrated into the marble walls and arched stone roof.

The obsidian tables and polished kimberlite floor created a stunning ambiance that Erik soaked up for a moment as he stepped across the threshold. At the front of the room, a stone platform made of a polished, high-olivine basalt stood out from the wall, with unbordered obsidian sheet steps that matched the tables.

By the time he arrived, the man onstage had already been speaking for several minutes, prattling on about credible threats. The crowd clearly wasn't buying it, and several people were booing his every word. Eventually, he shouted, "We're all screwed!" before walking off stage.

Yikes, Erik thought, sliding slowly into a seat near the back in case he felt the need to get away quickly. As soon as the next speaker walked up, he immediately realized his mistake. The timid voice of the scrawny, bespectacled little man could probably barely be heard from the front row. From the back, it sounded like complete gibberish.

"We must evacuate now!" the speaker shouted emphatically.

Deep within the crowd, one man shouted, "You're a tool!"

The speaker seemed unfazed by this, replying, "And you are a fool," then walked off the platform.

The next speaker promised to be just as interesting. A burly forty-something man stepped up onto the stage, looking very much like he had just walked in from his job at the quarry.

His speech started well, but quickly descended into paranoid delusion.

"That's what the government wants us to believe," he shouted. "They want us to run so they can take our homes and our businesses and sell them to the Terran government."

The crowd murmured, wondering whether the man was a genius or a lunatic, then apparently concluded the latter as they started jeering him.

"Get off the stage, you drunk!" a man shouted.

Probably the same guy, Erik noted.

Finally, a speaker arrived at the stage who was neither a politician nor a theoretician nor a raving lunatic. A young woman in her thirties climbed up the steps and walked to the podium at the front of the stage. Her dress and overall appearance gave her an immediate air of authority, at least when compared with the rather poor personal hygiene of the first two speakers.

"My fellow Tularians," she began.

Good so far, Erik thought.

"Today, we must make what may be the most crucial decision of our lives. We must choose whether to run—to allow the infiltrators to take our land, our possessions, our hard-earned lives away from us—or stay and fight."

Not so good.

"Earth may come at us with phase pistols and nuclear warheads and fighter ships, but we will come at them with upright morals and a spirit of victory."

Not good at all.

"Our fathers built this planet," she continued, "and I'll die before I'll leave it. I say we stay and fight. We have nothing to lose but our dignity. Who's with me?"

The crowd cheered uproariously.

We're screwed.

With that realization, Erik quietly slipped out the back and walked home as quickly as his feet could carry him.

***

MARC walked into the research lab as Kristen was walking out.

She doesn't look too happy, Marc thought.

The moment he entered, Trent stood.

"Here for our weekly check-in?" Trent asked.

"Yeah," Marc replied. "What's the status."

"Screwed," Trent replied. "We underestimated the power requirements for a full-scale deployment of Omega Dawn. A single portable nuclear generator can provide enough power for the actual full-scale test, but there's no power left for shields. The device would be destroyed before the test began. It wouldn't even make it through the corona...."

Marc heard the door open behind him, but decided to ask the obvious question anyway.

"So we need another generator," Marc replied. "Can't we just dig one up from engineering?"

"It's not that simple," Kristen replied.

Figures. There's always a girl around to hear it when I ask a stupid question....

"There's no room for a second generator in the outer casings we manufactured," she continued. "We need a more powerful generator. We can get one—better yet, two so we have a spare—from Central on Kinji, but someone will have to go pick them up."

I know where this is going, Marc thought.

"Please?" she asked, pouting.

Marc closed his eyes and gritted his teeth.

***

"How was the meeting, Papa?" Anna asked before his foot had even crossed the threshold into the foyer.

Erik struggled to maintain his composure. *Best not to scare the little one*, he thought.

"Nothing we didn't know already," he replied, preferring to remain vague.

"So when are we leaving, then?" she asked.

Despite his best efforts, his silence spoke volumes.

"We are leaving, right Papa?"

Erik sighed.

"Papa?"

Erik lowered his head. When he raised it again, he saw his wife, Sarah, standing in the doorway watching the scene from the kitchen. Erik sighed again.

"They want to stay and fight," he finally replied. "They think we can win. I think we can only die trying."

Sarah smiled a forced smile, then spoke.

"We can always take the nearest escape shuttle when things get bad," she said, nodding in Anna's general direction. "There's one about three kilometers from here."

Erik understood. "Yes, of course," he replied, smiling slightly, "the escape shuttles."

If only there were any... but no need to scare little Anna.

Erik sighed.

***

Marc and Kurt sat alone in the shuttlecraft Isis as it plunged from the sky over Kinji like a hawk diving for a fish—like a hawk diving at Mach 10 and reaching temperatures approaching the melting point of lead, mind you, but like a hawk nonetheless.

As the shuttlecraft shuddered and shook its way through the jet stream, Marc pulled back on the controls and brought it into a steep, but controlled descent.

Three minutes later, they touched down on landing pad C9 of Colonial Central Command. Marc could see Admiral Murrow watching them intently as the landing struts came gently to rest on the pad recessed deep within a mountain. He nodded his understanding when he saw Marc at the helm.

As they stepped out onto the pad, Admiral Murrow greeted them. Moments later, two huge, hemispherical doors slowly crept up and over the pad, blocking their view of the sky.

"Gentlemen," he began. "Come, come. Let me show you to my office."

Marc and Kurt walked out into a long, empty hallway, its functional, corrugated metal surfaces painted a dull gunmetal grey. Throughout the hallway, the recessed fluorescent lighting near the ceiling and floor cast harsh shadows that made everyone look almost inhuman.

As they reached the end of the hall and rounded a corner, the admiral steered them towards an open door, and they stepped inside.

***

The sound of an explosion in the distance woke Kimberly up from a deep sleep.

Shit, she thought as she rolled out of bed, threw on a uniform, and ran towards the bridge.

By the time she arrived, it was clear that they were under attack.

"What the hell is going on?" she shouted.

"The Terran military!" Walter replied quickly. "They found us somehow!"

"Raise the shields and scan for transmitters!" she replied.

"The shields are up," Walter replied. "We're detecting a small fold in space coming from the cargo bay. An isolation team is moving in to investigate."

"We're in trouble," Kimberly said matter-of-factly. "Send a coded transmission to Kurt and let him know we're falling back to the Tularis system. And get that damn beacon off my ship!"

Why did Kurt have to leave me in charge? she thought.

***

MARC shivered as he and Kurt followed Admiral Murrow into his office. It was appointed somewhat differently than the corridor, apparently cut into the rock structure of the mountain in which it resided, and thus felt about ten degrees cooler.

Next door, the admiral's private dining room was similarly built, its hardwood furnishings standing in stark contrast with the stone floor, ceiling, and walls. A couple of paintings were hung on the wall, but most of the decorations were either sitting on tabletops or bookshelves.

"So have you heard the Terran news?" Admiral Murrow asked mockingly. "Apparently we're under attack."

Kurt frowned.

"Make yourselves at home," the admiral remarked, "and be sure to have a look at the balcony across the hall. The view of Bellany just down the hill is truly stunning. I'm going to go get some coffee."

As the admiral made his exit, Kurt activated the viewscreen.

They immediately saw a full screen graphic showing red X marks—bombing locations, presumably—along with a caption that read simply, "Attack on Kinji".

"What are they talking about?" Kurt asked. "Do those guys think we're stupid or something?"

> "You're tuned to TANN, the Terran Alliance News Network," the reporter said. "In regional news, Terran Alliance troops have just captured Kinji's capital city of Tyrano, and are moving on Bellany."

"Do you see any Terran troops?" Kurt asked.

"I doubt there are any Terran troops within a hundred miles of here," Marc replied, scratching his beard. "I wonder if the Terrans know that their media is feeding them a load."

Kurt rolled his eyes.

"Your family doing okay?" Kurt asked.

"Yeah," Marc replied. "Tularis Prime is right in the crosshairs, but so far, they've muddled through."

"Let's see what's *really* going on," Marc said, changing the channel.

> "...after securing the capital city of Tyrano. Our embedded reporter, Gilbert McIlhenry, is standing by in Tyrano. Gilbert?" the reporter announced.
>
> "Yes, Annie," the man replied. "It looks like Tyrano was secured several hours ago, and Colonial Alliance troops are

> slowly pushing the aggressors back towards Worcestershire."

"Away from here," Marc noted. "That's why we don't see anything."

As he said this, air raid klaxons began to blare.

"This could get rough," Kurt said, sighing.

Overhead, the sounds of fighters flying cover created a rumbling sound that shook the stone walls. Kurt and Marc held their ears as the rumbling grew louder and louder. Silverware rattled on the countertop, bookshelves discarded their contents, and an antique picture frame fell from the end table, its glass pane shattering on the hard stone floor.

The rumbling slowly decreased and eventually subsided. Then suddenly, as quickly as they had begun, the sirens went silent.

"This is it," Marc said. "This is how it begins."

And silence still.

"Oh, yeah," he said, as he looked down at his watch. "It's January 14th. Happy thirty-eighth birthday, Kurt," Marc said.

"Yeah. Whatever."

A few minutes passed in silence, and still they heard no signs of an attack. When they walked out into the hall and stepped out onto the balcony, they were greeted by a dark sky with no signs of any activity whatsoever beyond the normal glow of the city lights in the distance.

"Where's the kaboom?" Marc joked. "There was supposed to be a Kinji-shattering kaboom."

Kurt rolled his eyes again. "Go get the generators," he said.

Marc nodded.

***

Wilson stared at the viewscreen as the news reports continued.

> "You're tuned to TANN, the Terran Alliance News Network. In interplanetary news, the Terran government has announced that they have found credible intelligence indicating that the disappearance of the entire population of Lenora Prime was in fact caused by a new Colonial Alliance weapon currently in development. In a statement before the press this morning, Secretary of State Millard Taylor said, 'We are certain that these weapons of mass destruction are located on Tularis Prime, and we are taking steps to secure that planet in the name of freedom and democracy.' The Colonial Alliance denied their claims."

He changed the channel.

> "You're watching CNC, the Colonial News Channel, with news updates three times a second. In colonial news, a new report has emerged from Kinji that implicates the Terran Alliance government in a test of a superweapon that obliterated all traces of the population of Lenora Prime nearly thirty years ago. Historical logs prove definitively that Terran Alliance military forces were involved in tactical operations in a secret facility in the cliffs above Lenora Station."

After what felt like hours, he pressed the "off" button and called Frank. A moment later, Frank's bald scalp reflected the lights like the headlamps of a starship on final approach. The look of horror on his boss's face told Wilson all he needed to know.

"I... didn't think it would be this bad," Frank stammered.

"You didn't..." Wilson replied.

"I thought the public had a right to know."

Wilson closed his eyes.

"Consider this my resignation," Wilson whispered, then closed the channel.

***

FRANK Oslow stood as the viewscreen disconnected.

So this is it, he thought as he sat down at his desk. *This is what the truth brings—death, destruction, war, desolation....*

He paused as he slid open the lower right-hand drawer.

All I wanted was for the world to know the truth.

With that, he slowly pulled the revolver from the drawer and brandished it in his hand.

Was that so wrong?

He slowly raised the weapon to his temple.

Father, forgive me....

***

THE portable base shuddered as the folding drive shifted them out of the Ouroboros Nebula. Another explosion rocked the ship as a torpedo crashed into the folding drive, sending pieces of metal floating away into space.

"Again!" Kimberly shouted as they rematerialized in orbit around Alpha Centauri V.

A moment later, they materialized in orbit around Proxima Centauri IV.

"Next!" she shouted.

About three seconds later, they entered orbit around the twin stars of the Lenoran system.

"Take us home!" she shouted.

With that, the ship shimmered. Then, an explosion rocked the ship.

"What the hell was that?" she shouted.

"Our folding drive failed midway through the fold," Walter replied. "The folding gate around Lenora gave us an assist and we're in a stable orbit around the Tularis sun, but the folding drive is fried. If trouble comes, we're going nowhere fast."

Kimberly sighed.

***

Marc rounded the bend into the admiral's office, pushing a cart containing a large generator and a bowl of fresh fruit.

"Building a piña colada machine again?" Kurt asked.

Marc rolled his eyes.

"Remember your orders," the Admiral said as Kurt walked towards the door.

"Only if we lose communication, sir," Kurt reminded him.

"Of course," he replied. "If."

Marc shivered.

They pushed the cart onto the landing pad and into their shuttle. The bay shields rose as the overhead doors opened slowly. Bright flashes of light on the shields told them that their position was being targeted already. Marc picked up the intercom and warned the admiral of what was to come.

"We're doing an atmospheric fold," Marc warned. "Prepare for the world's loudest sonic boom."

Marc watched through the cockpit window as the admiral covered his ears, briefly uncovering one just long enough to give him a thumbs up.

"Here we go," Marc said.

"Isn't folding inside a gravity well a bad idea?" Kurt asked.

"The laws of physics won't let us fold very far," Marc replied, "but the base has a folding drive that can fold us a few thousand feet—far enough to not be scorched before we can get our shields up. Besides, the landing pad is rad shielded."

Kurt's eyes widened.

The ship shook violently as it suddenly displaced about sixty thousand liters of air. A moment later, a hum told them that the shields were active. This was followed a moment after that by a sudden feeling of increased gravity as the ship accelerated with minimal inertial dampening.

Marc slammed the controls back and forth repeatedly, dodging debris, bombs, and the occasional surface-to-air missile as their craft ascended nearly vertically to the folding gate overhead.

By the time Kurt opened his eyes, they were rapidly approaching the Tularis sun, and with it, the portable base that had become their home.

***

Erik stood and gazed at the sky through the storm door. The dawn's early light crept over the horizon like a thief stealing the Crown Jewels, and yet even near the horizon—against the backdrop of its orange glow—he could still see the explosions flashing brightly—a constant reminder that a terrible space battle loomed just overhead.

Sarah was still outside milking the cattle and gathering eggs for their breakfast when Anna stumbled down the steps, her weary, sleep-deprived features showing a mere fraction of their usual energy.

"Would you like me to help gather the eggs, Papa?" Anna asked as she strode into the kitchen.

"No, hon," he replied. "Let your mum take care of it."

She frowned.

"Is everything all right, Papa?" she asked.

Her furrowed brow betrayed her trepidation.

"Do not be troubled, little one," he replied.

She scowled.

Odd. That always made her relax when she was younger.

"You haven't called me 'little one' since I was four," she replied. "What's going on?"

He sighed.

"A great battle rages overhead," he answered, trembling. "I do not know how much longer it will stay away."

"Should we evacuate?" she asked naively.

Again, he let out a sigh, then paused to try to find words that would soften the blow.

"There is no place left to go," he said finally. "Go. Go outside and help your mother."

As the door opened, he regretted those words. A sudden, violent shaking rocked their home. Anna shrieked in terror and ran to him. He wrapped his arms around her and held her close.

***

KURT sat alone in his office, staring out the viewport at the cold blackness of space. To pass the time, he switched on the Colonial News Channel.

> On the screen, a terrified news reporter stood in front of a large glass wall on what appeared to be a space station.

"As you can see," he said, "we are monitoring events on Kinji from a medical corps station in orbit."

Suddenly, the image shook violently and the reporter hit the ground rather hard. A moment later, he crawled to his feet and leaned against the window, clinging to the handrail for dear life.

"It... looks like some sort of explosion.... Oh, my.... Dear God.... It's burning.... The *entire* planet is literally burning! Oh, God! Oh, God! Oh, God! The humanity!"

Kurt wanted desperately to turn away, but could not muster the courage to shut off the viewscreen.

The computer's chime suddenly drew his attention to a blinking light on the console beside him. He pressed a button to view the incoming message. Admiral Murrow's face appeared on the screen—a welcome relief from its previous contents. Kurt relaxed visibly.

"Attention," Admiral Murrow began, "This is the weekly service bulletin for all officers with red-seven clearance or higher. If you do not have red-seven clearance, it is a crime to receive this broadcast. Disable your receiver immediately."

The admiral paused for a few moments, and Kurt took the opportunity to take a sip of hot cocoa from the mug he kept permanently on his desk.

Admiral Murrow tugged on his shirt, then continued.

> "As you probably know by now, Colonial Central Command has been under siege for three days straight. We are running short on supplies, and our shields are failing. If you do not hear from me again in 72 hours, your orders are to..."

With that, the transmission was replaced by static.

Kurt knew what this meant. With the press of a button, he severed all inbound and outbound communications.

This is it....

***

Marc stood up and smacked the side of the viewscreen after the image of the Colonial News Channel was suddenly replaced by static.

"May I have your attention please?" Kurt's voice announced through the comm system. "We are having some problems with communications at the moment. We'll try to get it cleared up as soon as we can. We apologize for the inconvenience."

Communication problems, Marc thought. *I'll bet....*

Marc walked immediately towards Kurt's office. As he rounded the bend, he saw Kim and Kristen walking towards him.

This can't be good.

"Marc," Kim began, "We have a problem."

"New calculations," Kristen interrupted. "With each test, we're getting a better picture of the load, and it turns out that the power requirements are exponential."

"Bottom line?" Marc asked.

"There's no way to maintain a shield long enough for the device to do the job without a full ship power plant behind it," Kim replied.

Marc raised an eyebrow.

"The only way this device can possibly work..." Kristen continued.

"...is to fly a ship into the star," Marc finished.

"More specifically, this ship," Kim added.

Marc thought for a moment.

"Kristen, do the numbers again," he said finally. "Let's make absolutely sure. Kim, you're with me."

Marc continued with Kim to Kurt's office, where they found Kurt sitting in his usual chair watching the news feed as it streamed into his private console.

> "The CEA capital in Mikarta was reduced to rubble today after weeks of air and space fighting between CEA and Terran military forces. Also lost was the Mikarta Central Intelligence orbital outpost above Proxima Centauri III. This outpost, also known as Athena Station, is rumored to have been the emergency base of operations for the CEA military. Word has it that Terran forces are currently moving on Tularis Prime."

He heard Kurt whisper something.

"Come again?" Marc asked quietly.

"No one left to surrender," he whispered again.

Marc grew pale.

***

When Erik pulled his granddaughter cautiously to the doorway, his heart sank. A pile of ash and rubble lay where the barn once stood—his prize-winning cattle, his chickens, and....

Sarah!

Erik ran out of the house.

"Stay inside!" he shouted at Anna as he ran towards the debris.

"Sarah!" he shouted. "Sarah!"

Desperately, he threw bits of debris out of the way, searching with vain hope for some sign of his beloved wife.

"Sarah?" he called, a little more quietly this time. "Sarah?"

And with every passing moment, his cries became more hushed, more whispered, until they were lost upon the breeze.

Slowly, he walked back to Anna and wrapped his arms around her once again. Then, they stepped into the storm cellar. Together, they sat huddled in an interior corner away from the vent windows and listened to the bombs fall—wave after wave, flash after flash, tremor after tremor. They held each other as the squeal of engines pierced the silence of the early morning. They prayed in terror as the air raid sirens wailed. They ducked for cover as the cellar door exploded in a giant fireball.

And through the day and into the night, they waited, hoped, and prayed, but mostly waited.

Chapter Fifty

January 17, 2391

THE crew was gathered in the mess hall for Kurt's announcement. As he stepped up to the microphone and began to speak, his voice wavered.

"I have an announcement," Kurt told the onlookers. "I've just received word that Terran forces are taking Tularis Prime. We can't risk this project being discovered, and after that last attack, we are unable to fold. We have to move now."

"I thought the StarKiller was never to be used except as a deterrent," Kim asked.

"The Tularis System has all but fallen," Kurt replied. "Terran forces have already shown a willingness to scorch the earth after they take control of a planet. At this point, you should assume that everyone on Tularis Prime is dead or soon will be."

"We have decided to show the Terrans that we are willing to use the ultimate weapon—that we are even willing to make the ultimate sacrifice—to halt their advance on our territory," Kurt continued. "Today, we black out Tularis, our sun."

Kurt paused for a moment to let this news sink in.

"Gather your belongings," he ordered. "You will all meet here in two hours for final orders."

***

Carson Peterborough stepped into his office at Colonial Investigations. His colleague in forensics, Judy Paulson, was on her way out the door as he walked in.

"Carson," Judy said, spinning to face him, "I think you're going to want to come along on this one."

Carson turned and looked up at Judy. For several seconds, they stood in silence, yet her eyes spoke volumes.

"It's Frank," she said finally.

Carson's face grew pale.

"How?"

"Self-inflicted," Judy replied, her voice quavering.

Carson nodded. "Hold on a minute. I'll get my gear and meet you at the van."

***

Two hours later

"My friends and colleagues," Kurt began, addressing the mess hall, "We are gathered here from planets scattered across the known worlds, with many tongues, many cultures, many hopes, many dreams... but we all have one thing in common. All of us share a tortured destiny—what we know we are supposed to do but have not done or perhaps cannot do. We each feel it in our own way—in our actions, in our words, in our drives and our ambitions—but we each feel it just the same.

"Today is a historic day, not for the reasons we might hope for—not because the war is won, not because the fighting has ceased—but because the war is all but lost. Today, we find ourselves on a narrow ledge, hanging on by nothing more than our fingernails and a tenacious desire to be who we were meant to be.

"But some of us will never be who we were meant to be. Our destinies are different. Some of us must stand in the face of certain defeat and hold back the looming darkness of the night that falls upon us. We must stand firm. We must stand strong. We must stand proud.

"Today, the forces from Earth have decided to cast their forces upon our soil. We have witnessed the devastation of their weapons in the aftermath of Lenora Prime, and we cannot—nay, shall not—allow them to gain a stronghold here beyond our ramparts. If Tularis Prime falls, then *we* fall.

"So, today, we destroy the sun that has given so many of us light throughout our childhoods. It is the only way."

The murmurs of the crowd told him what he needed to know—that in spite of their misgivings, they also realized that they had no alternative.

"The inhabited worlds of the Tularis system will quickly become uninhabitable as a base of operations, and the Earth forces will be forced to seek shelter elsewhere," he explained. "Make no mistake, without a working folding drive, this is a suicide mission, and thus, I will be flying it alone. The rest of you will leave in escape pods. Once someone picks you up, I would ask that all of you do your part in searching for survivors on the Tularis worlds and carrying them to safety."

The crowd murmured their acceptance.

"So ends my journey, friends, my tortured destiny fulfilled at last, so that you might continue on your journeys and your destinies might be revealed. May you be forever blessed."

The computer finished his speech for him with just a few brief words. "All hands, abandon ship. Please make your way to the escape pods immediately. StarKiller will engage in ninety minutes."

"Kurt," Marc said, "My family...."

"I heard it on the news a few moments ago," Kurt replied. "New Umbria was completely destroyed in a bombing raid. Even if they survived the initial attack, Tularis Prime is basically a war zone on the ground, with full military occupation. There's really nothing you can do for them. I'm sorry, Marc."

Marc gulped.

"At least the prototype will be destroyed," Kim said reassuringly.

Marc nodded.

"Make sure the plans go with it," Marc added. "This war ends today."

As Kurt turned to walk away, Kim shouted at him. "Kurt, whatever you do, don't push the button unless you're sure."

Kurt turned around and looked at her with a puzzled expression.

"Once the buffers reach 60 percent," Marc interrupted, "there's no stopping it. That takes about twenty seconds. Don't push the button unless you're *absolutely* sure."

Kurt nodded his understanding.

***

KRISTEN held the door to the last escape pod open with her arm as she waited for Marc and Kimberly to arrive. She knew they had to wait until the rest of the crew, staff, and civilians were clear before they could leave, and this pod was the last one remaining.

About ten minutes later, Marc arrived.

"Where's Kim?" Kristen asked.

"I sent her on ahead," he replied, stepping into the escape pod with her. "Didn't she get here yet?"

"Oh," Kristen replied. "I assumed she was helping with the shutdown."

"Yeah, an hour ago," Marc replied, smiling slightly.

Kristen nodded.

"According to the crew badge count," he added, "we're down to just the two of us and Kurt. Everyone else has checked into an escape pod."

Kristen nodded again as she released the door.

"I hope he's right," Kristen said after a few moments pause. "Kurt, I mean."

"So do I," Marc replied as the shuttle detached from Portable Base 3. "So do I."

***

KURT looked out at the empty mess hall. By now, the escape pods were well on their way to the folding gate at Tularis III, safely outside the battle zone. The dim glow of emergency lighting cast a pall over what had been a vibrant floating township just hours earlier.

As he walked to the bridge, he pondered the meaning of the universe.

Which is worse: to carry out the orders of a now-dead leader knowing full well that the battle is already lost or to ignore those orders and ensure it? I think Shakespeare put it best when he said, "To be, or not to be: that is the question: whether 'tis nobler in the mind to suffer the slings and arrows of outrageous fortune, or to take arms against a sea of troubles and by opposing end them. To die—to sleep, no more; and by a sleep to say we end the heartache and the thousand natural shocks that flesh is heir to...."

There's the rub, he thought. *We can end the war, but we will be killing our own people along with the occupiers... not that there are many of our people left, but if there is even one, is that not better than none?*

No, he thought, *one person forced to live in servitude in a land controlled by the enemy versus one person dying free... but what right do I have to choose for that one person? Is it really fair for me to exercise that right merely because I am the only one who has the power to do so? But then what of the lives that are saved by ending this now? Will prolonging the war cause even more harm? Earth already destroyed Kinji. Where will it end?*

No, it must end here and now. To be, or not to be? If it be not my right, it still remains my duty, and without my sense of duty, I am not to be, myself.

Kurt was in this mental state when he arrived on the bridge. The portable base had entered the corona moments before, and was rapidly proceeding into the chromosphere.

Thirty seconds to the core, he mused. He quickly went over the checklist in his head.

Dispose of research data? Check. The research team wiped all their data, and the only copy left is on the data chip in this ball-point pen. It will go up with the ship, but I'd better keep it with me until then in case something goes wrong, he thought, tucking the seemingly innocuous red pen into his shirt pocket.

Systems check? Done. The StarKiller is armed, and the power systems are online and reconfigured to handle the immense power drain of solar insertion.

Evacuation plan? Check. My personal portal is set to send me to Proxima Centauri III a moment after detonation... assuming the antenna array lasts that long.... If it doesn't work, at least death will be quick.

Everything on the list is done, he thought.

With his checklist complete, Kurt uttered some words from Dickens: "It is a far, far better thing that I do, than I have ever done; it is a far, far better rest that I go to than I have ever known." Then, he pressed the button and prayed.

The power buffers in the StarKiller began to charge rapidly.

At 60%, there's no stopping it, Marc had said. 50 percent now. Fifty-two. Fifty-four.

Then the incoming message light began to blink. Kurt put it on the viewscreen.

"Abort!" Marc shouted through the comm link. "We're getting rumors of a new cease-fire."

Kurt looked down at the console.

60%

His heart sank.

Detonation in five... four... three... two... one....

And as the room and its contents were suddenly bathed in white light, Kurt faded to grey.

***

ERIK Hanssen huddled under the heavy wooden table. Around him, the ground shook as wave after wave of missiles struck the barren desert, bringing pieces of brick and mortar down from the wall above his head. His granddaughter, Anna, huddled next to him.

"It's gonna be okay, hon," he said as she cried on his shoulder.

"I'm scared. Where's mommy?" Anna asked.

Erik cringed. *How do you explain death to a nine-year-old?*

"She's in a better place now, sweetie," he replied, fighting back tears. "She's with God."

"Will we see her soon?" she asked.

"I don't know, honey. I don't know."

Another explosion shook the house, bringing bits of the ceiling down on their heads. Anna screamed at the top of her lungs.

As Erik held her tightly, his granddaughter's terrified cry was drowned out by the sound of engines whining—*a fleet of landing craft settling to the ground outside, no doubt.* As the bright lights bathed their house, Erik and Anna covered their eyes and waited.

Any moment now, the troops would start firing, their pulse rifles obliterating anything and anyone in their paths.

As if on cue, the landing troops began firing at the oncoming soldiers—a deafening cacophony that left Anna's ears crying in pain—and all the while, air raid sirens blared in the distance.

Suddenly, an even more violent explosion rocked the house, sending a ceiling beam falling onto the table above them, and along with it fell darkness. As the power failed across the city, the sirens stopped, and their world fell into an eerie stillness—dark, silent, and cold....

***

By the time Kurt regained consciousness on the beach of Proxima Centauri III, the tide had already halfway buried him in the sand.

Kurt breathed a sigh of relief.

It is done, he thought. *I'm alive, the prototype is destroyed, and... but wait... who won?*

With that thought, he looked down at a data pad and skimmed its contents. The lead story described Earth's new weapon against terrorism, the "ground clearing bomb". The accompanying video clip showed a terrified reporter again saying, "The *entire* planet is literally burning!"

Three days ago, he thought. *Too early.*

And so, after seeing a few moments of the story, he skipped forward four days.

The headline for the next day read, "Billions killed as Earth Burns." In small print below that, it read, "Accidental Detonation Obliterates Population." As he watched, the headline faded and vanished. In its place, the headline now read, "Millions killed as star collapses."

And upon seeing this, Kurt slowly faded into nothingness; where he stood, a small, red ballpoint pen stuck innocently out of the sand.

***

COMMANDER Fuller sat in the command chair of the colonial frigate C.S.S. Hail Mary as it folded into an orbit around Tularis III to defend it against Terran invasion forces.

Built with expensive and bulky low-radiation-emission folding drives, the Hail Mary was designed for low atmospheric folding over enemy targets. The resulting sonic shock wave would incapacitate the ground troops, making them unable to usefully attack it during landing.

Too bad they can't make one that can jump more than a few hundred AUs at a time without a ten-minute cool-down, he mused. *Oh well. At least it gives me time to catch up on my reading.*

But as he reached for his novel, a blinking light brought that plan to a screeching halt.

From across the bridge, the communications officer turned and shouted, "Sir."

He turned. "Yes?"

"We're receiving colonial distress beacons from a debris field about 30 million km from here," the officer replied.

"Take us in, full thrust."

***

THE escape pod door creaked open. *Its rusty hinges were clearly not built to work more than once,* Marc thought, *and we used that up when we closed it.*

As his eyes adjusted to the dim lights of the shuttle bay, he could just make out the outline of a familiar face.

"Kim?" he mumbled. "Colonial ship, I trust?"

She smiled at him.

"Frigate," she replied. "We're going to Tularis Prime."

"Out of the frying pan," he replied.

***

ON Proxima Centauri III, Earl Watts and Chip Hardy stood in front of a media circus as they each picked up their ceremonial golden shovels.

"You first," Earl said.

With that, Chip drove his shovel into the ground. This ceremonial motion was followed shortly thereafter by the clink of Earl's shovel hitting concrete. Chip chuckled as Earl struck again and hit dirt.

They threw the dirt into a wheelbarrow waiting nearby, hitting an onlooker with overspray in the process.

"I'm so sorry," Chip said in horror.

The young girl smiled and brushed off the dirt.

"Natalie," she said, suddenly thrusting her hand in Chip's direction.

"Chip," he replied, smiling.

"You two have fun," Earl said as he walked over to chat with the waiting reporters.

"You went to school here?" Chip asked.

"No," she replied. "I go to Hollerith Academy."

"That's amazing!" he exclaimed. "That's where I'm going while they rebuild!"

"Cool!" she replied, grinning. "So we might be classmates soon."

Chip smiled. "You wanna go get some pizza?"

***

WILSON walked up to the Colonial Investigation main entrance. Seeing the place covered in crime scene streamers wasn't completely unheard of; it wasn't an everyday event either, though, so it was with some trepidation that he ducked under the police line to see what was going on.

"Nature of your business here?" the police officer at the door asked.

"I work here... or at least I used to. I'm here to clean out my stuff."

From behind him, a voice shouted, "You can't quit, Wilson."

He spun around to see Carson Peterborough of the CI forensics team staring him in the face.

"And why is that?" Wilson asked.

"You didn't hear?" Carson replied, his appearance growing suddenly concerned. "The police say it was suicide."

"Frank?"

Carson nodded.

How could this day get any worse? Wilson wondered.

"And the Governor chose you to be the interim head of Colonial Investigation."

I had to ask....

"And your home planet is a pile of rubble."

I really had to ask....

"Besides, I sure as hell don't want the job."

Wilson just chuckled and shook his head.

***

By the time Marc stepped off the landing ramp onto Tularian soil, he was already taking fire. He dove behind a large rock to get the lay of the land.

I don't get it, he thought. *There are no military targets in the Felton Mountains. This should have been the perfect spot for a covert landing....*

That's when he noticed that they weren't shooting at him; he was catching stray fire from two military forces, neither of which wore any obvious military uniforms.

The C.S.S. Hail Mary was perched on a plateau overlooking a small valley. Below him, a team of troops, dressed in black, seemed to be fighting to get out of an oddly designed building that descended into the side of a hill. The other team, dressed in blue, seemed to be near the entrance in strategic positions, preparing for an ambush.

But who are they? I can't tell.... Oh well, Marc thought. *Only one way to find out.*

"This is Commodore Marc Hanssen of the Colonial Command to any troops in the Felton Mountains," he said into his radio. "Please identify yourselves."

The lack of a response told him all he needed to know. *Neither one is Colonial,* he realized. After a few moments, he called for troops.

"Let's rock this place," he said.

With that, hundreds of Colonial troops ran out into the clearing and began taking up positions behind boulders, trees, and anything else that would provide cover.

Moments later, another transport ship sat down a few hundred feet away.

"Sir," a voice called over his radio. "We have a Terran troop ship at your three o'clock. Please be advised, over."

"Acknowledged," Marc replied.

The sound of gunfire from the oncoming Terran troops quickly followed and drowned out the gunfire from the unidentified soldiers below.

Marc's forces immediately began firing upon the Terran troops, who in turn immediately began firing upon both the Colonial forces and the ambush squad.

But not a Colonial ambush squad? Marc didn't quite know what to think.

"Commander Fuller, I need conclusive identification," Marc ordered into his radio. "Find out if we have a black ops team on the mountain."

Marc pulled out a pair of binoculars and began to study the fighting below. He could swear the building looked familiar.

That's when he saw them. A young man—probably twenty-six or twenty-seven—emerged from the building carrying a young woman in his arms. She looked seriously hurt, possibly dead. The look in the man's eyes chilled him to the bone. Beside him, another young man helped a young woman who looked like she had seen better days.

"They aren't ours," the commander's voice crackled.

"That's all I needed to know," he replied.

Terran rescue mission gone wrong, he mused, *and the men in blue aren't colonists and aren't our military. That means... they must be the terrorists we keep hearing about. So they* ***do*** *exist....*

"Men!" he shouted at his troops. "Target *only* the terrorists in blue down below and fire."

After a few moments, the startled troops in blue were lying face down.

"Ten hut!" he shouted as he began waving a white flag.

With that, his soldiers snapped to attention one by one down the line.

He then paused and saluted. One by one, the colonial troops followed his lead, lowering their rifles to order arms and saluting the fallen soldier.

As the Terran soldiers walked up the hill towards the two parked ships, Marc picked up his radio again. *To hell with the orders of dead men,* he thought. *Nobody in this area of space outranks me. It's time to end this.*

"Begin broadcasting on all standard channels," Marc said. "By order of the acting theatre commander, all colonial military forces are hereby ordered to stand down and await further orders."

"To all Terran personnel and all civilians," he continued, "we have come to help. In case you haven't noticed, this planet is dying. We are offering all colonial military ships at hand to assist with rescue efforts and evacuation to medical facilities on nearby worlds. We extend this offer not only to civilians, but also to any injured military personnel as well."

"While this cease-fire is temporary," he concluded, "I believe that the hostilities have gone on long enough. We have already seen Kinji burn and Tularis freeze. It should be clear by now that if this fighting continues unabated, soon there will be nothing left to fight for."

Marc then shouted to the men inside the ship. "Fly a medical flag," he ordered as he jogged behind his lines and up the ramp.

The men pulled out a medical rescue flag and hastily attached it to the side of their craft.

A few moments later, the two men helping their injured comrades arrived at the base of the ramp, and two members of Marc's team lifted the injured onto gurneys. As they rolled the injured women up the ramp, one of the men followed them.

"I'm afraid you can't ride with her," Marc said. "The transport is for the injured and their family members only."

"I'm the only family she has," the young man replied somberly, "and she's the only family I have, too."

Marc saw the pain in the young man's eyes and knew that he had endured much.

Poor guy must really love that girl, he thought.

He waved him in, then helped the other man with the injured blonde, whose friend kept calling her Jennifer.

***

Wilson's personal shuttle landed near where his apartment once stood on Tularis Prime, its charred remains more closely resembling a burnt-out warehouse than a home. He had hoped he might find something in the rubble, but it quickly became clear as he dug through the piles of ash by the light of a headlamp that there was nothing left to find.

"All gone, eh?" a woman's voice asked from behind him.

Wilson jumped what seemed like three feet into the air, much to the woman's amusement. One giggle later, he turned towards her, blushing.

"Hi," he began, turning his flashlight to see her face.

"Hi," she replied.

"I'm Wilson. Apartment 13."

"Naomi," she countered. "Apartment 17."

"W-w-wait," he stammered. "We've been living two doors apart for..."

"Seven years," she replied.

"I've been here for nine, so... yeah, seven years," he said. "So we've been living two doors apart for seven years? Why haven't I met you before?"

She smiled.

"Where are you going?" she asked.

"I guess I'll try to find a place near work on Alpha Centauri V," he replied.

The girl's eyes lit up suddenly.

"Really? Where do you work?"

"Colonial Investigation," he replied.

"Cool," she replied. "Third Centauri Bank. We're about three blocks away."

"Remind me to change my bank," he said coyly.

She giggled.

"Here's my card," she replied. "Call me sometime."

He smiled, took her card, and handed her his card in return.

"You know what?" he said finally. "I think I'm gonna get out of here and go someplace warm. You wanna go get some pizza? On say... Proxima Centauri III?"

She grinned and nodded. "Sure."

***

MARC stood in the hallway and watched as Jennifer walked into the hospital room. Joseph sat pensively beside Amanda's bed.

"Joe," she said. "How are you?"

He smiled and stood up to greet her.

"I see they have you all patched up."

"Yeah," she replied. "I think the phrase the doctor used was 'Swiss cheese'."

Joseph chuckled.

"I met a guy on the ship," she continued. "Do you remember that? No, I guess you don't. You probably don't remember much of anything."

"Yeah," he replied. "I saw him. Marc, was it?"

Jennifer's eyes widened and she grinned from ear to ear.

"Yeaaah," she said dreamily.

Joseph smiled knowingly.

"Anyway, his family was on Tularis Prime and..."

"Go," Joseph replied, quirking a smile.

"Are you sure?" she asked. "Are you sure you'll be okay here by yourself?"

"I have Amanda," he replied, nodding at the young woman's unconscious form sprawled out on the hospital bed.

"Not much of a talker, huh?" she said, smiling a sad half-smile.

"True," Joseph replied, chuckling. "She's not like you, Jen. She didn't regain consciousness and immediately start talking everyone's ear off."

Jennifer rolled her eyes, and in her best valley girl impersonation, said, "Like, what... evaaaah."

Joseph laughed.

Jennifer slowly, cautiously reached her arm out and gave him a sidelong hug.

Joseph smiled weakly. "Thanks, Jen. I needed that...."

The doctor walked in moments later and gave him the young woman's status.

"You know," Jennifer said, "a little prayer couldn't hurt."

Joseph nodded, then turned back to the young woman and stroked her hair.

Marc bit his lip.

"Be well," Jennifer whispered as she turned towards Marc and walked away in silence.

***

Two hours later

MARC stood with Jennifer and Trent outside the burnt out remains of Marc's home. The shuttle's spotlights illuminated its remains. The walls were nowhere to be seen, and parts of the ground floor had collapsed into the cellar.

And softly, in the distance, he heard a young girl's tearful cries of mourning.

"Anna?" he shouted. "Anna!?!"

Marc ran towards the source of the sound but could not see beyond the collapsed section of the floor. As he stepped near the edge of the hole, the wood creaked eerily, so Mark stepped back.

"We'll have to go in another way," he said, and ran to the cellar door.

He turned the handle and pulled, but the door would not budge.

"Get me something to pry with!" he shouted.

Jennifer looked around and, finding nothing, ran back to the shuttle and grabbed a pickaxe.

Marc swung the pickaxe at the door, splintering away fragments until the center of the door suddenly gave way and half of the door fell into the stairwell. Then, Marc swung the remaining half open to get it out of the way.

As they descended the rickety stairs, flashlights in hand, Marc saw his grandfather lying on the ground with Anna by his side. Marc ran to them and wrapped his arms around his little sister.

"He just stopped breathing," she said. "I didn't know what to do."

Jennifer scanned him with a medical scanner.

"Ruptured aortic aneurysm," she replied. "There's nothing you could have done."

"Mother?" Marc asked.

"She was in the barn," Anna replied in tears. "It... exploded."

Jennifer walked up and put her arms around the pair.

Marc's eyes welled up as he pulled Anna to him once again.

"It's gonna be okay, sis," he said. "You'll see. Everything will be okay."

***

THE shuttlecraft Peacemaker trudged its way from Tularis Prime past the artificial atmosphere of the outer colony on Tularis VII where dozens of shuttles were converging in preparation for the arrival of a temporary folding gate. In it, Marc, Jennifer, Anna, and Trent fled the darkness with a handful of refugees, many of whom had left behind family and friends who could not fit on the limited transports available—who had left their homes behind in the cold darkness of space, their planets drifting aimlessly without a star's gravity well to direct their orbits.

As the shuttle skirted the outer cloud, it moved into position in a line of shuttles with elevated priority heading towards a Terran battleship that was providing limited folding service for military and medical vessels on both sides.

After what seemed like an eternity, they reached the front of the line and waited for the battleship's folding drive to cool. And as the folding drive hummed to life, they received an old-style audio transmission, delayed by traveling through space for over three decades.

> *Sic Kend'hara i'michlus't vi yu grecht. Sic Kend'erus vi vey inacht. Frecas sol vey grecht. Oc'flieme, sepra, fliecht ste'gats frecasse. Ic nule vey carus. Ic Kend'hara fi erust.*

Marc looked at Jennifer with a puzzled look.

"What was that?" Marc asked.

"Don't ask," she replied. "Just... don't ask."

Chapter Fifty-one

Two months later (March 7, 2391)

WILSON greeted Naomi as she stepped across the threshold into his office. "Hey, Naomi!"

"I hear we have a new President," she said.

"Number five thousand, three hundred twelve in the line of succession," Wilson replied. "Marc somebody-or-other."

Naomi shook her head. "I hear he's military," she said. "Probably not the best person to run things...."

"On the other hand," Wilson replied, "he called for the cease-fire that ended fighting on Tularis Prime."

"After his forces blew up the star," she countered.

Wilson grimaced.

"True enough," he said. "Could be worse, though."

She looked at him with a puzzled look.

"I hear the next person on the list was a crack addicted homeless guy living under a bridge on Proxima Centauri III," Wilson joked.

"You sure that would be worse?" she replied.

"Touché!"

***

MARC Hanssen squinted his eyes as he stepped onto the brightly lit makeshift platform on Kinji. In spite of the worldwide firestorm, a few parts of Kinji remained relatively sheltered by mountain chains. This part was not one of them, however.

Around the stage, the charred remains of an old forest spread as far as the eye could see. A few scattered pine trees could be seen emerging from the ash nearby, but otherwise the entire landscape was a dull, grey-black dust that burned the eyes when the wind blew... but this spot was no accident; it was special to Marc. He just had to keep reminding himself of that fact as his nose and throat burned from the blowing soot and other particulates.

As he reached the podium, he looked out at the crowd of reporters and knew that elsewhere in the universe, hundreds of billions of men and women were watching him from the comfort of their living rooms. *Lucky bastards,* he thought. *Oh well. No point worrying about it now.*

"My fellow citizens of the Colonial Alliance," he began. He cleared his throat, then continued. "... of the Colonial Alliance, Citizens of the Terran Alliance, and citizens of unaligned worlds, welcome. My name is Marc Hanssen, and I am the acting President of the Colonial Earth Alliance. With me is the President of the Terran Alliance, Adam Fitzgerald."

"Adam," he continued, "while I am a citizen of the Colonial Alliance, my family tree began its colonial roots in an Earth-allied colony—my grandfather was born on Mars as the child of two Mars colonists—so in spite of our differences, I share many of your ideals. I hope that the relationship between our alliances will prove to be a lasting one, as I truly feel that we are more alike than we are different."

Marc cleared his throat and rubbed his neck symbolically again before continuing.

"I'm not one for speeches—my friend Kurt—now he could give speeches. In the last speech he gave us before his final mission, he spoke of tortured destinies—what we know we are supposed to do but have not done or cannot do. He said that we each feel it in our own way—in our actions, in our words, in our drives and our ambitions—but we each feel it just the same."

"Well, our two alliances have tortured destinies of their own. We were destined to live in peace, a peace that has been repeatedly broken by... madmen and monsters, a peace that has been tested by orders that contravene the trust that peace requires, a peace that has not been supported by the politicians and bureaucrats who should have instilled the desire for that peace in their people instead of getting them riled up for war."

"Well, that ends today. And what better place to end it than here on Kinji. The planet burned in war is beginning to blossom again, with a few daffodils poking their heads up through the ash alongside the nascent pine saplings. It is a place of rebirth, and thus a fitting place to sign these peace accords today."

"But this place means more than that. Here on this very spot, the first President of the Colonial Earth Alliance was inaugurated in 2360. Of course, as we all know, things didn't quite go as planned, and after the first Colonial Congress was firebombed at the inauguration, the government that took its place created conflict and division among our worlds, taking us to the brink of utter annihilation."

"My best friend Kurt would have particularly appreciated the irony, then, of signing the peace accords here, as his older sister, Kacey Watson, was the first Colonial President. She died that day along with dozens of other good men and women, and with them—at least in the minds of many Colonials—died the hope of peace and prosperity as well. It is particularly fitting, then, that in this place of rebirth, a hope for peace should spring anew today."

"Kurt would have loved to have been here to witness this, and I'm sure he could have written a much better speech than this one," he added.

The audience chuckled, so Marc paused to let the noise die down before continuing.

"...but in a way, he is here. When Kurt watched his sister die on this spot, thirty-one years ago today, he never imagined that some three decades later, his sacrifice would save the lives of millions—perhaps... perhaps even billions—of people by bringing this horrible war to a close."

Marc turned and looked out into the crowd and saw his fiancée, Jennifer, standing with Anna.

"And one of the people he saved was *my* little sister, Anna."

He smiled and waved at Anna. Anna beamed.

"Today is a historic day, not for the reasons we might have feared—not because the war is all but lost, not because the death toll is rising, not because more planets have fallen in this war's wake of destruction—but because the war is over—because the fighting has ceased and *peace* has fallen in our land."

"We found ourselves on a narrow ledge hanging by only our fingernails and a tenacious desire to be who we were meant to be, and we pulled ourselves to safety. We stood in the face of certain defeat and held back the looming darkness of the night that fell upon us. We faced our greatest fears. And we prevailed. But this peace will not be easy to maintain. We must stand firm. We must stand strong. We must stand proud if we are to achieve the lasting peace that we all long for."

"And so ends this great journey, our alliances' tortured destinies fulfilled at last, bringing peace... so that you may each continue on your own journeys of discovery.... May each of your destinies one day be revealed, and may you be forever blessed."

The crowd applauded, and as he signed a permanent cease-fire between the Colonial Alliance and the Terran Alliance, Anna Hanssen ran up on stage and hugged her big brother.

Chapter Fifty-two

Ten years later (2401)

THE sun shone brightly on Proxima Centauri III as Nicolette ran down the seashore. The eight-year-old had already skipped ahead two grades, and her parents adored her. Of course, her aunt, Anna, took care of her a lot until she left for college last summer.

I miss Anna, she thought. *I think I'll go look for shells like we used to do.*

Nicolette ran to a small tide pool that had about eight inches of water in it, then waded out into the deeper backwater beyond, slid her goggles down over her eyes, and put her head under.

This is where all the good shells wash up, she remembered.

But today, there were only a handful of sand dollars, which she dutifully collected. The only other thing she could see anywhere was something red down at the far end. She pulled her head up out of the water and waded down to investigate.

As she reached under the water again, her hand hit upon the shiny, red object.

A ballpoint pen? How odd, she thought. *I think I'll take it apart.*

With that thought, the girl unscrewed the top of the pen and found that it had a hidden compartment.

What's that? It looks like some kind of microchip, she thought.

"Nicolette! Dinner!" Jennifer shouted.

She screwed the pen back together and ran back to the house.

Ooh, I need to put these sand dollars in my secret place, she thought. *Mommy doesn't know about it. I've hidden lots of things there, including the rest of my shell collection....*

When she reached the back porch, she turned, opened the cellar doors, stepped halfway down the steps, and slid a brick out from the side of the stairwell, revealing a small chamber under the dirt.

...but the prettiest thing, she thought, *is this funny-looking red crystal. It was there when I found this spot five years ago.*

She placed the sand dollars alongside the crystal and her other shells.

But, she thought, *what should I do with this pen?*

She pondered this for a moment as she stared at the initials K.L. inscribed on its body.

I think I'll keep it with my shell collection, she thought, smiling, and placed the pen into the hole beside the crystal, then slid the brick back into place and ran inside to dinner.

Epilogue:

Eighty-five years earlier (2316)

"You may kiss the bride," the priest said, smiling.

The couple stared deep into each other's eyes across a small, candlelit kneeler and mouthed the words "I love you" to each other, then leaned towards each other and lost themselves completely for what seemed like an eternity before the organ woke them up from their dreamlike state.

Angela Rae Walker Hanssen smiled at Tim as they stood and slowly made their way down the aisle and into the adjacent fellowship hall.

After an hour of dancing, speeches, and eating way too much cake at the reception, the couple made their way to the main entry hall. The church doors creaked as the ushers struggled to open them, but they eventually gave way. Beyond them stood a crowd of well-wishers lining the sidewalks, throwing rice.

Tim marveled at his wife's determination to have rice at the wedding. *It will never grow in hydroponics,* he had thought. He was wrong. It took a year worth of water in the first three months alone, but it grew.

Yes, everything seemed perfect—his newlywed wife by his side, a cease-fire in the war, and plenty of jobs rebuilding the damage it had caused—but as he stepped out onto the cathedral steps with his blushing bride, a motion in the distance caught his eye—just a tiny speck, far out in the grounds of the nearby cemetery. Instinctively, he knew....

"A wise man once said 'Those who cannot remember the past are destined to repeat it,' and it's true," Tim said to the waiting crowd. "I've seen many mistakes made and remade over the past few years of my life."

"I've seen friends come and go, marriages and divorces, births and deaths... but one thing has remained constant—

steadfast and true", he continued, turning to his bride, "and that's you, Angela."

"And if I have learned only one thing from history, it is this: that I shall never leave you; as long as I live, and evermore thereafter, I will be by your side. But right at this moment, there's someone who needs me even more than you," he said, pointing and slowly walking with her across the gravel road and between the rows of markers.

"How long has it been?" Tim asked as he approached the tombstone.

"A year ago today," Joe replied somberly as he laid a single red rose upon the dew-covered grass.

"He was a good man."

Joe nodded.

"I hear your wife is pregnant," Joe noted.

"Yeah," Tim replied. "Let's keep that between us. Angela's mom wouldn't be happy."

Joe chuckled. "Do you have a name yet?"

"Erik," he replied, "after her grandfather."

Joe nodded. "Marcia named her first daughter Tommy after my brother. Poor kid's gonna be so screwed up...."

Joe chuckled.

"I understand you're back in school now," Tim said.

"Yeah. I decided to follow in my brother's footsteps and become an engineer," he replied.

"Tom would have been proud to see that," Tim began, then paused for a moment.

As Joe looked back up at him, Tim clapped him on the back. "Come on," Tim said. "I'll buy you a drink."

And for the first time in many long months, Joe smiled.

Closing Thoughts:

Thanks for reading the second book in the Patriots series of books. If you missed the first book, *Traitors In Waiting*, be sure to read it before you read the next book, *Beyond the Veil*. The third book tells the dark truth behind the events of the first book, revealing that everything you thought you knew is... well, not wrong so much as incomplete. Massively incomplete.

***

LIEUTENANT Pierre DesChambres could already feel the effects of the sodium thiopental as his wrist slipped free from its restraint. He struggled to release the other wrist restraint, then unbuckled the straps holding his legs.

The door opened easily when he approached it from the inside, much to his amazement.

The sick bay was not designed as a prison, he mused. *Wait a minute. Does that mean I could have walked out of here at any time for the last two days?*

His hope was short-lived, however; once in the hall, he found himself suddenly wishing he had a good place to hide when the doctors appeared at one end of the corridor.

He quickly ran away from them down the corridor to its opposite end, turned right, ran through a door into a larger hall, turned left, and finally ran through the double doors to his right.

Once through those doors, he found himself inside the Crew's Quarter, a large eating establishment. Were it not for his medical gown, he probably could have gotten lost in the crowd, but alas, it was not to be. About the only thing he could hope to do was to tell everyone what he knew.

"This is mad!" Pierre shouted across the room. "I demand to be heard. The Alliance is corrupt!"

Suddenly, the elite security forces crashed through the doors behind him.

"They're killing us!" he screamed. "They're killing us! Their own people!"

As the security team wrestled him to the ground, he continued to try to speak. "You have to believe me! There are traitors in waiting!"

Then, he felt the familiar jab of a stunner in his back, and everything went black.

About the Author:

David is an avid musician, writer, photographer, videographer, musical composer, and hard-core geek with a Master's degree in computer science and a Bachelor's degree in communications (broadcasting) and computer science.

In addition to writing this book, David also created various workflow tools used in its production, did all of the content production and design, redesigned many of the fonts, and drew the cover art.

His choral music has been performed by the Diocesan Choir of Monterey, California and the contemporary choir at Holy Cross Catholic Church in Santa Cruz, CA. He spends much of his spare time performing with musical ensembles in the greater Santa Cruz area.

http://www.patriotsbooks.com/

www.ingramcontent.com/pod-product-compliance
Lightning Source LLC
Chambersburg PA
CBHW030538310726
48979CB00010B/1957/J

* 9 7 8 1 9 4 0 8 0 9 0 3 8 *